PENGUIN VEER

SOLDIER AND SPICE

Aditi Mathur Kumar is a proud Indian Army wife, and this is her first book, based on the lives of army wives. As a civilian married to an army officer, she found a lot of stories from her life that she felt were poignant and the world needed to hear them. *Soldier and Spice* is a result of that. Aditi is also the only Indian Army wife to deliver a TEDx talk about the lives of army families. Aditi's other books are *Love, Whatever That Means* and *This Heartbreak: A Collection of Poems*. Apart from being an author of three books, Aditi works in advertising and can be found on Twitter and Instagram, @adicrazy.

T0158360

SOLDIER & *Spice*

ADITI MATHUR KUMAR

PENGUIN
VEER

An imprint of Penguin Random House

PENGUIN VEER

USA | Canada | UK | Ireland | Australia
New Zealand | India | South Africa | China

Penguin Veer is part of the Penguin Random House group of companies
whose addresses can be found at global.penguinrandomhouse.com

Published by Penguin Random House India Pvt. Ltd
4th Floor, Capital Tower 1, MG Road,
Gurugram 122 002, Haryana, India

First published by Westland Publications Private Limited in 2013
Published in Penguin Veer by Penguin Random House India 2023

ISBN 9780143459873

Typeset in Adobe Garamond by SÜRYA, New Delhi

www.penguin.co.in

SOLDIER & Spice

ADITI MATHUR KUMAR

PENGUIN
VEER

An imprint of Penguin Random House

PENGUIN VEER

USA | Canada | UK | Ireland | Australia
New Zealand | India | South Africa | China

Penguin Veer is part of the Penguin Random House group of companies
whose addresses can be found at global.penguinrandomhouse.com

Published by Penguin Random House India Pvt. Ltd
4th Floor, Capital Tower 1, MG Road,
Gurugram 122 002, Haryana, India

First published by Westland Publications Private Limited in 2013
Published in Penguin Veer by Penguin Random House India 2023

Copyright © Aditi Mathur Kumar 2013

ISBN 9780143459873

Typeset in Adobe Garamond by SŪRYA, New Delhi

www.penguin.co.in

This is for Chandan,
my Knight in crisp combats
And Gauri,
my lucky charm

This is for Chandan,
my knight in crisp combats
And Gauri,
my lucky charm

I'm a woman and an Army wife.
What's your super power?

Contents

chapter one

Happily Ever After. In a Theoretical Way, Of Course

'Are we there yet?' I ask for the millionth time, clutching my seat belt.

'We'll be there by eighteen hundred hours,' Arjun replies with a smile. His hands rest casually on the steering wheel and his eyes are steady on the road. He even has a relaxed smile on his face that immediately annoys me.

'But it's only—' I begin impatiently and look at my watch: it's 5.20 p.m. I start to calculate this into Arjun's preferred time format.

'Seventeen o'clock plus twenty minutes!' I wail, after doing the calculation twice, just to be sure. 'I have to pee!'

There's a slight twitch at the corners of his mouth which he attempts to hide by frowning at a truck dawdling ahead of us. So I made a mistake, I roll my eyes. Who cares? I mean, no normal person tells time in this prehistoric 'hundred' hours way anyway.

Except for Army officers, of course, and that's what Arjun— my husband—is.

Yes, I fell in love with and married an Army officer. Yaay me!

He sees me do the eye roll, laughs and pulls me to him. I stretch my stiff-from-travelling bones with some effort and rest my head on his arm uncomfortably. It's been one full month since our wedding, but we still crave every possible touch, the slightest brush of a hand and all quick cuddles.

Maybe a year-and-a-half of *super-secret* dating before tying the knot is responsible for this. Arjun, being in the Army and everything, was always posted away from Delhi; we met only when he was on leave, which, let me tell you, was never enough.

We were nothing like the couples I saw around me, who were constantly together; we were that crazy pair who was working on a 'long-distance relationship' and my friends either oohed and aahed over it, or thought it was the worst idea ever. Being subjected to crazy questions and gloomy predictions is not a fun thing, let me tell you.

'So. How does the only-talking-on-the-phone thing work?'

'Is there *giggle-giggle* phone sex involved?'

'Don't get too into it; you don't really know what's going on when he's a hundred miles away.'

'Erm, have you ever met him? Like, in real life?'

Annoying, I know.

Hence, the secrecy. The fewer people who knew, the fewer questions I had to answer. Also, I didn't need anyone telling me how Army men are unfaithful bastards who are always cheating behind their girlfriend's or wife's back—because, believe me, they do. I mean people. People do say things like that. So keeping it a secret worked fine for me. And then we got married.

And now, here we are—married for a month. And on the road for the past two days.

Despite the need to touch, I wriggle out of his arms. I wonder how people make out in cars. Even if you set aside the fear of someone pounding on the window while you're at it, it's just plain uncomfortable. Besides, it's tacky. Every time I see a couple make out in a mall parking lot or even in my society in Delhi (and you'll be surprised how often that happens), I give them my best 'Get a room' look. They never notice, though, obviously. But whatever.

I check my watch once again—still another fifteen minutes to go.

I can't wait any longer. First, I have to pee really badly, and Arjun says there is absolutely no place for that except home. And second, I am going to my own house for the first time ever!

My very own home.

Exciting, isn't it? I am about to clap my hands at the thought, *for the hundredth time*, but I stop in time. Clapping for no apparent reason seems to freak Arjun out. So I pretend to say a prayer with joined hands and he grins. Whatever, I'm not going to let him dampen my excitement.

Honestly, I never thought getting married would be such a thrill—even after the extravagant wedding shopping was over.

I know, I know—there's the togetherness part and the always-with-Arjun part, but I thought that would be *it*—and mind you, I was very happy with that. But turns out there is a lot more buzz to a marriage than one imagines. For example, the honeymoon was awesome. A-W-E-S-O-M-E. The dinners with numerous friends and relatives were pretty cool too—you get to dress up, put on a lot of makeup and just keep smiling.

The month after the wedding went by quickly and suddenly it was time to leave for Pathankot—that's where Arjun is posted.

Our home—*our own home*! Yaay! Maybe I'll daydream about it for the next fifteen bloody minutes.

The house is perfect.

Just perrrr-fect. Fifteen minutes in the house and I am still dumbstruck. It is overwhelming.

In a block of four houses, ours is the one on the left, ground floor. It has two bedrooms, an outhouse and a huge garden that lines the house on three sides. The garden is so awesome that I can already picture myself sitting on a comfortable chair, sipping hot coffee and reading some glossy magazine about smart gardening techniques.

Mesmerized, I walk through the house, running my hand over the stark white walls. Apart from the fact that my hands become all white and dry, it's a fulfilling gesture—caressing my house with love. Trying to get the paint off my hands, I float spellbound into the garden.

Honestly, I must have a natural knack for gardening or something, because I feel inspired; I'm already visualizing pretty trees and rows of lovely flowers.

Oh god, maybe I can get into bonsai, now that I have this huge space.

'Here you are!'

Arjun breaks my trance, and as I turn around to face him, my heart leaps. Arjun, all handsome and stunning, is smiling at me against the backdrop of our house. Oh, the scene is gorgeous. GORGEOUS!

I smile back at him. He leads me to the kitchen and asks if it is okay. I nod sweetly. What do I know about kitchens? I have never cooked anything in my life, except for boiling an egg and burning some Maggi for my little sister, Anya. I have a passion for not cooking. Tell me your favourite dish and I'll burn it for you. I've told Arjun about this a thousand times, but he is still going on and on about how the drawers are state-of-the-art and how the chimney (yes, those things actually exist) has been closed for safety purposes. I have a feeling he thinks I've been downplaying my cooking skills. Boy, is he in for a shock. But no problem—I've already married him, he can't change his mind.

The house has a few pieces of fauji furniture already—a couple of single couches in red, a few tables in every possible size, a small and sturdy olive-green almirah, and something I thought was a bedside table or a small wall-mountable mandir but is actually a shoe rack of some kind. The furniture is already arranged in the house and all we need to do is store our clothes in the wardrobes, put sheets on the mattresses and start living our lives. Wonderful.

After checking out every corner of the house and every tap in the bathroom, both of us settle on the couch and sit in happy silence. It's time to reach out and kiss him passionately, according to the plan that I carefully formulated on our two-day drive from Delhi to Pathankot.

I had decided that our *first* make-out session in our *first* house should blow his mind, in a good I-can't-get-enough-of-it way, you know? So I'd bought the latest *Cosmopolitan* from Jalandhar, where we had stopped for grub, and I can now recite the *How To Touch A Naked Man—16 Naughty Strokes That Will Send Him Over The Edge* article. By the way, did you know there are various erogenous spots in men's bodies as well—like the T-Spot and the R-Spot? Like the G-Spot mystery wasn't enough. Weird.

So anyway, here I am, quickly applying a fresh coat of my raspberry-flavoured lip gloss, about to grab his collar and start with a steamy kiss in the first ever living room of our life together, when a deafening scream pierces the silence, making me jump back in shock.

'*Jai Hind Saaaaaaaab!*'

It's coming from the front porch.

This can't be good, right? I feel a surge of panic. Arjun is being called for an emergency operation against terrorists right away! On our *first* day in our *first* bloody house!

'Don't go!' I whisper, my voice half-strangled by nerves.

'What?' Arjun says distractedly, getting up and running his hands over his barely-creased shirt.

'Don't go for the operation. Please,' I whisper, now clutching his arm.

'Huh?' He isn't even looking at me, just retying his shoelace in a hurry. Avoiding eye contact is definitely a sign that something is dreadfully wrong, isn't it?

'The voices . . . outside . . . who . . .?' I manage, nearly out of breath by now.

'Oh,' he says. 'They are my men.' He shrugs casually. 'They are here to meet me. Us, I mean.'

They are my men?

His MEN? That doesn't sound right, does it? What does he mean, *his men*? I look at him, uncomprehending, but he isn't paying any attention to me. Instead, he scoots over to the door. So much for first-time-in-house plan, I sigh.

A minute later, Arjun re-enters the room, and behind him are five tall, sturdy men in uniforms—and beat this—all have big furry moustaches. I giggle. FYI, I giggle a lot. A *lot*, really. Which is a good thing, I think. I mean, being happy is a good thing, right? And since Arjun has never said anything about it till now, I assumed he likes it. But apparently he does not, because this time Arjun shoots me a stern behave-yourself look. Maybe he's tired after all the driving, I think. He introduces all five men to me and each one greets me with a, 'Namaste Memsaab.'

Memsaab?

Me? Can you believe it? Maybe it's a joke. I want to giggle again, but Arjun is giving me that look, so I just nod and smile brightly. Doesn't Arjun get it? I've just been called 'memsaab', and there isn't a hint of a grin on his face.

I just *have to* share this with someone normal and get the reaction it deserves, so while Arjun gets busy talking to 'his men' about some strange stuff like BPET, falling in, papa battery, I grab my cell phone and text my sister.

Attention earthlings, I am now a MEMSAAB.

Anya replies promptly, within seconds, just the response I wished for.

OMG MEMSAAB? Where are you—16th century?

See? This is a *normal* reaction from a *normal* person. Stupid Arjun! I'll deal with him later. For now, let me revel in the glory of being a memsaab. No one has ever called me that, ever—okay, to be honest, no one has ever addressed to me as madam or ma'am either. I come from a completely civil family—civil, as in non-Army—and who in normal non-Army life uses words like this anymore? I've only heard it in old black and white movies. And now, suddenly I'm not just Pia, I'm something more—something magnificent.

Memsaab!

By now Anya must have told Mom and Dad, I'm sure. I know that no one in my family will ever believe it, ha!

I suddenly feel very pleased with myself and very memsaab-like. I like the Army already. Smiling in what I think is true memsaab-like fashion, I get up gracefully to do some memsaab-like thing—maybe throw a sheet on the bed? I glide towards my huge red suitcase to fish for the lovely green and white bed sheet set my aunt gifted us. I've barely unlocked the suitcase, though, when two of Arjun's men come running towards me.

'I'm sorry!' I yell and back away from the suitcase.

'I'll do it, Memsaab,' the taller one says. Arjun had introduced him as Ganga Singh earlier, but I'm not sure how to address him. Ganga ji?

I just shake my head and say, 'Nahi, I'll do it. Thank you.'

But he has already bent down and is now holding the suitcase open for me.

'Oh. Okay,' I mutter and dive in. It takes me some time but I successfully retrieve the bed sheets, along with a few clothes.

'Thank you,' I say to him, and he promptly reaches for the sheet.

'I'll do it, Memsaab.'

I have to admit, this is really intimidating for me. Never in my life has anyone wanted to do stuff for me so badly. It is so touching, I think I might cry. I am already warming up to this Ganga Singh person, in spite of his six-foot two frame and his moustache. I hand over the bed sheet and walk over to the couch smiling. I feel particularly celebrated. Arjun is still talking about some boring office stuff with the other men, and when he looks over at me, I beam beautifully.

'You want something?' he asks and immediately decides I am about to say something totally stupid like 'You!' so quickly adds, 'Coffee? Juice?'

It's annoying how he just assumes the wrong thing all the time. I so wasn't going to say 'You'. Honest.

Okay, maybe I wanted to, but I wouldn't have said it in front of these men.

'Coffee would be great,' I say.

One of the men scoots out of the house as if on cue.

'Wassup with him?' I ask Arjun. 'Did he just walk off?'

'He didn't "walk off", Pia. He's getting you coffee from the Mess.'

'Oh,' I say, and shrug as if someone rushing to get me coffee before I've fully articulated the desire for it is perfectly normal.

After our coffee and what seems like hours, Arjun's men finally leave after wishing me again. By now I'm totally exhausted. I just want to fall on the bed and sleep for two days, but Arjun—who is surprisingly upbeat now and not at all tired in spite of driving for so long—tells me that we have to go to the Officers' Mess for dinner at twenty-one hundred hours. I count; that's 9 o'clock.

'Oh no!' I cry. 'I don't want to eat! I just want to sleep.'

'I know you're tired, baby,' he sits next to me and tousles my hair—*finally!*—'but the Bachelors will be waiting for us. It'll be quick, I promise.' Bachelors are the unmarried officers who eat in the Officers' Mess every day. It's one of the things I know about the Army already, thanks to one-and-a-half years of dating Arjun.

But I'm really worn out, and it's not fair to drag me somewhere just because some people I've never met are waiting for us. I immediately want to throw a tantrum, or at least get out of the dinner somehow, but then I remember—I'm his wife now. I should be supportive and reasonable. Yes, this is the right time to make that important transition from a difficult girlfriend to a considerate wife. *It's only dinner*, I tell myself. No big deal.

'Okay,' I say.

'That's my girl,' he says, smiling happily.

'It's only eight o'clock now, though. What do you suppose we can do in the meantime?' I ask, in what I think is a seductive way, and a slow smile spreads across Arjun's face.

'I do have a few interesting things in mind,' he says, unbuttoning his shirt and walking towards me.

This is perfect. Maybe not exactly what I had planned—

Ooh. Mmm.

Actually, this is better than anything I could have planned.

chapter two

Discoveries of the Ultimate Party Girl

In my one week as an Army wife—commonly referred to as a 'lady'—here are the things I've learned:

- You cannot just waltz into the Officers' Mess if you are dressed in jeans and a tank top. The dress code for the Officers' Mess is *strictly formal*, which means that for the past one week, I've been wearing either a saree or a salwar kameez every night. Not that I mind. I love dressing up.
- Apparently officers are not 'men'. Officers are 'officers', and only other ranks—OR in short—are referred to as 'men' or 'jawans'.
- I cannot call the 'men', i.e., jawans, i.e., ORs (as explained above) 'men' or 'jawans'. I have to call them by name, adding 'bhaiya' or 'saab' depending on their rank (which is something that isn't quite clear to me as yet). So Arjun's buddy or helper or sahayak—explained below—is to be called Ganga bhaiya.
- The buddies / helpers / sahayaks are trained soldiers who have generally been with an officer for a long time. A

'helper' is an old term for a soldier who is an officer's combat buddy—his radio operator, his bodyguard and partner in war-times. In no-war times, he helps the officer arrange his various uniforms, games dress, name tags, stars and other accessories (or accoutrements in Arjun's language) that go on those various uniforms. He is also the runner that conveys orders from officer to subordinates, and also the officer's drivers under combat conditions. He helps an officer so the latter can devote maximum time to the responsibilities of command. In most cases, the sahayak-officer relationship goes back longer than the wife-officer one. Hmmph.

- As a 'lady', I have to get accustomed to being addressed as Mrs Arjun or Mrs Mehra by other officers' wives, 'Ma'am' by all the officers and 'Memsaab' by all the men. Good lord.

- Calling other officers and their wives by their first names is a no-no. So even if a couple of Arjun's fellow officers are really nice and we hit it off well, I have to still call them by their rank and last name.

- The food cooked at the Officers' Mess is *awesome*. It's like dining in a five-star hotel with super service. The cook in Arjun's Mess makes especially yummy Continental food.

Quite a list, huh? A bit overwhelming for a regular non-fauji girl like me, but I'm learning fast.

Arjun tells me that I'm going to be officially welcomed in the Unit next week; there's going to be a party. Yaay! Everyone, including the Commanding Officer (the CO), and all the wives will be there. I haven't met any of the ladies yet, or any officer senior to Arjun, so I am extremely excited.

The welcome party is called a 'high tea'—yes, 'high' and not 'hi!' like I thought at first. I think hi! tea would have been better—you know, saying 'hi!' for the first time and having tea together? When I found out it was actually 'high' I was quite disappointed. I'm just a normal civilian, spoilt even more by a job in a TV channel, where 'high' would have meant joints after the tea party. Highly unlikely in fauj.

When I announced my engagement to friends and colleagues, a lot of them came up to me and said thing like, 'Way to go, hot Army wife, you!' and, 'All set be one of those sexy Army wives, huh?'

I now wonder if they were being sarcastic.

Or ironic, maybe.

Don't get me wrong. Army wives *are* stylish. But there's no chance at all for them to be sexy, or even remotely hot. Army wives have to dress up in formals (sarees or salwar kameezes) at every occasion, since every occasion is formal in fauj. The slightest show of skin is a no-no, and even a sleeveless blouse can bring you grief sometimes—true story (more on that later).

Then what is it that makes civilians see Army wives as style divas, I wonder.

I remember the excitement generated in my physics tuition class when the very ordinary-looking new girl stepped out of an Army Gypsy (a uniformed man opened the door for her). Instantly threatened, all the girls broke out into a major bitching session, picking on her frizzy hair and messy handwriting. The boys were slack-jawed over the girl. I don't know what it is—perhaps there's a sense of mystery surrounding everything connected to the Army.

I also remember noticing Army moms in my school PTAs and thinking they were bold dressers. After Arjun proposed, I often pictured myself in an über cool short dress, sipping on a lemon soda and laughing a sexy throaty laugh instead of my pathetic high-pitched giggle—the dream Army wife life.

Reality, however, is completely different.

Before the high tea, Arjun lectures me endlessly about the importance of appropriate attire in the Army, leaving me extremely nervous.

'Does "Formal Dress Code" include Western formals?' I ask, remembering my perfectly-cut blazer and pencil skirt.

'Formal means Indian formals,' he says gently.

'*Every* party?' I ask, heartbroken.

'Yes, I'm afraid,' he replies in an apologetic tone, like he's the one who came up with the rule.

I am nonetheless irritated with him.

'Then when do I get to wear my normal clothes?' I wail like a child who's been told she cannot wear her pink fairy wings to her math exam.

'There are informal parties, like Social Evenings,' he offers.

'Um. Can I wear *anything* for those?'

'Well . . . mainly salwar kameezes. But in winter you can wear jeans and a long coat, yes,' he says happily, unaware of my heart breaking into tiny pieces.

'All my clothes are going to die unworn,' I say, miserable.

'You can wear *anything* when we're on holiday!' Arjun says brightly, really happy to have found a solution to my woes.

'Yeah? And when will that be—once a year?' I retort.

'Twice,' he smiles innocently and even looks quite pleased with himself. Good lord.

Later, I found out that an Army wife has a lot of rules to follow—and I mean a *lot*. But the one I learn fastest is that an Army wife has to be dressed properly at all times. Here you are subjected to constant scrutiny, largely because of the constant presence of jawans around you and your house. You have to dress properly (read fully covered) in their presence, and they're almost always around—to clean, or garden, or get your signature for various Ladies' Club circulars.

Anyway, before going to the high tea, I am both sad and anxious. I try on three sarees and two salwar kameezes before settling for a subtle caramel saree in Italian crepe, with elegant cut work on the border. For some reason, I find myself wishing I had a high-neck blouse to go with it, just to be safe.

'Who were those women wearing skirts with slits to my school PTA meetings?' I say to no one in particular.

'Hmm?' mumbles Arjun, who is trying to figure out his tie. I look at him—in the confusion of finding the perfect outfit, I hadn't noticed how hot he's looking in the dark suit he's wearing.

'Those Army moms from my school gave me entirely wrong ideas and were a very bad influence on my innocent mind,' I say, knowing I am being totally unreasonable. But it's hardly my fault, right? Think about all the sexy tops I've splurged on for after the wedding. What a waste! I shed a silent tear for them.

'Those bitches,' says Arjun, and an unwilling grin spreads across my face.

When I am done dressing up, I am extremely pleased with myself. I've paired my saree with extremely high-heeled nude sling backs and hope some lady at the party will notice and compliment them.

No one does.

We are back home and I am taking out the various safety pins I'd stuck into my saree, and feeling deflated. No one noticed. No one even commented on the saree, which I think is totally un-cool behaviour. Yes, I accept that I didn't quite get the draping right, but then I'm not used to tying a bloody saree every day! A little encouragement would have been nice.

Also, the high tea thing was nothing like a party. Not even *close* to a party.

I mean, it isn't a party if you can't let your hair down, drink and eat as you like, laugh a lot and maybe dance a bit, right?

In fact, it was not even the non-party type party at your close friend's place where you can turn up in your old sweatpants, eat loads of ice cream and gossip all night. Nope. This was a *very* formal affair, like the morning prayer session in my school— totally unnecessary, completely despised and yet followed religiously for some unknown reason. I was super bored, to say the least.

Among the few good things about it though, was the finger-licking array of snacks and meeting the other officers' wives, who were all cool as cucumbers, dressed impeccably in beautiful sarees and perfectly made up. The elegance quotient in the room was sky high. Everyone spoke gently, even the women— quite contrary to those I've known till now, including myself.

While no one seemed particularly excited or curious about me, they were all extremely pleasant and welcomed me warmly.

Arjun had warned me before coming to Pathankot not to expect people to hug and air-kiss in the Army circle; they are a different crowd altogether—almost alien compared to my friends back in Delhi. But their politeness was genuine and the gentlemanlike behaviour bowled me over.

By the end of it, I decided I'm okay with formal and pleasant; I have enough crazy, shouting and hugging people in my life already. I could use some civilized folks, right? So I guess no compliments are all right. For now.

I learned another thing to keep in mind while I'm in the Officers' Mess—Do Not Get Up From Your Chair.

Why, you ask?

Well, if you don't want every officer in the room—some of them almost the age of your father—jumping to their feet every time *you* get up, you better glue your ass to that chair, girlfriend.

Yes, it's true.

During the high tea, when I got up for the first time (to go to the ladies' room), all conversation ceased and all laughter died in a snap. Every officer in the room got up, their eyes on me.

I froze.

It felt like I'd accidently stepped on forbidden territory and now everyone was ready to pounce on me. Arjun quickly grabbed my arm before I could start blabbering incoherent apologies, and said, 'I'll show you the ladies' room.'

The ladies' room was labelled 'Queens' and was stacked with everything a woman could need in a washroom—from three types of hair brushes to lipsticks, fresh towels and even a packet of Whisper kept discreetly inside a drawer. *Of course*, I opened every drawer; what did you think?

I found it all very fascinating. But then I returned to the dining room and every officer got up *again*. Again, there was silence. I could feel my cheeks growing redder and redder. I almost told them to chillax, seriously.

The major letdown for me, however, is the realization that I'll never find a friend, a true companion amongst these women. Sure, we'll be friendly and we'll share anecdotes over coffee, but there won't be a close gal-pal equation with anyone here. I might as well kiss goodbye to all hopes of long bitching sessions and any girls-only shopping trips.

'What do you want a friend for?' Arjun is a little shocked when I tell him.

'Why not?' I reply at once. 'I'm not asking for a best friend. Not a soul sister. I have plenty in Delhi thankyouverymuch. Just someone who will laugh, gossip and have fun with me. Maybe go for walks together.' I am sulking now.

'Come on, baby. What difference does it make anyway? We'll be moving from one place to another every other year. In fauj, you'll make more friends than you can handle, just take it easy.'

He doesn't understand, of course. This is his profession. He isn't emotional about it, like I wasn't at my job with the TV channel. Fair enough, I think, suddenly seeing some sense in what he's saying.

'Also, you have me. And you know how much I love gossip,' Arjun says and winks. He hates gossip. In fact, he is hopeless when it comes to discussing other people and making fun of them. Gossip with him is no fun. But he's super cute, especially when he winks and tries to make me feel better.

I giggle. And just like that it goes from bad to sweet.

chapter three

Combating Temptation and Competition

Did I tell you how handsome Arjun is?

Not to show off or anything, but he is *extremely* good looking, and when he smiles, he is dazzling. My heart melts every time he smiles and winks at me. My stomach gives a nervous flip each time his eyes meet mine in a crowded place. I figure I'll get used to his charm eventually.

Obviously this is not what he wants. Because he dresses up in combat uniform every morning. I find myself numb at the sight, every bloody time. Numb with desire, of course.

It's embarrassing, really. It's all I can do to stop myself from wildly tearing the uniform off him right then.

What is it about Army uniforms? Especially combats. They are just drool-worthy, if you ask me. In fact, I think I might have a crush on Arjun in combats, and it's so strong that I want to put my personal stamp on him when he's wearing it.

So, one morning, just as he is kissing my forehead before leaving for work, I strategically kiss him on his collar. He smiles, ruffles my hair and leaves, unaware of the hot pink

SOLDIER & SPICE 21

lipstick mark sitting proudly on his collar. I feel quite pleased with myself. He will notice it sometime during the day and it will remind him of our deep passion. Maybe I should be ready for an intense make-out session when he comes back for lunch.

Arjun comes for lunch at about two in the afternoon and my excitement instantly dies. On his collar, instead of my perfect plump lip-mark, sits an ugly blotch that isn't even close to my perfect hot pink shade! It looks like dirt.

'Where is my lipstick mark?' I ask immediately.

'What?' he says, and then realizing that I'm staring at his collar, he says, 'Oh, that. You saw it?'

'Saw it?' I echo incredulously. 'I put it there!'

'You put it there?' he looks puzzled. 'Why?'

'Because . . .' I gulp. 'I like this uniform.'

I know it doesn't make any sense *now*, but it did when I decided to plant that kiss-mark as a sign of my love. I love the uniform, and I love him in the uniform, and it seemed like a logical thing to do. Arjun is looking at me curiously.

'I thought you'd see it while you're working and that it would make you happy. And loved,' I say quickly.

'Pia!' he says with an amused smile. 'And I thought it got there by mistake!'

Which means he didn't think anything was out of the ordinary when I suddenly decided to slather on hot pink lipstick while still wearing my nightdress. How depressing.

'Where did it go?' I ask.

'I had to get it off my uniform, so I rubbed it with a wet

cloth,' he says, craning his neck to look at the smudge. 'Didn't come off easily,' he tells me. 'Everyone saw it, even the CO.'

'Oh.'

It hadn't even occurred to me that other people would see my piece of art, I swear. That must have been a little awkward for him.

'Sorry . . .' I say, and run a finger over the mark. Wasn't the lipstick supposed to be long-lasting?

'No sweat,' Arjun takes my hand and weaves his fingers through mine. 'Don't do it again, though. I feel loved plenty.'

Despite my complete indifference, my kitchen is all set up. We have got everything required, and the ration allotted to Arjun has started coming. There are, among other things, eggs, pulses, flour, condiments (spices in normal language) and a packet a day of milk and bread. If I were an enthusiastic cook, I assume I would be thrilled about all this. But I am no cook. Anything I cook—after long phone calls with my irritated mother explaining a recipe to me—ends up burnt.

The good thing is that Arjun doesn't make a fuss about black scrambled eggs or pasta.

'No worries baby,' he said when I burnt my fingers trying to handle a hot pan and declared that the kitchen was haunted. 'I'll make you some Maggi and we'll go out for pizza in the evening.'

Did I tell you that I love him?

However, I know this can't go on forever, so I've devised a plan. My agenda for the next few weeks includes taking care of the supplies, buying boxes and containers, and taking a shot at making at least one thing every day.

With the help of my hysterical mother-in-law, who is an extremely good cook, I have put up a chart on the refrigerator door. It's secured by very cute magnets. I placed a bid on these adorable little wooden magnets on eBay and I won! They're bright and instant mood-lifters. There's a smiling blue whale that I particularly love and . . . oh yes, the chart.

BREAKFAST

Omelette: Break eggs in a bowl, beat. Add salt + pepper. Add chopped green chillies, onions. On a flat pan, pour over heated butter. Turn once and heat until cooked. *Experience: Measure salt ALWAYS. Pepper has to be crushed, or better, BUY BLACK PEPPER POWDER. Butter should not be heated so much that it turns blackish-brown, the burnt taste doesn't go. Never pour the entire egg mixture on the flat pan all at once, it could splash and get on your favourite white top. (Note: Send white Zara top for dry cleaning.)*

French toast: Break eggs in a bowl, beat. Add salt + pepper. Dip a slice of bread in egg. Shallow fry on a flat pan in butter. *Experience: Bread slice will always break; use salt with precaution as it can always be sprinkled on top if less, and pepper powder doesn't dissolve on its own—if not whisked properly, it just sits in a big lump, and the big lump tends to come in one bite of one slice. Also, use very little pepper, just in case.*

Scrambled egg and toast: Easy-peasy. Heat butter in a frying pan. Break eggs directly in the pan and immediately begin scrambling them like crazy. They stick a lot, but will eventually be okay. Add salt + pepper. Can also add chopped onions, green chillies, tomatoes, etc., if you have time. *Experience: Really easy. Make every day.*

Bread and butter + jam: Cancel jam from the to-buy list, there is a surplus from ration anyway. Also, check the expiry date on jam bottles and cheese tins; two are already ten days past the date.

Cereal with milk: Use the huge packets of cornflakes that have come in ration and are taking up a lot of space in the kitchen.

Sprouts: Buy ready-to-eat packets from the vegetable truck.

Lunch / Dinner

Pasta: Instant pasta. Follow instructions on the packet.

Sprouts in spices: Use the sprouts from breakfast, heat oil and add salt, red chilli powder, etc., and stir.

Dal-rice: Call Mom for dal tadka.

Fried rice: Use rice from the previous meal, heat oil, add onions/tomatoes/garlic, etc. Add rice + spices.

Everything seems to be under control.

The only issue is Ganga bhaiya. He's invariably around the entire morning and every evening, politely telling me what 'Saab' would prefer and what 'Saab' will not like. 'Memsaab, that earthen vase Saab got from Bikaner should be painted black. Saab likes black.' Or, 'Memsaab, should I move the couch to the left of the room? Saab likes to sit next to the balcony.' *Or,* 'No, no Memsaab, don't cook cabbage. Saab never eats it except in Chinese food.'

I *am* grateful for Ganga bhaiya: he doesn't talk much and is very resourceful. He has 'connections' in the Military Engineering Services (MES in short, responsible for our house maintenance) and has thus managed to get us the best furniture available, *and* brand new fans (which, I'm told, is a big deal). He has a special interest in gardening as well, so my kitchen garden has been dug, seeds have been planted, and we are now waiting for garlic, sweet pea, spinach and tomatoes to grow. Imagine having my own supplies to conjure up delicious food for my Army man to eat and marvel at. Sweet.

Anyway, initially his constant stream of suggestions was fine with me—I was getting useful info about Arjun, which one can learn only when you live together. So the vase was painted black instead of gold, and Arjun loved it. The couch was indeed moved to the left of the living room, and though Arjun didn't seem to notice it, he did sit on it for five minutes last week so maybe it counts. And of course I didn't cook any cabbage; I hate it too.

But now it has gotten uncomfortable. The moment Arjun comes home in the evening and I'm busy giving him a download of everything that happened during the day, Ganga bhaiya quietly slips in and asks—'Saab, coffee?'

It is unacceptable! I am the wife. I will get the damn coffee for Arjun, not him! And what is he doing here anyway, behaving like a dedicated wife, trying to steal my thunder?

And that isn't even the end of it.

He insists on getting Arjun's dry clothes in from the backyard and folding them neatly before taking them to the iron-man. The man who irons the clothes, I mean, not *the* Iron Man. (Which reminds me, don't you think Gerald Butler would have made a better Iron Man? Right?)

Anyway, the entire clothes situation is really awkward for me because hanging in my backyard with Arjun's clothes are usually my clothes too—you know, lingerie and everything, which I generally hide under Arjun's tees. The whole purpose of not letting them dry in full view is completely defeated when Ganga bhaiya mechanically picks up Saab's clothes.

So after a weeklong drama of running towards the clothes the moment I see him there or trying to dry my lingerie inside my room, under the fan (not recommended at all—unless you're ready to wash all your lingerie in Dettol every weekend and wait two days for a bra to dry), I finally ask him to stop. I will give him a bag of clothes every second day for ironing, I tell him. He looks like I've just asked him to stop breathing.

Arjun laughs it off when I complain about Ganga bhaiya's zealousness.

'He's been with me for a long time. Maybe that's why,' Arjun says.

'It's very strange,' I say.

'He's a good chap,' he shrugs.

'But he has to let go!' I protest.

'It's just clothes,' Arjun says mildly. 'Let him do it.'

'It's not *just* clothes!' I wail. 'And he has to realize I'm your wife!'

'Don't overreact. It's nothing,' says Arjun with a grin. 'Pia—' he reaches for my hand, but I pull it away.

'*I'm* overreacting!' I exclaim. I just can't believe it, this is ridiculous. 'He thinks I can't take care of you and your stupid clothes?'

'Relax Pia. He's just doing his job.'

OMG. Arjun's so naïve!

'If it's just his job, then why is he so possessive about you?' I ask morosely.

'He is not.'

'He so is,' I say in a defiant tone. 'He doesn't let me do anything for you. It's like dealing with a vindictive ex-girlfriend who is still trying to win you back.'

Arjun sighs. He really is clueless.

It comes to you when you're not looking. . . . That's what they say about love, isn't it? I met Arjun when I wasn't looking for a relationship, let alone an always-and-forever one. I'd recently gotten out of a shitty relationship where the boyfriend will be referred to as bastard and me, the sufferer. I had been going out with this particular bastard for over six months and he was driving me crazy with his huge ego. I'd never been too good with relationships anyway, so I ended it one day—only to have him stalk me for a month.

As a result, I'd sworn off men at the time I met Arjun, and like a cliché—before I knew it—I was falling for him. He claims it was love at first sight for him, but I doubt that very much. I was smoking a Navy Cut when he was introduced to me by a colleague at some random wedding, and I was wearing the most unflattering flat chappals. If I'd only known I was about to meet my soul mate at that blessed wedding, I'd have put on some heels and not been taking deep drags from a cigarette like a junkie. I still smoke sometimes, rarely, but Arjun has managed to upgrade me to Marlboro Lights. And honestly, I plan on giving up soon. If the Army has a list of all things un-ladylike, smoking would be in the top three, just after stripping down at a social evening.

Back to the you-find-it-when-you're-not-looking thing: You remember how I'd given up hope of finding an Army-Wife-Best-Friend-Forever—in short, AW-BFF—since I'd met the wives of the other officers that day at the Mess. I decided to content myself with hour-long phone conversations with my sister and my friends in Delhi. I was, in fact, talking on the phone to Anya, my younger sister, when Ganga bhaiya announced that tiny spinach leaves had appeared in our kitchen garden. Excited, I hung up immediately and ran to check them out.

Such an emotional moment! My first ever spinach leaves in my first ever kitchen garden. I felt ecstatic. I immediately filled a frying pan with water so I could water the plant. It was a great moment in my new nature-loving environment-friendly avatar—except for Ganga bhaiya telling me to be careful and not overwater the plant. Um. You can never overwater a plant, can you? I mean, there's mud there; all the water will be absorbed, eventually. Right?

So anyway, here I am in the evening, standing beside the spinach patch with a cup of coffee, trying to soak in all the nature and half-wishing someone would teach me how to cook it once it's fully grown—when suddenly my ears catch parts of a conversation from somewhere nearby and I snap to attention.

'—and if they don't listen to you babe, just tell them to fuck off and resign. You'll get a better job anytime you want babe, you know you rock!'

My heart stops.

Someone is speaking in my language.

I look around and spot a petite girl in the adjoining garden, talking on the phone. I stare at her for a second; my heart is now beating faster and my skin is all prickly. I take a few steps towards her. She looks up, our eyes meet and I know I have indeed found a friend—peeping from her shiny brown curly hair is a gleaming strand of bright red lying proudly on her shoulder.

I can already picture the two of us getting pedicures together and encouraging each other to buy an orange lipstick. I smile at the image in my mind, my eyes misty, and she waves at me with a bright smile.

chapter four

My Elementary Education: Guide to the Army-Wife Life Part 1

It's about a week since my first meeting with my AW-BFF.

Aka Mrs Sharma.

Aka Naina.

(She insists I call her by her first name even though Captain Sharma is a year senior to Arjun. 'I have a name of my own, you know,' she said the first day we met. So I call her Naina.)

We're chatting over a cup of coffee in my house. Our husbands have had lunch, an hour's nap, and are off to the office again. Her husband is in another Unit that I don't care to *and* cannot even-if-I-want-to remember (the names and number of Units are really just random and make no sense to me whatsoever), and she's my next door neighbour. She's from Pune, has been married for almost a year and is completely my soul sister. That red strand in her brown hair was truly a sign from the universe. That had to be someone like me!

Being married in the Army for about eleven months now, Naina has way more experience than me, and she instantly assumes the position of my mentor. She says that it's okay to be overwhelmed by the Army-Wife life in the beginning—she had loads of trouble too. Understandable: any normal person would be overwhelmed; I know that by now. But the important thing, according to her, is to realize and appreciate the power vested in an Army wife's hands, the perks that only we enjoy. Perks, I am familiar with by now. But powers . . .?

'What kind of powers?' I ask.

'Like helping people and stuff,' she says in a matter-of-fact way.

'What people?' I ask.

'You know, people,' she gestures vaguely.

I nod, pretending to understand. You don't want to come across as a complete fool to your mentor, you know. At least, not this soon in the relationship.

Instead, I say, 'It's *so* different from regular life!'

'Yes, it is. It is very different,' she nods in agreement. 'The people, the vast social circle, the culture—everything is quite different from civil life.'

'Yes, the people! I mean, what's up with the ladies? So dull and un-happening!' I say with exasperation.

'Now, Pia,' she leans in a bit, in an about-to-reveal-a-secret way. I lean in automatically. 'You never talk about Army ladies like that. *Never.*'

'Oh,' I say. I feel a bit shamefaced: I should not be talking to a potential BFF in a manner that sounds outright bitchy. It is not a quality one looks forward to discovering right away (though of course we will get to it eventually!). I look sheepishly at her. She doesn't appear upset by my stupidity.

'In fact,' she is saying, 'you should never talk about the ladies.'

'What?' This, I don't understand. What is left to talk about then? The crop of extremely bitter spinach in my backyard? Ugh. I don't even think it's spinach. It's just some gross weed unsuitable for consumption by any living being.

'Don't worry,' Naina says. And then breaks into song. '*Main hun naaaa*!' she sings in her shrill voice.

One thing you should know about Naina, is that she's obsessed with Bollywood; she invariably inserts random movie dialogues and songs in general conversation. I'm still not used to it.

'I'm there for you, no, Pia! I'll tell you everything you need to know about this life—from my own experience,' she says, looking like her life's purpose has suddenly dawned on her.

'Great,' I say, keeping up with the excitement.

Wasting no time, she starts giving me pointers that, she says, are mandatory for an Army wife to know and/or follow. Personally, I'm not sure how much of this is correct gyan, but here's the download anyway:

- Never say 'no' to any task given to you by a senior lady, until you become friendly. (These tasks can vary from dancing to a filmy number at a Ladies' Meet, participating in a salad competition, or inspecting the various vocational course classes that are arranged for the OR wives.) After you become friendly with the senior lady, never say 'no', just suggest your discomfort or inability to do the task and hope like hell that she won't force you.

- Never talk about the ladies. Never discuss one lady with another. Army is an extremely small world where everyone talks about everyone, nothing is a secret and hence, gossip can get messy. It might get you in trouble with the senior ladies, and really, that's the last thing you want.

- Needless to say, never bitch about any lady. If you are completely delusional, have an I-don't-care attitude and go around bitching anyway, than you should be forewarned that you are walking into a potential minefield. The I-don't-care routine works in civil life, yes. Not in Army. Here, it will *always* come back to hit you like a boomerang.

- Remember the rank structure like your last name. Army is nothing without its structure, its hierarchy. Army chief is the senior-most officer in the Indian Army. The general officer commanding, or the GOC, is a major general in rank and is the top officer in a division. The commander, a brigadier in rank, commands a brigade and the commanding officers, or COs, command a unit. Never confuse GOC for JCO; the latter is a junior commissioned officer, which is between an officer and a jawan. Apparently Naina made this mistake once and shudders at the memory. When she sees that I'm still confused about the ranks, she says, 'Haven't you seen *LOC Kargil*? Or *Border*? They're not accurate, but they give you an idea. And, you'll learn with time.' She pats my hand and hums *Sandese aate hain* in a low voice.

- The CO's wife is called the First Lady of the Unit and requires your full respect and attention at all times. Stand when she's standing, sit after she sits and eat only when she tells you to. She's usually a complete bitch, but if you're lucky, she'll just ignore you.

- *Never* text the CO's wife inquiring about maids. Or about electricity at the gym. Yes, Naina did this when she was new—sent an SMS to the CO's wife asking if the maid, who worked at both houses, had come yet. The rest, she says, is written in the history of her husband's Unit and his personal performance report. And yes, there is a Unit history that is maintained religiously.

- Always wish the senior ladies. Never pretend not to see them—they notice *everything*. Naina once tried to hide behind a row of Tupperware in the Army Canteen when she saw the deputy commander's wife—only because she was having a bad hair day (which, according to me, is a very good reason to hide). She got a phone call from her CO's wife the next day, demanding an explanation for her appalling behaviour, followed by a lecture on decorum.
- When in doubt, wear a saree to all fauji functions. A few senior ladies are very particular about dress code, and defying it will be seen as bad behaviour.
- If the senior ladies think you're a complete bitch, their husbands will take it out on your husband through his performance report. (Scary, this one!)
- When attending any Ladies' Meet, wish everyone, even if they have no idea who the hell you are, and then try to be invisible.
- Never expect to win any raffle/lucky draw prizes at the Ladies' Meet. It is heartbreaking, but Naina has noticed that, generally, only the CO and commander's wives get lucky and win prizes. Hmm.
- But no reason to fret, because the prizes are not worth lusting after anyway—they're either boring crystal stuff (the Army is obsessed with crystal) or fancy candles made in fauji workshops. There are exceptions, of course, but don't get your hopes too high.
- When attending meetings organised to plan an upcoming Ladies' Meet (the planning and practice meetings), keep your lips zipped at all times. Do not offer any help, any suggestion or any bright idea that you might have—if you do, you'll have to execute your bright idea all alone, and

from that day onwards, you'll find yourself doing the same thing *forever*. Also, your CO's wife will get very upset about the 'wastage' of the Unit's time and resources, even if it's only *you* who is doing everything and no Unit resources are being utilized.

'That's priceless info, Naina,' I say earnestly, while sipping my herbal tea—herbal bloody tea! Look what's happened to me!— 'You're a rock-star,' I say.

'Yeah, I know,' she shrugs and flashes me a smile. 'I wish I had someone like me when I was new here.' She then proceeds to sing a line from some old song, '*Koi hotaaaa, jisko apna hum apna keh sakte yaaron . . .*'

This time, I don't mind. One does need special guidance sometimes.

Arjun takes me out for a lavish dinner at a new Chinese restaurant after I blackmail him with the you-are-not-giving-me-enough-time thing. It's unbelievable how it always works. Every time Arjun succumbs to this routine, I can't help but feel a little guilty. Of course we spend enough time together—we have all our meals together, including lunch, which I think is great because I haven't seen anyone from the corporate world ditch work and come home for lunch, right? Plus we go to so many parties and lunches/dinners together. So, no, time isn't an issue with me; I just play that card to get out of cooking.

After eating yummy food and getting some packed as well, we drive back to the Army Residential Area, which is huge and green and—somehow—strange to a new-to-Army girl like me.

I mean, the roads are in the best possible state—all shiny black and gleaming. It is always properly lit, and the street light poles have speakers on them, from which music emerges in the evening. Pretty damn cool, right? They call it the Walking Plaza. The Army residential area also has many alert guards, shouting 'Jai Hind Saaaaaab!' along with a crisp salute whenever an officer passes them. It is all well kept and managed, and yet it seems a bit dull to me. Where are the people? Where is the noise? Where are the meandering cows, or the terrifying stray dogs running after cars with faulty silencers? There are about fifty married officers' accommodations here, along with outhouses for maids etc., and yet there are just four people that are visible to me right now. Four!

Maybe I can shake things up a little bit, now that I live here—like, say, loudly play some Maroon 5 in the late evening to get people in an upbeat mood? I imagine standing in my garden with *One More Night* playing at maximum volume and passersby doing the moonwalk as they pass my house, after giving me a grateful 'Thank you for the music' nod. Super cool, I think and smile in Arjun's direction as he parks the car in front of our house. I've hung a huge bamboo wind chime near the door. For some reason, Arjun seems to hate it. I think it's the fact that he has to duck an entire foot while entering the house, but I don't care, it looks nice. (Plus it will add to the jazz-up-the-street plan with its shrill tinkle, right?)

Ignoring his frown at the wind chime, I ask him if he's game for a walk. There's a great children's park right outside my house, complete with brightly coloured swings and slides. He agrees and so we stroll around the park, talking about Major Rathore, an officer from Arjun's Unit, and his wife. Apparently they had a huge fight last night and today she packed her stuff and left for Jaipur, her hometown.

How do we know this, you ask?

Come on, have I taught you nothing so far?

The Army is a small world, and a Unit, even smaller. Things go around, even if they're totally unimportant bits of information, and of course, if something is supposed to be super hush-hush, it spreads like wildfire. The culprits can be many:

1. The sahayak bhaiya who is almost a permanent fixture in your house and is invariably a witness to pretty much everything that happens.
2. The housekeeping men—they go to every house every day to clean, and some can get, well, chatty. You never know.
3. The driver. He is there if the officer is late from work, he can hear the officer talking to his wife on the phone, and when the wife leaves, he is the one who drives her to wherever. Knows everything, this man.
4. The ladies. If one lady happens to have a weak moment and tells another about her troubled married life, the entire Unit will know it before you can clap your hands.
5. Wine. Some Army wives are fond of wine. And combined with marital troubles, it results in much blabbering. The truth is out within three goblets wine.

So, back to Major Rathore and his wife. Arjun thinks it isn't that big a deal and that she will return as soon as her anger subsides. I find myself wondering what if Arjun and I face a similar situation and shudder at the thought. At the same time, we pass a man, accompanied by a young boy, walking their Labrador.

Arjun immediately stops to wish him and introduces us. He is Col. Walia and he lives nearby. His dog is adorable and I instantly try to pat him on his shiny head when he attempts to hump my leg. Gross.

I jump back and shoo him off. Labradors are always horny, I've noticed. Especially Army ones. Col. Walia comes to my rescue by throwing a stick and shouting, 'Get it Bozo, get it!' Bozo runs away purposefully. I wonder how women would take it if men were also so easily distracted, quitting a lovemaking session for a stick (or an XBOX 360).

I am lost in that disturbing thought, when suddenly, it happens.

Col. Walia says to his little kid: 'Oye! Did you wish?'

Hearing this, the five- or six-year-old boy immediately snaps to attention and sings—'Good evening, Aunty.'

Very cute, I think and smile. Then I turn around to see the aunty he is wishing so sweetly. There is no one, the road is empty.

'Is someone there?' I say, squinting at the road.

'Good eveninggggg, Aunty!' he recites again, his wide eyes set on me.

I don't understand.

Could he be, like, calling me an aunty?

I freeze. I couldn't be . . .

Aunty?

This stupid kid has to be blind to call me . . . that. I think I'm glaring at the little devil when Arjun's elbow pokes my arm. 'He's wishing you, *Pia*,' he says, with extra emphasis on my name, and I see a twitch at the corner of his mouth. He is enjoying this.

'Me?' My voice comes out as a croak, my eyes wide with disbelief.

'Yes, Aunty,' the kid says, smiling sweetly. That little bastard.

By now Arjun and Col. Walia are both starting to get a little uncomfortable and Arjun jabs his elbow at me again. 'Erm . . . Good evening . . .' I manage.

'Good boy!' says a clearly delighted Col. Walia, and after wishing me himself, the father-son duo leave with Bozo running behind them.

'Aunty?' I look at Arjun when they are out of earshot. I am only twenty-six! No one should call me Aunty.

Arjun is having a fit of laughter, almost choking himself. He has no heart, really. I mean, look at me—do I look like some old constipated aunty? I'm young, I'm smart, I'm reasonably good-looking (and also very sexy, if you believe Arjun)—and I'm far from being someone's aunty. I am enraged!

'To Army kids, every officer is an Uncle and every wife is an Aunty,' Arjun says, trying to conciliate me. 'Even if the "kid" happens to be only a couple of years younger than us.'

'That is wrong on so many levels,' I say, shaking my head.

'It's Army culture. I actually think it's a good thing—kids learn manners and to respect elders. Don't you think?'

'If anyone calling me Aunty is culture, I'm going hippy and culture-less,' I hear myself saying defiantly.

'Okay,' Arjun says nicely. 'But you do know that hippies also had a certain culture, right?' I really hate him. I'm in no mood for this discussion right now anyway.

'Whatever,' I say in a dejected tone.

chapter five

I'm Coming Up, So You Better Get This Party Started!

A couple of weeks after my high tea welcome, I am busy packing away my trendy clothes (skirts, hot tops and shorts that I had planned on wearing casually at home while doing my homely chores; sigh). I'm hugging my tomato-red Mango dress, whispering promises to wear it soon, when a man in uniform knocks on my door. I need to sign something, he says very politely. Politeness is something that scores high with me, you know. And I'm the type of person who commands politeness, I think—like certain people who command respect? Hmm? Sure, my snooty boss at the TV channel was never polite to me, but then he was a moron and he doesn't count. Everyone else I meet is nice to me in general, and I like it.

The man at my door has a circular placed neatly in a folder, inviting me to a Ladies' Meet. My first ever Army Ladies' Meet! Happily, I sign against Mrs Pia Arjun Mehra, allowing myself a brief smile on reading my new name before checking out the colourful circular.

Ladies of the Victory Brigade

Invite you to share an evening of joy with us
To celebrate the miracle
That a woman is!
Theme: *The six yards of emotions—women empowerment*
Dress Code: *Saree*
Competitions: *Most interesting saree drapes. Participants will walk the ramp with sarees tied in different styles inspired by various states, cultures, trends or even Bollywood.*

Note: Every Unit should give the names of the ladies wishing to participate in the competition by Monday.
Let's Celebrate Womanhood.
See you there!
Venue: Victory Officers' Mess
Time: 1700 hours

I'm so excited! Maybe I can finally wear one of my designer sarees, which Arjun always rejects for Mess functions, saying they are too bling, and hence, inappropriate. Which they are not. Someone needs to sit him down and explain the inspiration behind a Sabyasachi saree and a Ritu Beri creation. Also, he doesn't know how much they cost me.

I run to my wardrobe to select a saree for the event, when 2IC's wife, Mrs Bhandari, calls me (2IC is second-in-command, a lieutenant colonel generally, and is just below the CO in seniority) to ask if I would be willing to participate in the saree-draping competition. Now, wearing a saree casually is one thing, but walking the ramp in it is totally different. And scary. I want to shout 'NO FREAKING WAY' instantly, but then I remember Naina's lessons.

Never-Say-No-To-A-Senior-Lady.

Plus, she says that I would be perfect for a fashion show, which makes me happy. She must think I'm fit to walk the ramp, like them models, yo!

So I agree. How tough can it be anyway? Plus, Mrs Bhandari thinks I'm pretty enough to walk a ramp, yaay!

I decide I will ask Naina to help me tie the saree. Unfortunately her husband falls in a different brigade and so she won't be attending this ladies' meet. And no, you can't hop brigades as you like. Sad but true. I asked Arjun the day I found out that Naina was not in ours, and he had a hearty laugh.

So that is it. I am participating in a ramp-walking saree-draping competition at my first ever Ladies' Meet. Some might say I've completely lost it, but I say I'm getting into the groove, yeah!

The day of the meet comes quickly.

It's a Wednesday. I'm told they generally organise these things on a weekday so as not to disrupt any weekend plans you might have.

I've chosen my super-cool, brand-new Ritu Beri chiffon plus crepe saree. It's red and black with big yellow flowers—very

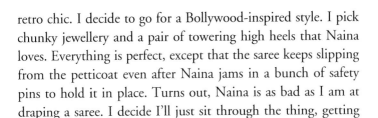

retro chic. I decide to go for a Bollywood-inspired style. I pick chunky jewellery and a pair of towering high heels that Naina loves. Everything is perfect, except that the saree keeps slipping from the petticoat even after Naina jams in a bunch of safety pins to hold it in place. Turns out, Naina is as bad as I am at draping a saree. I decide I'll just sit through the thing, getting up only to walk for the competition, so as not to disturb the drape too much.

Mrs Bhandari and I ride in the same Army vehicle. We reach the venue, and I am told that I will have to introduce myself to all the guests. As if walking on a ramp in a saree that is threatening to fall isn't enough! I look around in bewilderment. There are not less than eighty women around, and I am petrified, to say the least.

'Mrs Bhandari,' I whisper in her ears after buying tambola tickets. 'Um, is there any chance I can skip the saree-drape thingy?'

I might as well have told her I'm a cross-dresser, considering the reaction I get. She turns towards me with a jerk, absolute terror in her eyes. 'Nooooooooo,' she says. 'No, no, no. Don't even think about it, Pia. The First Lady will be *very* upset.'

'Oh. Cool,' I say in a deflated tone. 'I was just checking.'

'Besides, you look good. Relax,' she recovers. And smiles.

Okay. Maybe it's not that big a deal, but I feel good about it. This is the first compliment I have got from a woman since I've set foot in Pathankot station, and it means a lot. Everyone knows that compliments from a woman are a million times better than from a guy. Right? So it lifts my spirits a few notches.

We enter a big palatial hall, decorated with a lot of flowing sarees—sarees hanging from curtain rods, tied around window frames, twisted around a picture of the Goddess Kali. It is so vibrant and grand that it scares me. This is nothing like your regular kitty party that civilians have, no sir. This is something close to your prom night (if you were in the US, that is) or your annual school function (if you were in India), but better.

Mrs Bhandari then subtly separates herself from me and proceeds to sit on a couch in the fourth row. The first row comprises shiny red couches meant for the senior-most ladies— the GOC's wife, who is the chief guest, and the brigade commander's wife. The next two rows of red cushioned single sofas are for the wives of the COs who fall under the Victory Brigade, like Arjun's Unit. This is followed by another row for 2IC wives of all these Units. After these are rows and rows of plain plastic chairs for the remaining janta—like yours truly. On these plastic chairs, I spot two officers' wives from Arjun's Unit, Mrs Jyoti Singh and Mrs Soma Sengupta, both of whose husbands are majors. They wave at me and I sit next to them.

'What were you staring at?' Mrs Singh asks me as I attempt to balance my clutch, my tambola ticket stapled to a piece of cardboard, a pencil and a raffle ticket on my lap.

'The empty couches in the first row,' I answer.

'They are for the VIP ladies,' says a bored-looking Mrs Sengupta.

'What if someone like me goes and sits on one of those— theoretically?' I ask.

'Nothing. They'll politely ask you to take a different seat,' Mrs Singh shrugs.

'That's it? I thought there'd be more drama.' I am disappointed.

'There will be. Later. The CO's wife will take up your case nicely,' Mrs Sengupta says.

Hmm. Doesn't sound good. Our Unit CO's wife, Mrs Nair, is a teacher, and I've never liked teachers. 'Ah. Army!' I sigh.

'What Soma, don't scare the poor girl,' Mrs Singh says. 'She's exaggerating,' she tells me. 'Army isn't all that bad.'

'Arrey bhai, I'm not saying Army is bad at all!' Mrs Sengupta says, picking up a cup of almond soup from the tray a waiter has just offered us. 'I love the Army. What other profession in the world lets the wives party on its expense?' She has a point. 'I may make fun of the Army life sometimes, but God knows I cannot even think of living any other way,' she winks.

'Sach mein, Pia,' Mrs Singh says. 'It's truly a rich life. Our standard of living is much higher than most of our friends in civil.'

'This soup sucks,' Mrs Sengupta makes a face, and slips the cup on the peg table next to her. I look at the cup in my hand. It really does look revolting. I slip mine, untouched, next to her cup and sit down only to be dragged up by Mrs Singh.

The chief guest, the GOC's wife, has arrived—exactly on time, obviously. She waves at the crowd (us) and gestures for all of us to sit down. No one does. After greeting the ladies in the first row and hugging a few, she finally sits down, front row, centre couch, and the others begin to settle down too. She is adjusting her lithe frame on the couch when a waiter chaperoned by a nervous-looking lady brings an assortment of drinks for her to choose from. She picks a glass of coconut water, and as if on cue, the emcee starts the programme.

After a short speech by the host Unit's CO's wife, the new members of the Ladies' Club are asked to introduce themselves. This is the custom, Mrs Singh tells me. I was planning on skipping the introduction, considering how no one knows me outside my Unit and it wouldn't matter anyway, but then I see Mrs Nair's head turning back 180 degrees towards me from her couch in row two. She jabs her thumb towards the stage.

Damn, I think, I should have ducked for five minutes.

I walk towards the stage grumpily. As luck would have it, I seem to be the only new member this time, so absolutely no use trying to be invisible—all eyes are on me.

I take the cordless microphone from the lady hosting the show.

'Hello,' I say. 'Er, I mean, Good Evening everyone.'

I'm a confident person, really. But something about fauj just gets to me. I feel nervous.

'I am Pia Mehra. From Eighteen Twenty-Two Regiment, Artillery. Thank you.'

I am about to run back to my chair, but one of the ladies from the front row says, 'Lovely name, Pia. When did you get married?'

She is smiling and suddenly everyone is interested in what I'm saying.

'Thank you,' I mumble into the microphone. 'I got married on . . . um . . . almost two months back.'

The ladies clap and cheer, and I rush back to slump in my chair.

'Hahaha,' Mrs Sengupta is laughing heartily.

'That bad, huh?' I ask her.

'Nahi, nahi. Probably the only good thing about this evening will be your introduction,' she says happily.

'The damn wedding date wouldn't come to me!' I exclaim, annoyed at myself.

'Relax,' Mrs Singh pats my hand and the lady with the microphone announces that we will be playing a paper game now.

My first thought is that they're going to have us make stuff out of paper, and I feel a little happier. I can make a pretty good paper rose. But of course, that isn't it. Every Ladies' Meet has a 'paper game'; it's some kind of unwritten rule. This one requires us to pick the odd one out from a list of names. For example:

1. Kalpana Chawla, Rakhi Sawant, Indira Gandhi, Madame Curie
2. Medha Patkar, Mamata Banerji, Madhuri Dixit, Arundhati Roy
3. Parveen Babi, Helen, Malaika Arora Khan, Ayesha Takia

Not easy, let me tell you. For instance, in the first line, you might choose Rakhi Sawant, but then, if you think again, it could be Madame Curie too. She's the only non-Indian in the list. Mrs Singh is sure it's Madame Curie.

The second one is tricky too. It could be Arundhati Roy, because her name starts with an 'A'. But Madhuri Dixit could also be the answer.

And the third one! I think it's Parveen Babi because she's dead and the others are still alive, but Mrs Sengupta says it's Ayesha Takia because the other three have hit songs to their credit and she doesn't. Ayesha cannot be an item girl even if she wants to, Mrs Sengupta adds. She's cute and all that, but too busty. These are the times of stick figure girls.

I'm still feeling disappointed with my performance at the paper game when they announce the saree-draping competition.

I'm no longer feeling as upbeat about it. The pleats of my saree have come off twice, and the safety pins are doing nothing more than making big holes in the delicate material.

'I'm going to fall on that damn ramp,' I announce to both ladies before getting up and heading backstage.

'Come on, Pia,' says Mrs Singh warmly, 'you'll be fine.'

'Don't worry, even if you fall, everyone will be busy talking amongst themselves. No one will even notice,' Mrs Sengupta tries to cheer me up in her own way. I smile weakly and totter towards a line of sexy women in sarees. There are women in the most beautiful sarees, draped with such style, that I immediately begin to regret my participation. I spot a stunning size-zero (or stick-figure, in Mrs Sengupta's words) girl standing in the line, writing her name in the participation register. She is wearing an ivory silk Assamese mekhla chador, and boy, she looks gorgeous. I am sure she will win this thing and I look up at her face to see if she's pretty too.

Damn, she is, and she's also scaling me—giving me the once-over. I straighten up to my full height and run a hand through my hair.

And then it is my turn to write in the register, and while taking those two steps towards it, I step on my saree. The delicate material gives out a faint screech and there is a huge hole at the top of the pleats next to where the safety pin was. Disaster.

I cannot go on stage with a visible hole in my saree, right? Size-zero sniggers and walks off. In a panic, I gently remove the safety pin, whisper a silent apology to my saree, yank half the pleats out and fold the now very long pallu around my neck. Twice.

I am on next.

And like divine intervention, it dawns on me that everything that could have gone wrong *has* already gone wrong—how bad can it get now? I feel relief spreading slowly.

I walk the ramp smiling widely and thankfully it is over soon. I go back to sit with Mrs Singh and Mrs Sengupta.

'That is a new type of drape!' Mrs Singh exclaims, looking impressed.

'Yeah, straight from the runway of Milan,' I say, rolling my eyes.

'No one was paying attention, I told you,' Mrs Sengupta says and I find it strangely comforting. If no one noticed, I might have dodged months of being secretly laughed at.

I begin to relax and Mrs Singh starts to explain how simple it is to drape a saree if you remember the everything-on-the-left-side rule.

The hostess, or the emcee in fauji terms, recites a poem on women power and everyone claps enthusiastically. She bows sweetly and proceeds to announce the results of the saree-draping competition.

Dear reader, say hello to the runner-up!

Yes, yes, yes!

I have won second prize!

I walk up to the stage again, my pallu still around my neck, and as I accept a brightly-wrapped gift (a crystal bowl, I find out, once I reach home), I glance at size-zero who hasn't won anything but is still lingering near the stage for some reason, and feel a little dart of triumph. She looks utterly deflated.

'I told you, you looked quite pretty with the pallu around your neck. Plus your blouse is very sexy,' Mrs Singh says when I get back. 'The judges must have liked it.'

'Really?' I ask with delight.

'The judges are so old,' Mrs Sengupta offers. 'They probably thought it was the latest fashion statement amongst young people these days.'

I think she is right. Almost all the VIP ladies are oldies. Maybe they think it is some hot new style, and that I am some kind of a fashionista. Which I am. Really. Don't go by my fauj-forced look.

Mrs Bhandari gives me a thumbs-up from the front and Mrs Nair seems to be in a good mood through the evening.

After some time, we move to another hall for refreshments. I am enjoying a second helping of yummy Tipsy Pudding when Mrs Singh asks me—'Pia, your blouse is so deep from the back, how do you keep the bra strap from showing?'

For the second time that day, I feel awesome.

'No bra,' I say enthusiastically. 'This baby is padded.'

'Arrey, nahi!' she says, clearly impressed. 'Where did you get it made?'

'Can I touch?' says a suddenly interested Mrs Sengupta.

And so our snack time is spent gleefully talking about my tailor and my super cool, padded blouse. And Mrs Sengupta wanting to touch my blouse to make sure I am not lying.

chapter six

Cultural Shifts and the Art of Learning Fast/Pretending

'And how are you finding the Army life so far, Pia?' Mrs Bhandari asks me casually on our way back.

'It's different,' I say, careful not to crib.

'Hmm.'

'And it's a bit overwhelming,' I confess.

'Yes,' she nods. 'Yes. It can be a bit too much in the beginning. But don't worry, you'll learn.'

I like her. I really do. I mean, somehow she seems quite approachable, like I can tell her stuff, you know? So I say—'It's too formal for a regular person like me.'

'We are all regular people, Pia,' she laughs. 'But we are not regular wives.'

We are not regular wives.

The statement echoes in my head a few times. There's a nice ring to it.

'Our husbands are in defence. That's a whole lot different from a husband who, say, works in a bank, right?' Mrs Bhandari says.

I nod in agreement. I can't imagine Arjun working in a bank. Don't get me wrong, I like banks. I really do. It's the people in the banks that I don't like—rude, most of them are. And all that banking stuff, filling out numerous complicated forms and giving the same detail twice on each for a small thing like depositing money? Thank God for internet banking.

'We deal with different situations and entirely unique problems,' Mrs Bhandari says. 'The situations we Army wives have to deal with are not normal ones at all. The nomadic life we lead, moving from station to station, being separated from our husbands for long stretches of time, and the constant fear that we live with if our husbands are anywhere near the sensitive areas in the country . . .' she looks at me with bright eyes.

She's right, isn't she? I mean, it really is a different and difficult life for us, but we manage it all because we're so competent and skilled. I'm feeling these virtues grow in me as she speaks. 'True,' I say, and nod gravely.

'Not to forget the social responsibilities, the children and their education, and a hundred more things. The OR wives look up to us for guidance and help.'

'Wow,' I say, my voice all dreamy. I'm sure I'll be great at guiding and helping others. For one, I give awesome relationship advice—just before I resigned from my TV channel job, I successfully hooked up a colleague with the muscular bouncer-type guy from the tenth floor and they're still going strong. Plus, my opinion on the anchors' outfits and makeup was always welcomed by the studio staff.

'And God knows how different our lives are!' she continues cheerfully. 'Our husbands' uniforms cost five times more than our clothes. We set up a new house after every two-three years. We have more bed linen than Big Bazaar does, and we learn to sleep through the sound of tanks, planes and artillery simulators.'

I have goose bumps on my arms and I'm a little teary-eyed now.

'We are special, Pia,' she says.

'We are special,' I repeat.

'An Army wife always keeps her head high, her voice low and her heart open,' she says in a proud voice. 'And always remember, Pia—we Army wives laugh instead of crying at things that are out of our control, at situations that are challenging and tough,' she concludes with a flourish.

Have I said before that I like Mrs Bhandari? I really do.

When you are in an Army circle, surrounded (only) by Army people, you are bound to come across certain terms that are either not very common in civil life, or have a totally different usage outside fauj.

The Army has its own lingo—words and phrases that only those associated with it will understand. If you are a non-defence person or are a newbie like me, you will often wonder at a few unusual names and phrases, trying not to giggle at some, and frown at the others. They also use bizarre short forms for various things which are, like, super confusing. I'll tell you what I mean.

My list of Top Ten Army Twisted Terminologies and Phrases:

Civil: We know what the word means according to the dictionary. In the Army dictionary, however, it means someone who does not belong to the Army, an outsider. If you are not in the Army, you are a civilian, or in short, 'civil'. The word is used in various ways.

- Noun: Used like a name or a label. Usage—'Oh, he's civil! He doesn't know a thing about golf!'
- Adjective: Used to enhance the meaning of a noun or a pronoun. Usage—'This was almost like a civil party. It sucked.'
- Abuse: Most commonly used. Usage—'Don't behave bloody civil with me now!' one officer said to another and, 'You civil people have no clue!' Might as well replace it with stupid. Or useless.

Tambola: It's more commonly known as housie, but in Army we insist on calling it tambola. Most ladies will look at you blankly if you ever, by mistake and out of habit, call it housie. A round of tambola is a permanent feature at every Ladies' Meet and most social evenings, and is adapted to Army lingo. Eighty-eight is 'Two Fat Majors—eight—eight'. Sometimes, the hosts will take a lot of pain to make it relevant to the theme of the party. For example, at the Women Empowerment Ladies' Meet, the tambola tickets were numbers as well as the names of famous Indian women. But—it's called tambola.

SF: This is the short form for 'Separated Family'—that is, wives and children staying at a station away from the husband. Reasons can be the sudden posting of the husband during the child's school term, forcing the wife to stay back for a few months, or the posting of the husband to a no-family station, like the Valley, or because the wife works and isn't willing to move every two years. Anyway, the point is, how bloody cruel is this term! I mean, they could have called it something less painful, like, say, 'Officer Out' or 'Independent Lady' or maybe even 'Home Alone'—you know, to make it a little fun. Anything but Separated Family.

Forced Bachelor: This one is sort of funny. A forced bachelor is an officer who is married but stays alone for reasons like the ones mentioned above.

Show the snacks: Every time I hear this phrase at a party, I have to try very hard not to laugh. When the waiter comes up with a tray of snacks, he doesn't offer them to you, he 'shows' it to you. At dinner parties, you'll often hear the hostess whispering to waiters, 'Bhaiya, show snacks to the ladies.' Or, 'Pia, have the snacks been shown to you?' Once I asked Arjun, 'Am I supposed to just "look" at the snacks or am I allowed to take them too?' He rushed into a long explanation and I giggled.

Pudding: Any dessert is referred to as 'pudding'. It could be a chocolate soufflé, Spanish Crème, fruit custard, apple pie or even gulab jamun, but it will be called pudding. 'What's for pudding?' someone will ask at a gathering. And, 'There's chocolate mousse for pudding!' will be the answer.

Miscellaneous: Terms like paper game, which is used for every game and/or quiz that is played on a piece of paper; eats—used as a collective term for the food or the menu; ladies and VIP ladies for, well, the wives, etc.

Quite a list, isn't it? And it isn't even half of what's out there in the Army world.

The evening after my first Ladies' Meet, right after Arjun leaves for office, Ganga Bhaiya politely says that Saab would probably prefer the new crystal bowl on the centre table, filled with water and flower petals. Honestly, I'm a million times more than just annoyed. I ignore it and instead request him to give a message to Naina's bhaiya (oho, sahayak bhaiya!), asking Naina over for a coffee-'n'-cookie session. I want to discuss my first Ladies' Meet experience, plus I have a new crystal bowl to flaunt, tee hee hee.

'Fauj hai, yaar, things are always grand,' Naina says when she comes over, dressed in her favourite sweats and a tee. 'Like the sets of a Karan Johar movie. In Army, we never do anything simple.'

'Mmm . . .' I mmm-ed in agreement. Everything about Army is over-the-top and grand. From four-course dinners to theme parties, so much effort goes into almost everything.

'Have a separate showcase made for all the crystal you're going to collect over the years,' Naina says, looking at the bowl, unimpressed. 'You'll collect shitloads of crystal in fauj.'

Then we go on to do the unspeakable—we discuss the ladies.

'It's like any other ladies' club in the world,' Naina says. 'There's a lot of conspiracy, and some amount of bitching is almost inevitable when there are us women involved, ha ha—but if you know how to have fun-fun-fun, you'll be all right,' she finishes triumphantly and winks.

'Really?' I say, stuffing my mouth with the delicious handmade chocolate I picked up from the FWO shop. Maybe she has a secret formula that helps her have fun at all these meets. 'How?'

'Just think of it as a source for future sessions of juicy gossip,' she says. There isn't a flicker of humour in her eyes. 'And when things get really bad at these Ladies' Meets—and trust me, they will—just remind yourself that it's just one inconvenience to all our benefits.'

'Like not worrying about buying groceries!' I exclaim. It

really is fab and a huge relief to me. Not buying groceries myself, I mean.

'Like never worrying about your husband's job security. And other more important stuff like . . .' Naina breaks off when she sees my face. 'I mean, regular ration supply is important too!' she adds hurriedly. 'Imagine going to the market and actually haggling over rates, gosh,' she shakes her head for effect and eyes me. I feel slightly stupid now. Must say something smart. But what? Ah, genius!

'Exactly,' I say firmly. 'And come to think of it, the Army is probably the only profession where you can run a household with only one salary.'

It's true. Unless their family business is selling oil, most couples I know both work if they want a comfortable life. Everyone is running after money, sacrificing time that could be spent in love and togetherness for soulless jobs. It's cruel, really. I click my tongue, and shake my head in dismay.

'Sachhi yaar, everyone is working nonstop to make money in civil,' Naina says, looking as distressed about it. 'In the Army, the highest career position wives can achieve is that of a harassed Army school teacher, dealing with rowdy fauji kids.'

I laugh, but I actually think Naina misses her job. Or jobs. In the two years after she graduated and before she got married, she worked at five different advertising agencies. I, on the other hand, don't miss my job at all. Seriously. It is ridiculous! I've shocked myself by not even once longing for the so-called glamorous life I had in TV. Maybe it's too early—I've only *just* got married after all.

'Fauji kids are the worst kind of kids,' Naina is saying.

'And Army daughters married to an Army officer? There are quite a few of them, right?' I ask, suddenly remembering something I have always wondered about. Life must be easy-breezy for Army daughters who marry in Army, I reckon. It's like their home ground, no confusion and hence no constant terror of making a mistake.

'Haan, loads of them! They are really sophisticated. And why wouldn't they be? They've got it really easy, same childhood, same married life. No difference,' she says and sips her coffee. I nod.

Between the two of us, we finish all the chocolates, lick the wrappers clean and then she leaves, promising to bake a shepherd's pie the next day. I see her off to the door and then place the crystal bowl on the window sill in the living room. It looks gorgeous.

chapter seven

Tales of the Lucky

Weekend arrives quickly, and it's time for an impromptu lunch with the Unit ladies at Mrs Bhandari's place. After a lot of thought about what to wear, I settle on jeans and a bright red wraparound top. It's a casual thing so I pair it with flat tie-up sandals.

Sitting on a comfy chair in Mrs Bhandari's garden, all of us are discussing a recent scandal: a bachelor officer's alleged affair with the commander's daughter. Apparently the commander found out only after they had broken up over a question of career: she wanted to be an air hostess, the officer didn't want to marry a career girl.

'But when it reached the commander's ears,' an animated Mrs Singh says, 'he wanted to patch them up. The officer in question is doing well and is said to be ambitious—what more does an Army officer want for his daughter?'

'Good for her,' says Mrs Sengupta. 'No girl needs an idiot to weigh her down in life with prehistoric thoughts about education and career.'

I nod in agreement. What a chauvinist pig that officer is, I think angrily.

'That she'll end up marrying an Army officer anyway is another story,' Mrs Sengupta continues. 'But kudos to the girl.'

'Maybe she won't marry an Army officer,' I offer. No offence, but there are more choices out there, no?

'Oh puh-leez,' Mrs Sengupta sings. 'She's an Army daughter, what else will she do!'

'Ouch!' An offended looking Mrs Singh says. Yes, she is an Army daughter. 'That's unfair! Army daughters can marry anyone!'

'Yes, they sure can. But do they really?' Mrs Sengupta shrugs. 'You married an Army officer, didn't you?'

'But I fell in love!' Mrs Singh says in a high, brittle voice. Legend and gossip has it that her husband was in her father's Unit a long time back and they fell in love over dances at parties.

'Same difference,' Mrs Sengupta says, waving her hand dismissively and putting a piece of garlic bread in her mouth. Mrs Singh makes a face.

'Sounds like some kind of a rule,' I say to Mrs Sengupta, warming up to the topic now. 'Army girls marry Army officers.'

'Unwritten rule,' Mrs Sengupta nods. 'Army girls are born and brought up in the comfort of an Army household—there's a gardener, an Army vehicle with a driver, and by the time they grow up, their fathers are really senior officers, so they have a small platoon of people ready to make anything happen. It spoils them.'

'Excuse me?' Mrs Singh looks hurt. Yet not completely surprised.

'And they know the only way to have the same lavish lifestyle is to marry an Army officer,' Mrs Sengupta continues, ignoring her.

'*So* not true!' retorts Mrs Singh. 'We have to deal with transfers, constant good-byes, adjusting with new schools, making new friends. You have no idea how difficult that is.'

'Oh come on Jyoti. Moving is good. Who wants to get stuck with the same losers all through school?' Mrs Sengupta says, in her typical blunt style. 'Besides, this is one reason Army daughters are able to have more boyfriends than any civil girl. You'll move away in a year or two anyway, so who cares!' she winks at me.

I laugh. Mrs Singh sighs, but her mouth twitches slightly.

Right after the lunch and a cup of hot tea in the garden, Mrs Sengupta excuses herself, saying she has to go shopping with friends, and I make a mental note to do the same with Naina soon. All we ever do is walk around the blessed park or sit at home and drown ourselves in herbal tea, which is *so* not me. Maybe I can buy a new pair of heels. Red! I can wear them with pastel sarees, like a statement piece. Already excited about my stunning new red heels, I thank Mrs Bhandari a little too cheerfully for the awesome lunch and am about to walk down to my house, when the Army daughter stops me and tells me a story.

Mrs Singh tells me that she has been all over India—twice.

Her Army officer dad insisted on the entire family moving with him to every family station he was posted at, and her mother was only too glad to be with him. This meant that Mrs Singh was constantly changing schools, sometimes mid-session.

Mrs Singh was a shy kid, often labelled a snob in her teens. Obviously she had a lot of trouble striking close friendships when time was always an issue, and if she did manage to make good friends, she was heartbroken every time she had to leave. She would cry secretly at night when she was a kid. She learned to deal with it later, but it was always difficult.

Mrs Singh hated the idea of dating an Army kid, and hence never did, on principle. She thought it would be way too complicated. The civilian boyfriends she made—she insisted there were very few—always seemed to secretly like the fact that she would soon be leaving town for good. Mrs Singh didn't like that, and so none of these boyfriends lasted long enough to see her leave town anyway.

Things played out differently when cupid struck her as she met a young officer in her father's own Unit. She was finishing collage, had never been in a meaningful relationship—not in retrospect, at least—and this officer was smitten by her. He was charming, agreeable, crazy about her—as much as an Army officer can be with all his job commitments and his Army officer-ness—and though it was against her principle to date within the Army, she now realized that they had in common the most important part of her life—an Army background. It started with dances to Army band songs at parties and soon moved to coffee invitations to her house. They got married within a year of the coffee-at-her-home ritual.

'*Meri mummy ne tumhe kal chai pe bulaya hai . . .*' I wanted to sing. Yes, I'm spending way too much time with Naina.

The topic of Army kids lingered in my mind longer than usual. I had a few Army daughters studying with me in school, but as Mrs Singh pointed out, none ever stayed long enough to really get to know them. I knew practically nothing about these kids, and obviously I never cared until now. Though it is far-far-*far* away in the future, it dawned on me that my kids will be Army kids too, and they will grow up in a completely different environment from the one I did. Hmm. Just this thought requires some getting used to. And some research.

A few days later, I find myself attending a party at the Unit Mess. Now here's the thing about formal parties and kids—no matter what age the kids are, if it is a formal party, they're either left behind at home or brought to the party only to be sent into a hall that has a television set, a regular supply of snacks and all the other kids. The mothers check on the kids from time to time, but I shudder slightly at the awful impression these kids must have about parties. I bet half of them think all parties are boring, which just breaks my heart in pieces. Someone's got to tell them it's not true, right? So I go to the hall to cheer them up a bit.

Inside the hall—total commotion. Three girls are sitting on the couch bang opposite the TV, completely lost in a movie while eating popcorn and fish fingers. Two other girls, slightly older than the ones watching TV, are reading from what looks like someone's diary, and both look up when I enter—their lips pursed in disapproval that a non-parent adult is in their territory. Two boys are fighting across a table with cloth napkins.

'I'm the Jedi!' barks the pudgy boy, dressed in jeans and a striped shirt.

And I'm the Mummy!' roars the other one, dressed in cute yellow shorts and a shirt.

'Hey, aren't you guys eating?' I ask nervously, trying to get them to stop fighting.

'Mummies *never* eat! They're dead!' yellow-shorts boy says, giving me a 'not so bright, are you?' look, while the other one yells, 'Aunty, I'll eat only when I kill the Mummy! Yaayyyy!' and they launch into another napkin-attack.

I look around, avoiding the two diary-reading little monsters, and spot a teenage girl sitting in a corner on an armchair, calmly reading a Nancy Drew novel, as if there were no one else in the entire building.

Then I look in the other direction and clasp a hand over my mouth. There, in a slightly dark corner, a boy not older than six or seven is holding an imaginary stethoscope against the chest of a fully-naked-except-for-a-pink-strawberry-print-underwear girl of the same age.

'We're playing doctor-doctor,' the girl tells me happily, while the boy continues the 'check-up'.

Embarrassed for no reason, I quickly go back to the dining room and whisper to Mrs Sengupta about the doctor-doctor game.

'Major Pandey, Nakul is at it again,' she says to the boy's father, loud enough for all to hear. Perfect. Now I'm even more embarrassed, being the bearer of the news and all that.

'That little rascal!' Major Pandey says and runs toward the kids' room, his wife following him. And from the corner of my eye, I see Mrs Nair—the CO's wife—slam her drink down on a table and run behind them. Apparently the girl being examined is her daughter.

'Weird,' I mumble.

'Not anymore for us,' Mrs Sengupta says coolly. 'That boy is horny before hitting puberty.'

I giggle.

'Typical Army boy,' she continues, smirking in Mrs Singh's direction. Mrs Singh pretends not to hear, like she does most of the time. I giggle some more.

I've noticed though, that Army couples are pretty serious about cultivating manners in their kids, and it shows. Although

I still wince when I'm called Aunty, I have to say that I've never met a five-year-old kid outside Army who's wished me with as much as a smile, let alone a 'Good Morning, Aunty'.

'Being an Army kid is definitely different,' a colonel's teenage son tells me a day later, during my evening walk. 'We go through situations that require us to have courage and the ability to handle pressure. And you have to be responsible and prepared—to move, to tackle a non-family posting, or even worse . . .'

I know what he means. Though no one says it out loud, Army kids and wives live under the lurking fear of the 'worse'. It's one subject I can't even think about. I quickly change the subject.

'There must be some hitches in normal life . . .'

'Yeah,' he says calmly. 'There are missed birthdays and unattended school functions. But as you grow up, you either understand or learn to deal with it. It's cool,' he spins the basketball in his hand skilfully.

'Are you proud?' I ask. I'm proud that Arjun is in the Army. I want to know if the kids feel the same way, or is it just a way of life for them.

'Hell yeah!' he replies like I've asked him the most stupid question ever. I smile sheepishly. 'I'm going to NDA too, like dad,' he says, his young face glowing. Stupidly, I feel proud of him.

chapter eight

My Elementary Education: Guide to the Army-Wife Life Part 2

Dear Reader, I may have failed to mention it, but there is a particularly strange couple—a certain Mrs James and Major James—in the Unit. They're recently married, just a couple of months before Arjun and me, and Mrs James and I are both often referred to as the 'new brides' of the Unit.

Major James is about five years senior to Arjun, so I address his wife as the rule dictates—Mrs James. She repeatedly asks me to call her Jincy because we are friendly and because she assumes we are of the same age. Which we are not. Of the same age, I mean. She's past thirty and I am still at a stage where thirty seems pretty old. Okay, okay, I'm twenty-six, so just four years away from thirty, but she is thirty-two! So I never call her Jincy; anyway, I've already become used to 'Mrs James'. And about being friendly, well, we do get along; sometimes sharing a cigarette that she steals from her husband's laptop bag, which is where he hides his stash.

Apparently both of them used to smoke and they collectively decided to quit after their wedding. But of course neither has really done so. He secretly smokes in the office, and she steals cigarettes from him and secretly smokes when she's alone in the house.

'I'm sure he knows I'm stealing cigarettes,' she tells me, 'but he can't really say anything because, you know, he's not supposed to have them in the first place.'

I know. Too complicated.

As I said, they're a strange couple—and in true Army fashion, everyone talks about how different they are from each other. Mrs James hates cooking Indian food, and has lived her life on homemade pizzas and cakes. Major James, on the other hand, will eat nothing but fresh, homemade, traditional south Indian food. And then, Mrs James is the kind of person one would describe as a 'free soul', with not the slightest idea of what 'formal' means. Major James is a proper, fully-bred fauji, with formal fauji mannerisms running in his blood. There are other issues, and because of this, they fight plenty. Mrs James tells anyone who has ears how badly it is going for her.

Oh, and yes, theirs is a love marriage. Just letting you know. Not that it's important or anything.

Both the husband and wife tend to get quite wasted at parties. Post which, Mrs James immediately starts talking about the fabulous job that she had to quit after the wedding (she worked for some art gallery and claims it was ultra glamorous; she says she knows a lot about art, which everyone, including me, doubts—I mean, they have a huge embroidered hot pink sparrow hanging over the dining table; super creepy).

Often, she also says how the Army has slowly 'killed her jazz' (she hates to wear sarees and is extremely uncomfortable in one; apparently Major James loved her in dresses and shorts before the wedding, but now he won't let her wear those clothes and the Army is to be blamed for it).

Once, at a dinner party, she began wailing in front of Mrs Nair and Mrs Bhandari, saying her husband wouldn't let her shop (Major James is known for being, erm, cautious with money). At another event (I told you, the Army entertains a *lot*), she walked up to the CO and asked him to tell her husband to come home early every evening like everyone else's husbands. (Her husband is known—oh screw it, it's too boring.)

The point is, they behave in a way that is abnormal by Army standards, as per seasoned Army wives (aka Mrs Nair, who has no qualms in publically declaring Mrs James as the uncouth lady of the Unit).

I have actually quite grown to like her, over all those stolen cigarettes that we've shared. At least she's different.

One evening, Mrs James invites the other ladies of the Unit and their kids for a fast food fest—she makes really good cake, you have to give it to her. The husbands are all working late for some very senior officer's visit to the station, so the ladies agree. Mrs James lives in fauji accommodation like me—a two-bedroom house comfortable for two, but obviously not large enough to hold a party for eight women and their children. Result—total chaos.

She is handling it as well as she can, and a couple of us are helping her with the arrangements, but by now you should know that Army standards are higher than anywhere else, even the White House for all I know. The CO's wife—Mrs Nair—doesn't look too impressed when Mrs James offers pizza slices to everyone in quarter plates of different colours.

'I only have two dinner sets,' Mrs James explains happily. 'And both are for six. So . . .'

I feel sorry for the poor thing; she really doesn't have a clue. In fact, I probably know more than her about Army customs and expectations by now, and she has been here a few months more than me! I say a silent thank-you to God for Naina and her education, and instantly miss her. This is Unit-ladies' gathering so she's not here, obviously, but I wish she were. She could Army-train Mrs James as well, who is really getting into deeper shit today. I shake my head slightly when, instead of following Army protocol of asking each lady what she wants to drink, she points towards a table on which are glasses, bottles of juice and wine, and says with a flourish: 'Grab your poison, ladies!' The ladies in question are shell-shocked, and stare back at her with blank expressions.

By now everyone's pizza slices are over but the pasta is not ready yet because a short circuit has caused a problem with her microwave. Not wanting to (or not knowing how to) cook it on a stove, Mrs James desperately opens several packets of Maggi Instant Pasta and drowns them in water on the stove. This is all obviously taking time, and more heads are shaking in displeasure in the living room.

The kids are allowed to rummage around in Mrs James's bedroom since—according to Mrs Nair—no 'activity' was arranged for them, and the mothers are relieved to be alone for a while.

When the instant pasta finally arrives and is being served/shown, two kids rush out of the bedroom gripping a Kamasutra Jumbo Pack and wave it in front of Mrs Nair's face. One of them, her daughter (the patient from the doctor-doctor game, remember?), asks, 'What is this, Mom? It says strawberry!'

Mrs Sengupta giggles hysterically as Mrs Nair practically snatches the shiny packet from the girl and scolds her for behaving badly.

'But it says *strawberry*!' the girl wails and sits next to her mother, sulking.

Mrs James runs towards the bedroom and emerges out of breath, ushering all the kids, who then sit down and eat the Maggi pasta. Phew.

By the time everyone leaves and it is only Mrs James and me, she collapses on the couch and says, 'Remind me Pia, why did I invite them? What was I thinking?'

Aww. She's feeling quite a misfit after today's fiasco and I feel bad for her. Maybe we're both misfits, both 'new brides' out of place as Army wives, and though I've somehow been able to manage better than her in the whole new Army wives world, I feel a connection to her. I hug her and tell her to relax.

The following week, all the ladies of the Unit are summoned to the Officers' Mess to discuss and finalize the theme, menu and games for an upcoming Ladies' Meet that we are hosting. I am having so much fun! I *love* planning parties and a really cool theme has been picked out—'Back to the'80s: Total Bollywood'.

In between cups of tea and plans, Mrs Sengupta looks at me and says, 'Pia, you can wear your saree Mumtaz-style.' I think she really does believe that I won the saree-draping competition because of my cutting-edge sense of style. Ha! But I feel I should let everyone know that it was a fluke, so they don't expect me to dress in a different style every damn time.

'No, Mrs Sengupta,' I say, my voice firm. 'I don't know one bloody thing about tying a saree.'

Some women turn in my direction with a start, while others stiffen a bit. Somebody coughs. Maybe they think I'm kidding. Or worse, that I'm deliberately shying away from a task.

'I cannot tie a bloody saree to save my bloody life!' I say again, emphasizing every word.

Mrs Bhandari shudders visibly and Mrs Nair (yes, yes, you remember—the CO's wife), looks at me, her eyes narrowed.

'I have no idea why they gave me the bloody prize because—'

'Don't worry Pia, you'll learn,' Mrs Sengupta quickly cuts me off. 'And ladies, what about the menu?' She looks around at the others, and then, with great interest, down at the menu. Rude, I think, but at least she has saved me from further explanation.

As soon as we leave the Mess, Mrs Sengupta says, 'Too much "bloody" today, girl!' She is laughing and it takes me a couple of minutes to understand—it is a reference to my language, my bad bloody language! How stupid can I be?

'Is it, like, bad to use that word?' I ask, mortified.

'Bad enough for you to be pulled aside and lectured,' she replies coolly. 'I'm surprised Mrs Nair didn't do it right away.'

It is my turn to shudder.

Dinner time. Ganga Bhaiya has just left unwillingly after I ignored his comment that Saab would prefer paranthas instead of puris to go with the choley. I narrate the entire 'profanity' fiasco to Arjun who listens quietly and then shrugs.

'Relax. No one's going to lecture you,' he says.

'Really?' I want to believe him, but I saw Mrs Nair's face, and now that I know the reason behind it, I'm sure she's going to come after me. Oh God, why did I have to be so stupid! The numerous horror stories I've heard about the result of a lady's bad conduct are already doing rounds in my head. Is it possible to court-martial an officer's wife, I wonder. I hope not. It would be awful to see Arjun ashamed of me. I sigh heavily.

Arjun hugs me. 'Don't do it again though. Abuse isn't taken lightly around here.'

'*What?*' I can't believe it! He has got to be kidding now! 'Since when? All you officers do is abuse people left, right and centre!' Which is true. Various cuss words form an integral part of the men's language. And in the Army, there are a few customized swearwords to go with the regular ones. Once, at a gathering, I overheard Colonel Bhandari, the 2IC, say, 'Don't cut a Charlie out of him, yaar!' and everyone laughed heartily. In Army terminology, A is Alpha, B is Beta and C is Charlie. If you haven't understood yet, I'm sorry I cannot explain further. I'm trying to sanitize my own language here, aren't I?

'When have I abused in front of you?' Arjun is a little taken aback by my accusation.

'You haven't,' I say. 'But I know you do when I'm not around. And most of the others do. I've overheard them loads of times.'

'When?' he asks, quickly on guard.

'Whenever, Arjun!' I say impatiently. 'The point is, why this double standard?'

'Ladies should not abuse—that's the theory behind it I guess,' he shrugs.

'Like I said—double standards,' I say in an accusatory tone, as if it is Arjun who's responsible for it. He mock-sighs.

It is now a few days after my slip-up in the Mess, and no one has called me yet. Aal izz well, I believe, and am dreaming about baking a perfectly moist and spongy cake (much simpler than actually making one), when Mrs Singh calls me on the fauji phone.

'CO's wife has requested a short meeting with all the ladies. Be at the Mess in two hours,' she says in an odd voice.

'But I haven't made the invitation card yet!' I say. I'm supposed to make a sample invitation card for the VIP ladies being called for the Ladies' Meet. I have loads of ideas that I'm sure will totally blow everyone's mind, like a hand-painted movie poster from the '80s, or a movie ticket for a film like *Qayamat Se Qayamat Tak*. But that is scheduled for next week. I feel panicky.

'This is about something else,' she says in a tone suited to the secret guardian of the Holy Grail. I hear faint alarm bells ring in my head.

And rightly so.

It turns out be an 'Etiquette Class'.

A bloody Etiquette Class! Can you believe it? For a bunch of educated women, all over the age of twenty-five! I feel disgusted. Also, responsible. It might seem farfetched, but I think I may have something to do with it. There is of course Mrs James' eccentric pizza-pasta dinner-hosting, and I have heard that Mrs Sengupta's sarcasm isn't always well received, so those are probably the main reasons. But—a tiny doubt niggles in my brain—maybe my slip-up with language triggered Mrs Nair's decision to hold the class. Possible, right?

My heart starts to thump in panic. Torn between outrage and terror, I try to maintain a calm face and deal with whatever the hell it is going to be. All the other wives settle down in the hall which is dimly lit as if for effect. Wasting no time, Mrs Nair announces that since there are new members in the Unit, she feels a strong need for a short session on etiquette and asks Mrs Bhandari to start.

Mrs Bhandari takes the podium—yes, a bloody podium to add to the drama!—and starts telling us things about protocol and an Army wife's conduct. She basically just reads out from a sheet of paper, not looking at anyone in particular, but let me tell you, it is pretty intimidating. We have been asked to write down the main points, which I think is stupid, but I take them down anyway in case Mrs Nair checks our notepads, or worse, asks us to get them framed or something.

Pia Arjun Mehra.
Mrs Mehra.
P.I.A.
~~Pretty Intelligent Angel~~
Etiquette Class.

- *Never use foul language, especially in the Mess.* (This is obviously for me and I have never felt so humiliated in all my life. Every other woman in the room is kindly avoiding my eye right now, but I am already imagining them whispering and nudging each other later: She cussed! She cussed in the Officers' Mess! This is a nightmare.)
- *Never wear jeans in the Mess.* (Four women, including Mrs James and I, instinctively cover our denim-clad legs with handbags, scarves or sweaty palms.)
- *Three things are never to be discussed in the Officers' Mess: Women, Politics and Religion.*
- *When you invite someone to your place, take as much care of them as they take of you when*

*you are at the Mess. Offer everything on trays,
and politely, by bending a bit.* (Clearly
directed at Mrs James and her fast food fest fiasco. She
is, however, in a trance, staring at her lap so intensely
that I'm half certain she'll burn a hole in her jeans.)

- *Never wish a senior lady with a 'Hi' or 'Hello'.
  It should always be 'Good Morning', 'Good
  Evening', etc.—which is the proper respectful
  greeting.* (Again, directed at Mrs James, who once
  said a cheery 'Hiya!' to the deputy commander's wife.
  I didn't think she'd mind—the deputy commander's
  wife seems laidback—but apparently she's the one
  who told Mrs Nair, so you never know.)

- *Do not wear clothes that are revealing.* (I
  don't know if this one is for anyone in particular. For
  all I know, they could be targeting someone's low-rise
  jeans or something else equally normal.)

- *Be careful of what you're wearing when the
  bhaiya (the sahayak, why do you keep
  forgetting?) is around. There have been
  unfortunate incidents in the past.* (What
  incidents? With bhaiyas? Really? How come no one's
  told me about these cases? *Note to self: Ask Naina
  and/or Mrs Sengupta about the bhaiya
  incidents.*)

- *Do not consider your husband's bhaiya as
  your personal helper. He is only supposed to
  take care of your husband's uniform. He
  must not, under any circumstances, be asked
  to do domestic work. He's a soldier and it is
  not his job.* (In short, don't expect him to cut veggies

for your dinner or entertain your kids while you are resting. Which suits me—I am not a fan of Ganga bhaiya's perennial presence in the house anyway.)

So, that is pretty much it. I look at my swirly handwriting, read a couple of points again and stifle a yawn.

This is *so* boring. Next thing they'll do is appoint etiquette police and start filing complaints against people.

Why are they so interested in other people anyway? I mean, how does it matter if someone is bending thirty-five degrees instead of forty-five while offering, erm, 'showing' the snacks?

And while I'm on the subject, how the bloody hell is it anyone else's problem how I dress? I mean, all of us are adults here; I'm sure no one is going to waltz into a formal party wearing a bikini, right? No one gives a flying fuck about such petty stuff in civil, I think and chew my pen angrily. Bloody hell.

Oh. Okay.

I remember the point that was obviously meant for me—my language. Panic replaces anger all at once. Sitting in the Army Gypsy on my way back home, I bite my fuchsia-painted nails. How did I end up in an Etiquette Class so early in my Army life? What am I doing wrong?

God, this is bad, *really* bad.

I yank out a Body Shop facial wipe from my clutch and rub it on my face—Aloe Vera soothes you, and I could use some soothing right now.

'You need to calm down, you know. Everyone was targeted,' Mrs James tells me later. 'We'll be careful from now on. What else can we do, yaar?'

We have just shared a smoke in her living room and now, to cover up the smell, she is chewing gum, blowing it in big bubbles every now and then, and I wonder if Army wives are allowed to chew gum. . . .

'I am *so* ashamed that I featured in that list! It's humiliating,' I wail.

'Just let it go. It wasn't a big deal, really,' she shrugs.

'But it was,' I say, feeling dejected. 'It was awkward. I'm lying low for a couple of years till everyone forgets about it.' I mean it. It was embarrassing.

'You're crazy,' she says now, looking at me. 'That was nothing. Awkward is what happened to Vini.'

Vini is the wife of an officer from another Unit. We often meet at Ladies' Meets and parties. She's a quiet woman, very pretty and we chat and laugh a lot, and I have no clue what Mrs James is talking about. 'What happened to Vini?' I ask her.

'She once wore a low cut sleeveless blouse to a party. Apparently her CO's wife doesn't approve of any kind of skin show, so the next day Vini's husband was called in by the CO himself and lectured endlessly in front of all the other Unit officers.'

'Fuck,' I whisper and then immediately cover it with a fake cough. Damn, my language really is bad. Mrs Nair would have died of shock if she'd heard. Or have me arrested by the etiquette police.

'Chill,' Mrs James says, waving her hand. 'But imagine Vini's husband getting grilled because she was wearing a sleeveless blouse!'

'Ridiculous,' I agree. 'Vini is too good-looking for her own good.'

'True. And her CO's wife is a jealous old hag,' she giggles. 'But bottom line is: take it easy. Shit happens.'

True. Shit happens. Bloody hell.

chapter nine

Meet the Foodie, the Loser and the Winner

It's a few days after the dreadful Etiquette Class and I am done sulking. Both Arjun and Naina have convinced me it's not a big deal, so I'm back to normal. That is, except for mentally going over every word before saying it out loud. No point dwelling in the past, right? I enjoy a lot of things about the Army and so, I guess, it's okay to have to deal with the few not-so-pleasant things. And, it's not like they singled me out—if anything, Mrs James should be spending a month underground. But is she even slightly upset? Nope, not one bit.

Besides, I'm an Army wife now, the epitome of strength and character; I shouldn't get so hassled by such inconsequential issues. So I'm just putting it all in my jar of experience and moving on. Like a grown-up.

A lot goes on around you when you are living the Army life, and I am feeling a lot more mature and grown-up over the past few months. I'm even managing to focus on my cooking skills. With the help of two cookery books and a very supportive audience—Arjun—I'm making good progress. In fact, some dishes turned out so yummy, I'm sure my true calling in life is cooking and baking. I baked a perfect apple pie (in my very first attempt!), and though the peanut butter cookies I made didn't set or harden (at all, actually), the dough tasted heavenly. So I'm pretty confident about exhibiting my talent to an unsuspecting Naina. Wait till she tastes my awesome corn cutlets and a slice of hot apple pie. Just wait!

'I can't believe you made these,' remarks a clearly impressed Naina, examining the apple pie's soft, crumbly crust. The expression on her face—and the fact that she polished off four cutlets in one go—tells me that I have arrived in the great domestic world, and how!

The main reason for my relief is the Army dinner culture.

You know by now that the Army people have a lot of parties (you should also know by now what those parties are like, so I hope no one's dying to get in). When we're not going for elaborate parties, we are invited by or inviting some family or the other over for dinner. This is the Army dinner culture. These dinners aren't casual affairs either—you show up in formal attire (well, semi-formal at least), eat yummy food (Army food is always yummy) and talk about . . . stuff. And now that I've been to almost everyone's place for dinner within the Unit, I have to start inviting people over. Do you sense the magnitude of this thing? I will have to cook a main course along with snacks, soup and a dessert. You see now? It is *very* important for me to learn cooking.

Thankfully, Arjun is a supportive husband. He eats whatever I put on the plate and always appreciates it. Or the effort. In a world where fussy husbands throw plates full of food at the walls (Major James, for example; true story), I feel incredibly lucky to have Arjun.

Okay. Perhaps I spoke too soon about Arjun and his apparent support for my cooking. All I can say is, he has really let me down big time. My heart is so heavy, I can barely explain what happened without getting mad.

But I'll try.

So. My delusions about Arjun were shattered the day Mrs Sengupta and I went to Mrs James' place to finalize the menu for the upcoming Ladies' Meet, for which the three of us are responsible. The selection done in five minutes, we quickly moved on to much more important issues, such as what is up with Mrs Nair, the CO's wife.

To tell you the truth, apart from a lingering resentment about the Etiquette Class she arranged, I don't really have anything against Mrs Nair. However, this is apparently because I'm new and therefore don't have a clue. That she's the CO's wife is reason enough to dislike her, the other two tell me. All CO wives are mean, forgetting their time as a junior officer's wife and constantly pressurizing others to perform or participate or—in Mrs James and Mrs Sengupta's case—to behave.

I have to say, Mrs Nair has been good to me so far, but who am I to interrupt a gossip session. So, after rejecting the 'She's uneducated' and 'She's jealous of us' arguments (she's an M.Phil, and let's face it, what have we three got that she'd be jealous of), we go on to discuss the possibilities of her being sex-starved, frustrated and thus this stuck-up, when Mrs James jumps up and excuses herself to do some cooking.

'At this time?' I ask her. It is way past lunch.

'Yeah. For the hubby,' she says, cutting frozen fish into bite-size pieces. 'I send evening snacks over to the office.'

'*Why*?' Mrs Sengupta and I scream together.

'Because,' she says with a woman-on-a-mission expression, 'if I don't send him home-cooked food, he gorges on the Mess food, which is oily and too spicy. It's messing with his system.'

'Ah,' Mrs Sengupta nods wisely. 'The Mess food syndrome. Honestly, Army officers are really the worst of all men when it comes to food. They're critical of anything that is short of being a dish served in a five-star restaurant.'

'They're so used to the cooks in the Officers' Mess, that's the problem. And *they've* been trained in five-star hotel kitchens,' Mrs James agrees.

'So we wives have to work really hard to make them eat home-cooked food, both for our satisfaction and for their health.'

'True. They can't eat chilly chicken, butter naan and chocolate cake every day just because it is delicious!' Mrs James says and bangs shut the microwave door angrily. 'What about healthy eating habits? What about cholesterol levels? Hmm?' she asks me.

'Um. I don't know,' I say, a little confused. For one, Mrs James is someone who lives on pizza, hardly the healthiest food. And for another, what is all this talk about officers and Mess food? 'I never thought about it,' I add.

'About health, you mean?' Mrs Sengupta asks.

'Yes. I mean, no. Not *health*. I make healthy food,' I say quickly, thinking of the butter-soaked chicken curry I made the night before. 'Arjun eats all his meals at home so I never really worried about the Mess food,' I clarify.

'Oh ha ha!' both of them laugh in synchronization.

'Aww, sweeti,' Mrs Sengupta says. 'Aww, honey, how do I break it to you—you can take an officer out of the Mess, but you cannot take the Mess out of the officer.'

They are laughing and shaking their heads in amusement. I feel like a college fresher who's just been told that there's no uniform in college. I feel stupid.

'*All* our husbands eat from the Mess, Pia,' Mrs James says to me. 'So my husband might give me a hard time about the food I cook and Captain Arjun might eat everything at home, but then they both go and eat their favourite tandoori chicken and butter naan in the Mess.'

'Really?' I ask, shell-shocked.

She nods. 'In fact, I know for sure that Captain Arjun eats breakfast with my husband in his office—super oily bread pakoras and cold coffee.'

'But Arjun leaves home after having his breakfast!' I say. By this point I am fairly alarmed. I don't know how to react to this news. If he's really eating food from the Mess, it must mean he doesn't actually like my cooking, right?

'That does not mean he doesn't like your cooking,' Mrs Sengupta seems to have read my mind. Or my pathetic I-am-a-lousy-cook-after-all expression. 'But we wives have to come to terms with the fact that we will never beat the Mess cook in this battle of the kitchen.'

'Yes,' agrees Mrs James, packing the cooked fish fingers in silver foil.

So there. This is the story of how Arjun has no heart and how he broke mine over some greasy bread pakora.

Later that day, still reeling from the betrayal, I corner Arjun and confront him directly.

'Have you been eating bread pakoras from the Mess?'

'Oh yes!' he exclaims, his face instantly lighting up with the memory. 'And baby, you should try them. They're just out of the world. Out of the world! Wait, I'll send some over to you tomorrow morning.'

I'm not sure, but I think his mouth is watering. Oh gross, I think miserably.

So there is Mrs James, sending a regular supply of home-cooked food to her husband's office in order to keep him away from oily Mess food. And there is cool Mrs Sengupta who, in her own words, 'Has given up entirely on the effort of outdoing the Mess cook'. She confesses she herself prefers the Mess food to what she cooks anyway. And here I am, somewhere between the two—feeling quite numb.

'The bread pakoras really are out of this world,' I say to Mrs James. We're chatting on the fauji phone.

'Oh please,' she retorts. 'Not you now! I hate those damn things.'

'You should try one! For breakfast tomorrow?' I suggest with my mouth half full of that delicious thing. Seriously, how incredible are these bread pakoras? I intend to get the recipe from the cook bhaiya—might as well learn how to make it before he gets posted out.

'No thanks. I'm trying to reduce my oil intake as much as possible. What about healthy eating? These things are a disaster, don't you think?'

'Mmm . . . I think I'll ask for these things every day for breakfast,' I say happily.

I am now sick of the bread pakoras. Too much oil, really. And potatoes! Killer carbs! I've asked Arjun to stop eating them as well.

'They're oily and we have to start thinking about our health,' I recite Mrs James' words.

'Arrey, we're young!' he says throwing his hands up in the air. 'And they're yummy, you know it!'

'But what about healthy eating?' I ask in my most solemn voice.

'Screw it,' he says. 'We're healthy.'

Doesn't sound quite right, that. And his undying love for the Mess food isn't impressive. It suddenly dawns on me that this cook is stealing my husband away from me. You know, pleasure-of-cooking-food-for-him wise. Here I am, a cooking-challenged girl who overcame her fear of frying pans and spices only to be outdone by some five-star trained man. I hate the cook, I decide.

Also, just think about it for a moment: first the possessive bhaiya (sahayak, and next time I'm not explaining!), and now the Mr Perfect Cook.

How many more people should I be looking out for? Jeez!

I stand in the garden, my expression disgruntled, lamenting

the unforeseen invasion of the cook in my happy married life, when Arjun calls from the living room.

'Baby, can you make some cheesy fries and the red dip?'

I smile.

No damn cook in the world can cook the fries my way—the way Arjun likes it—because it's my own recipe!

Yes sir, Mrs Pia Arjun Mehra's own invention. Mainly because I read about a hundred versions of the thing and couldn't remember any while actually cooking it, so I just mixed up steps from various recipes. It turned out to be mouth-watering. It basically involves rolling sliced potatoes in corn flour, deep frying them till crispy, lying them on tissue paper for a couple of minutes and then lining them side by side on a plate and pouring loads of Amul cheese spread over them. Sprinkle salt, pepper and oregano over them, and you're done. I 'show' it with a homemade salsa dip, comprising flame-roasted or grilled tomatoes and green/yellow bell peppers.

Feeling like Nigella Lawson, I am happily done in about twenty-five minutes and as Arjun attacks the plate and kisses me afterwards, I say a silent 'Up yours' to the Mess cook. Our battle will go on, but now I know one thing—it is not going to be an easy win for him. Hmmph.

I kiss him back with enthusiasm and at the same time attempt to pat myself on the back. Not that he notices; I'm a pretty good kisser.

chapter ten

The Truth, the Lies, the Scandals and the Ridiculous

All the ladies are gathered in the Officers' Mess. Three ladies are in 'casual' sarees (that's what simple cotton sarees are called) and the rest are in salwar kameezes. I am wearing a deep V-neck kurta with leggings which are giving me a sense of perverse satisfaction. It is probably the only act of rebellion I will get away with after the Etiquette Class.

Discussions about the upcoming Ladies' Meet are going on (I know! It never stops!). This is a Brigade-level meet again, so only the Units that belong to our Brigade will be attending it. Seriously, when will Naina and I ever be a part of the same Ladies' Meet?

Anyway, though this will not be a big gathering, the party still needs to be grand, and duties are being allocated right now. I am to 'show' drinks to the VIPs as soon as they arrive, and then distribute paper for the paper game. Easy-peasy.

As it always happens when a bunch of women are sipping coffee together, the conversation quickly moves from the Ladies' Meet to the latest gossip. Someone mentions how embarrassing the recent Army scandal is: an Army couple falsely accused a very senior officer of sexually abusing the woman to get even with him because he had given the husband a bad performance report. The accusations were proved false by an inquiry board last week and it was all over the news.

'And they have done this exact thing before!' says a wide-eyed Mrs James. 'The same couple filed a similar report against another officer five years back!'

'Ambition,' sighs Mrs Sengupta. 'People will do anything to get ahead.'

'Sabotage someone else's life, even!' Mrs James shakes her head angrily. By the look on her face, you'd think it was her husband who was falsely accused.

'Pia's channel was even holding a debate on "The Fall of Morals in the Army",' Mrs Nair says, and I have to say, I am surprised that she remembers the channel I used to work with. I didn't think she paid any attention to anyone's pre-Army life.

'That was before it was proved false,' Mrs Singh offers in my defence, and gives me an assuring I-got-your-back smile. I nod seriously at her as if I care about the channel and what people think about it.

'They just need news to break,' I say calmly, looking at Mrs Nair.

'Oh don't blame the channels!' Mrs Sengupta says. She is stirring her apple juice a tad enthusiastically. 'Army likes a scandal anyway. If there isn't anything fresh, Army will dig up old ones or imagine new ones.' She flicks her silky hair and looks at each one of us. No one argues. Mrs Sengupta then makes a show of checking her wristwatch. The meeting is dismissed in the next five minutes.

'Yaar, it is tricky,' Naina says. We are on our evening walk around the children's park and I have just told her about Mrs Sengupta's 'Army is full of scandals' statement. 'Army couples go through much tougher situations than civilian ones. Every few years our husbands move to some field posting, away from us,' she says. 'Things happen sometimes.'

'Things?' I ask, looking down at my new sneakers and wondering whether I should have bought the turquoise ones instead.

'Dekho, when husbands stay alone for two-three years, meeting their wives only occasionally, some amount of infidelity is possible . . .'

I forget about my sneakers and shudder. The mere idea of having Arjun cheat on me is horrible.

'That's awful.'

'It is, yes,' she says, stopping to catch her breath. We're trying power walking today, and it's not working quite like we expected it to. For one, neither of us feels powerful even after three rounds of the damn park. 'And it's most common with officers posted in the Northeast.' She looks at me meaningfully.

'Because most of the Northeast is not a family station?' I ask.

'Yes. And also because the girls are stunning,' she says and starts singing the Bollywood song *Kanchi re kanchi re . . .*

'Have you known this to happen to someone?'

'No, no one I know personally. But I've heard . . .' She continues to sing the song. She even knows the stanzas. How old is this song? How does she know all the lyrics? What if Arjun gets posted to Northeast?

'They're most probably just rumours,' I say. I want them to be baseless rumours, otherwise I'm never letting Arjun go anywhere without me, I swear.

She shrugs. Her husband completed a two-year tenure in the Northeast before their marriage.

Mrs James is over at my house, getting my opinion on the VIP folders she has designed. These are folders in which pens, blank paper, programme schedules, etc. are placed for VIP ladies at the Ladies' Meet. They have to be special, though, because they are for the VIP ladies.

'Do you think Army relationships are tough?' I ask her.

'Of course,' she says, trying to stick a ribbon on a folder. 'Very tough. Take the food for example.'

'Food?' I ask. Food? She can't get off the food topic ever! 'No no! I am talking about the husband-wife relationship . . .'

'Haan, I know,' she cuts me off. 'And food is the first area where differences crop up.'

I look at her, at a loss of words. Food sure is a sensitive topic for her.

'Pia, you know how my husband hates the food I cook? He prefers the Mess food. It was the first thing we fought about and it only got worse from there,' she explains with a straight face and I want to laugh.

'Come on Mrs James!' I say. 'You're exaggerating.'

'No Pia, I'm not. You should see the way he reacts to my food. All his, "This curry doesn't go with rice", and "That fish is overcooked"—it drives me mad. Last night I told him if he wanted a cook, he should have married one.' For the first time, I notice traces of sadness on her face.

'Um,' I say. 'I'm sure he doesn't mean to hurt you.'

'I know he doesn't mean to, but he *is* hurting me. I used to work full-time in an art gallery before we got married—it's not like I was sitting at home taking cooking lessons all these years!' She trembles a bit and I suddenly realize I am being subjected to my first-ever domestic-fight vent. I should not be too logical about it, or too critical, I tell myself. I should just keep quiet and listen to her, be patient and maybe let her cry a little on my shoulder. Also, I'm feeling a tad sorry for her. I mean she is trying her level best here, isn't she? Maybe I should offer her some chocolate.

'He is always busy, never gives me time, hates my cooking and wants me to stop drinking wine,' she says, clutching the VIP folder. 'I gave up my career for this?' She looks at me for an answer. I offer her a piece of dark chocolate and hope it gets better for her.

The career woman who gave it up for love, only to discover that the husband doesn't appreciate it. She tries hard at everything domestic and wants to be respected for trying, which is only fair. But when the husband doesn't seem to notice, she feels cheated: she slowly become bitter and jaded.

Is there a simple solution? I don't think so. I put a piece of chocolate in my mouth and hope I never have to look for the solution.

I am obviously now Mrs James' confidante. She calls me up on the fauji phone and says, 'I will never understand how people manage to make relationships work in the Army.' Her voice is a little strained and it's safe to say that she was probably crying before she called. 'My husband doesn't want to eat what I cook! We fight all the time and we never go out for shopping or lunch or freaking dinner like you and Captain Arjun. And it's only the first year of our wedding!' She tries to camouflage a sob with a fake cough.

'Maybe he's just stressed because of work,' I offer.

'Bullshit!' she says. 'I don't even think he works. I checked his laptop history the other day—he is on Facebook the entire day from office. And Orkut.'

'Orkut?' I blurt out. Really, who uses Orkut anymore? *Who*?

She isn't listening, of course. 'I'm sure he is chatting with girls.' She is now sobbing openly. 'Oh Pia, what should I do?'

'First of all,' I say in a whisper, 'hang up the fauji phone and call me on the mobile.' The fauji phone is a parallel connection to the husband's office phone, and for all we know, her husband might be listening to the entire conversation. Happened to Naina, when her husband accidently overheard a new mom from their Unit telling Naina how comfortable feeding bras are. Awkward!

'No,' she says. 'Let him hear all he wants to. He should know that I know. I am not Major Sengupta who will take this shit lying down!' she practically shouts, and thus emerges the story I can scarcely believe—the story of how Mrs Sengupta fell in love with a younger officer a few years back, when Major Sengupta was posted to the Valley, to some no-phone connection, no communication kind of a place for two years. Apparently a lonely Mrs Sengupta fell for a particular single officer, and vice versa. Almost everybody claims to have seen the officer at her house constantly, and by the time Major Sengupta returned, everyone was talking about the affair openly.

Well, no one can really know what happened then between

the husband and wife, but people said she denied it completely, ditched the lover and went back to being the loving wife.

I simply couldn't wrap my head around this one when Mrs James told me the story. Mrs Sengupta? No way. I don't believe it one bit.

And for the record, from what I've seen so far, Major and Mrs Sengupta seem to have a very warm relationship. They hold hands while entering parties, wink at each other when making jokes about people, and they both have a dry, quirky sense of humour that I completely adore.

I'm a hundred per cent sure it's a rumour started by some jealous wife with a crappy husband who cheats on her, or someone Mrs Sengupta has unknowingly or knowingly (which is more likely) offended with her sarcasm. To be honest, it's possible; it's such a small community, there's no one else to talk to or talk about!

I've realized that despite the accepted code of conduct for the wives, there's a lot of bitching and politicking among the wives in Army, which if you ask me, is totally unnecessary. I mean, I'm new and everything, but I'm not stupid enough to imagine that my scheming against someone else will benefit Arjun's career in any way. But then some women just don't get it, and most of this politics is just a power game, and over the most trivial things. You know, like who's got an extra gardener or a better vehicle or who's closest to the commander's wife? It's the Army version of office politics, I guess. I knew people at the channel who would not hesitate to sabotage someone's image with an outright lie just to get into the boss' good books. I've never understood office politics, or the need for it. And one would think Army would be free of that stuff. Unbelievable! I refuse to believe such malice-infected gossip, no sireee!

Also, Mrs Sengupta and an affair? No freaking way.

Several days later I find myself in the same Army vehicle as Mrs Sengupta, going for a little gift-shopping for the upcoming Ladies' Meet.

Hoping to somehow get a subtle confirmation that the gossip about her is nothing more than a stupid rumour, I ask her with a straight face, 'Are Army officers crappy husbands?'

'Maybe,' she says. 'But they're excellent lovers.'

She winks at me.

chapter eleven

Tell-a-Tale

When you're a part of the Indian Army family, you attend a lot of events and meet a lot of people. In fact, if someone does a survey of who meets the most number of people in one lifetime, I bet the results will show Army officers in the top three. They'll probably share the position with the guys who write the Lonely Planet books.

It goes without saying then, that Army wives also meet a lot of people. Now, meeting new people is all very well, but think about it—how many topics of conversation can you come up with, when you've just met the other person.

Imagine this: You've been introduced. You've asked about each other's previous postings, home towns have been discussed, you've said a sentence or two about the snacks—and the soup hasn't even arrived. Now what? Here I am to your rescue—ta da!

Topics guaranteed to trigger long, involved conversations: *(Researcher: Pia Mehra)*

• Talk about the various courses that the Army offers for officers. For example, in Artillery, just mention the word

'Deolali' to a group of people and then sit back, sip your drink and enjoy the number of anecdotes that unfurl—everything at the mere mention of the city. Ladies will get nostalgic about the awesome time they had, officers will have funny stories to tell about their comparatively easy days, and if you are lucky, someone will tell you how Deolali is considered to be a 'fertile' place for all Artillery families. It is said that every Artillery officer has at least one Deolali child—a child conceived during their Deolali tenure.

- Travel. Just drop the name of a random city. In every Army gathering, there are always at least two people who have visited the city you mentioned—no matter which goddamn city it is. Then the reminiscences and will start and if you can manage to pay attention through this, you could gather some useful tips for shopping and eating out. My attention tends to drift, but I'm working on it.

- Difficult times they've seen in the Army. This could result in memories ranging from not getting food for a week because of landslides, to the ration not including Milkmaid.

- Music and movies are other topics that will help you have a rich and meaningful conversation with people. Talk about the golden days of Hindi music and you'll have someone humming *Chalo dildar chalo, chaand ke paar chalo* instantly. Foreign bands can be mentioned, but stick to The Eagles and Abba. Never, under any circumstances, bring up a Dido song, a Lady Gaga controversy or anything that has taken place in the last five years. You will be met with only blank stares and the awkwardness will be too much for you to carry for the rest of the evening.

- Kargil. Introduce this subject only if you are up for some serious, emotional conversation, because when you hear about it from an officer who was there or the wife who wasn't, but would have given anything to be there with her husband, it is impossible not to feel tears stinging your eyes and pride filling up your chest. You might even want to stand up and salute them both, but don't, because it is not what wives are supposed to do.

The Ladies' Meet that we so frantically prepared for is finally happening. The theme, like I told you, is *Back to the '80s: Total Bollywood* and, a good one hour before I actually need to leave, I am trying to figure out how to wear my saree in the famous Mumtaz style.

Arjun calls on the fauji phone.

'What's happening?' he asks cheerfully.

'Getting ready for the Ladies' Meet,' I reply.

'Oh okay. By what time will you be done?'

'Around seven-ish?' I reply, and poke myself accidently with a safety pin. 'Fuck.'

'No F-word at the Mess, remember?' he says and chuckles. Like it's very funny.

'Yeah. Whatever. Okay bye,' I say crossly.

'Listen, I'll pick you up from there and we'll go grab a pizza?'

'Sure!' I say happily. And then say a rude bye just so he knows I'm not that easily won over.

I reach the Officers' Mess, which is where the Ladies' Meet is being held, a good fifteen minutes early and find that most of the Unit ladies are already there and last-minute checks are going on.

The place has completely transformed from a masculine dining room to a gorgeous Bollywood-type lounge bar. Posters of Bollywood films hang on the walls and a huge golden gramophone sits elegantly in a corner next to the stage. I tell you, the men in the Army would be wonderful in event management! They are so organized and quick, work happens like in Harry Potter. Like magic, I mean.

Mrs Bhandari arrives soon after me and looks pleased to see that even Mrs James, who is perpetually late for everything, is there before her. Mrs Nair arrives last, gives everything a final look and smiles in approval. Mrs Bhandari exhales in relief—she is after all the second senior-most lady, and hence answerable for all shortcomings to Mrs Nair.

We all gather around the main entrance to welcome the guests. I quickly take position next to a giant silver trophy which I hope completely hides me, but am anyway called over and introduced to a bunch of women I've never seen before. Soon there is a huge, colourful group of ladies in the hall, and while we wait for the arrival of the VIP guests and the chief guest—the commander's wife—I look over the happy, chirpy group in retro prints, wide headbands and some even with pointy, conical bras.

I spot a petite girl clad in a Mumtaz-style (like me!) super glittery hot pink saree (not at all like me, thank god), with a huge bright pink artificial flower in her hair. Her husband is from some other Unit, and her name is Hina. Her husband is probably junior to Arjun, because she addresses me as Mrs Mehra—a first for me. I have to try really hard not to look smug. I am a senior lady to someone, at last.

Hina seems nice, but a little too loud for my taste. 'Everyone calls me H,' she says right after we're introduced.

'H for harassment,' whispers Mrs Sengupta.

H talks mostly in Punjabi-Hindi, backslaps other ladies from her Unit, and laughs hard at *everything*. And, for some reason, she addresses her CO's wife as 'my new mommy'.

Mrs Singh sits next to me during the paper game—we are waiting for the guests to finish—and tells me H's story.

H met her husband in Delhi through common friends and they fell in love instantly. However, their parents were against their marriage. When H's husband (then boyfriend) returned to Pathankot, H couldn't take it anymore. One fine day, she showed up at the Unit gate, demanding to see him. She was let in after a few phone calls and amused looks from the men at guard duty at the gate. Yes, she had run away.

I found it quite funny and filmy. I mean, who runs away from home these days?

Anyway, like the vindictive parents from some '80s movie, her folks registered an FIR with their local police and in a day or two, the police called up the CO. You can imagine how all hell broke loose. But our H, of course, refused to go anywhere.

Since she was an adult the police couldn't do much, and she stayed on with the officer for a couple of months, eating in the Mess and attending the Unit's official functions. This is when the entire Unit decided that it was better to marry them off rather than be in the constant eye of the public (read: other Units). So the CO and his wife performed the ceremony. Hence the CO's wife being referred to as the 'new mommy'.

Phew.

But it somehow makes sense when you see her. No, no—I'm not judging anyone! It's just that her personality somehow goes well with the ran-away-from-home-to-stay-with-and-then-get-married-to-the-guy story. She oozes the kind of over-confidence that only comes to people who wear deep red lipstick and sparkly tissue sarees in bright daylight. I look at her blatantly cheating from her new mommy's paper on the Bollywood movies quiz, and lick whatever is remaining of my pale lip gloss.

The evening is quickly edging towards an end and awards for winners of the Bollywood quiz, best costume and the mandatory game of tambola are given away. Everyone is ushered to the dining area, which has been set up in another hall. Our guests eat and talk while we hosts mingle, making sure everyone is comfortable. I walk unsteadily in my bloody Mumtaz-style saree from one group to another, striking conversation as directed by Mrs Bhandari, when H approaches me. 'Soooper party, Mrs Mehra. I loved it!' she says.

'Thank you,' I reply. 'Though I haven't done much.'

'Hai rabba, don't be saying like this,' she says in a hushed voice, leaning towards me. 'In Army, always say "I Did Everything", thik hai?'

I laugh, thinking that she is actually quite funny.

'Arrey, don't be laughing Mrs Mehra. Sachhi, always take credit,' she says, deadpan.

'Huh?'

'That is my mantra, Mrs Mehra. Keeping the CO's wife happy,' she says, sipping her tea. The rim of her cup has red lipstick smudges on it at three different places. She has to be the most unclassy Army wife I've come across so far. I stare at her intently.

'Waise, Mrs Nair is very nice,' she continues. 'I wish I was in your Unit, Mrs Mehra. Mine CO's wife is a nightmare, sachhi,' and she jerks her head not so subtly towards her CO's wife, who is just a couple of feet away from us.

'Shhh!' I whisper. What if she overhears?

'Oho don't worry, she won't listen. The woman is half deaf,' she laughs merrily, and attempts to give me a high five which I miss because I'm looking around uneasily to check if anyone heard her. This woman is mad!

'Hai rabba!' she says and lowers the hand that she'd raised for a high five. 'Insult, Mrs Mehra! I will take revenge, hahaha!'

Mrs Sengupta was right, H is indeed for Harassment.

Then she sobers up and says, 'But, by god Mrs Mehra. You are lucky to be having Mrs Nair. I am so tortured by this buddhi,' she says and indicates her CO's wife with her head *again*. I don't know how to react to this. Part of me wants to ask her the story she obviously wants to tell, while the other part of me—the sensible part—is telling me to abort this conversation right away. I finally go with the former. A girl needs her dose of gossip after all.

'But she seems to be fond of you; don't you call her your new mom or something?' I ask her casually, and pick up a cup of coffee from a waiter passing by, so I have something to do with my hands. It is silly, but I'm excited at the prospect of having something spicy to tell Naina for a change. H also looks excited at the prospect of a new set of ears for her dramatic story. She jumps at the opportunity and, grabbing my hand, drags me to the far end of the dining area.

'I *was* fond of her, Mrs Mehra!' she says, 'until I found out that she is bitching about me with everyone, you know, about how I fell in love and didn't care about duniya,' she says, her eyes dancing. 'I mean, I don't care what duniya says but kam se kam don't do my buraayi behind my back!'

I nod seriously.

'And Mrs Mehra, don't go by the sweet-sweet way she talks—she every time insults me in front of people. Jaise, last week only she told me to dress up like a new bride—not to wear jeans in front of other people. Socho aap!'

'Oh.'

'Jee haan! I was toh about to say that choro jee, you are not my saas.'

'Did you?' I ask, curious.

'Na baba, I have to be thinking about my hubby also, na? And her husband is equally evil. Makes my hubby work till late hours so that we can't spend time together. I hate her, sachhi.'

I gulp down my steaming coffee and burn my throat, but it saves me from having to react.

chapter twelve

General Complications

The Ladies' Meet was a big success, Mrs James tells me the next day. We are downing glass after glass of cold coffee in her garden, talking about how the commander's wife congratulated Mrs Nair before she left. 'She told Mrs Nair, "You've raised my expectations!"' Mrs James reports happily. When it comes to eavesdropping, she is as talented as they come. She can hear a conversation from across a room, over the wide fauji gardens even!

Just then, I notice the house next to hers—which has been empty so far—is buzzing with activity.

'Looks like you're getting new neighbours,' I say.

'Oh yeah. The house has been allotted to Captain Sood from our Unit,' she tells me. Captain Sood is junior to Arjun by a couple of years and has just gotten married.

'Cool. So we won't be the new brides of the Unit anymore, huh?' I joke.

'Thank God for that!' she laughs. 'Plus I can be the Army-wife-life mentor to the newbie. How super cool is that?'

Mrs James, a mentor. Yeah right. This is going to be fun, hee hee.

'I'll teach her all the rules of the game. The dos and don'ts,' she says seriously. 'I don't want anyone to end up in an Etiquette Class ever again.'

'Don't remind me,' I shake my head. 'Being summoned to an Etiquette Class at the very start of our Army-wife life? We must be the worst of the lot; real misfits in this fauji wife world.'

Mrs James nods so enthusiastically, she spills some cold coffee on her hand. She licks it off and then, realizing this isn't lady-like at all, she rolls her eyes and says, 'Oops!'

We laugh loudly. We really are misfits.

'Oh well, we might not be perfect ladies, but we are two very cool girls,' I say and we giggle some more.

'Aw Pia, it's so good to have you around,' she says.

'Ditto,' I say. 'I'm glad you're here.' And I mean it. Mrs James can sometimes get so caught up in what she thinks is wrong with her life—her husband or the Army or her sahayak bhaiya—that she barely notices the other person. I sometimes think she's as stable as Dr Jekyll! But she can also be really warm, and I do appreciate that.

The same evening, I am getting ready for my evening walk with Naina when she walks in. Ganga bhaiya is folding Arjun's clothes with a little too much care when she enters the living room and flops down on the fauji sofa. 'Namaste Memsaab,' Ganga bhaiya wishes her, but she's absently tugging at her hair and pouting. I think I know what is going on.

'What did Mrs Sahdeva do now?' I ask.

Dear Reader, meet Mrs Sahdeva—Naina's husband's CO's wife. She is known to be a tyrant, and is the reason behind all of Naina's foul-mood spells.

'She's unbelievable!' Naina says in an angry hiss.

'Talk to me,' I tell her encouragingly. Ganga Bhaiya leaves, as if on cue.

'She's horrible, dude!' she says in a whisper. No one is here, we're inside my house, but we're just in the habit of whispering things like this. Discussing a CO's wife or any senior lady is against the Army wife etiquette, obviously.

'What happened?' I ask gently.

'We were in the Mess today, discussing an upcoming Welfare event, and she tells me to wear a turquoise saree.'

I nod.

'You know I don't have a turquoise saree?'

I nod again.

'So I said, "Mrs Sahdeva, I'm sorry, I don't have a turquoise saree. Can I wear a royal blue saree instead?" And she said,' here Naina imitates Mrs Sahdeva's deep voice, quite well, I may add, '"When I say turquoise, I mean turquoise, green-blue, not royal blue!"'

Before I can say anything, Naina continues. 'I felt so insulted; I mean, all our Unit ladies were there! So I said, "Yes Mrs Sahdeva, I know what turquoise means, but I don't have a saree in that colour. Then she shouted at me, Pia! Like I've challenged her authority or something! She said, "Stop acting smart, Naina! There is a dress code and everyone has to follow it. If you don't have one, borrow it or something, but I want to see you in a turquoise saree that day. Is that understood?"'

'What?' I say, surprised. 'Really?'

'Yeah, really.' Naina says. 'It was so humiliating, Pia! I mean,

I'm an adult! No one talks to me like that! And it's not the first time; she always does this, to everyone. Others can keep quiet if they want, but nothing is above my self-respect, Pia,' Naina says, and adds dramatically, 'Nothing.'

She stops to take a sip of water.

'So this time I didn't keep quiet. I looked at her in the eye and said, "Sorry, but I don't do outfit-borrowing".'

'You did?' I'm impressed.

'Damn right I did!' Naina says. 'She couldn't believe someone had spoken back to her. She looked surprised, and then she said, "Naina, the dress code has been decided by the CO, and he was very clear that the ladies should wear a turquoise saree. Now, do you—or your husband—want to go against his wishes?"'

I gulp some water too. Mrs Sahdeva brought out the big guns here, not-so-subtly suggesting that wearing anything but turquoise would be seen as disregarding the CO's command, not just by Naina, but Naina's husband as well.

'You see what she did there, Pia?' Naina asks me.

I nod quickly, my eyes wide with shock.

'She practically threatened not just me, but also my husband.'

'Did you say anything?'

Naina nods. She looks a bit taken aback at her own courage. 'I said, "Oh, since when is the CO deciding what the ladies should wear, Mrs Sahdeva?" In front of everyone! But she started it,' Naina says, trying to sound cool, but there is a tremor in her voice. 'She said, "Naina, this is unacceptable." Ha fucking Ha! She couldn't think of anything better!'

Now I am really concerned. This has turned serious.

'"Naina, this is unacceptable!" Naina mimics Mrs Sahdeva again. '"Well, you pushed me too far Mrs Sahdeva," I said.

"Screw the dress code, nothing gives you the right to be rude to people," I told her firmly. She couldn't breathe—she was so pissed! Then she said, "My husband is definitely going to hear about this, Naina. You can't talk to a senior like this." Imagine! She thinks she is my senior! I said, "Mrs Sahdeva, you are *not* my senior. Your husband is my husband's senior at work. I don't work for fauj. You can't force me to do anything." Everyone else was staring at me in horror, but Pia, there is a limit to being insulted and today was my tipping point.' Naina is breathing heavily. 'Mrs Sahdeva shook her head and said, "I'm not forcing you; but you have to follow the rules. I did it in my time . . . everyone does." Then I just got mad, Pia. I also shouted. I said, "This is the most ridiculous argument I've ever heard! You'll do it because I've done it too? Really? Is that your reason to be so mean to everyone? Well, Mrs Sahdeva, if you did it, it was your choice. Too bad. I am not going to do anything that I don't want to and no one can make me do it".' Naina is now slightly shaking, as if reliving the scene. I might be shaking too, I think.

'Then?' I ask in a whisper.

'Then she said, "The Unit has done so much for your Naina, and this is how you repay it?" I was exhausted by then, so I just shrugged. "This is unacceptable," she said and left. I left quickly, too. Now let's see what the evil couple does,' she says, looking pale.

I'm worried. What next, I wonder. Maybe the GOC's wife will summon Naina for a lecture. Naina's husband could receive a reprimand too, who knows. God, this is horrible.

Naina is trying to sound cool but she's sweating heavily and I can tell she's thinking the same thing.

'What next?' I can't stop saying to no one in particular.

Naina shrugs wearily and hums '*Toh fir aaoo mujhko sataoo . . .*' in a worn-out voice.

After a couple of days we're at Arjun's Officers' Mess for high tea, welcoming Captain Sood and his new wife to the station. The new bride—dethroning Mrs James and I—is called Kanika and is, well, strange.

She's very fair and is wearing a heavily-embroidered salwaar kameez in extremely bright shimmery red. Her hands are covered with an intricate mehendi design and she has green and red glass bangles till her elbows.

And she has nose hair, peeking out of her pale white nostrils.

Once I've noticed the nose hair, I just can't look away. Really, it's all I can focus on, like I'm under a spell or something. How is it possible to have nose hair so rich and flourishing?

'Hi!' Nose Hair says to me, and the hair trembles a little. Oh God, I'm going to throw up.

'Pia?' Mrs James, who has just introduced us, says and looks closely at me as if to check whether I'm about to have a seizure or something.

'Yes, hi,' I say quickly, forcing my eyes away from Nose Hair. There is an awkward silence for a second and then Nose Hair laughs loudly.

'Your friend looks like a lost puppy, Jincy,' Nose Hair says to Mrs James.

'No, um, I'm just distracted,' I say in what I hope is a calm tone, forcing myself to look into her eyes. Did she notice me staring at her nose hair? She *is* aware of her nose hair, right?

'Pia is our quirky sweetheart, she's so funny!' says a smiling Mrs James.

'I can see that,' Nose Hair says. She is looking at me as if sizing me up for a duel or something. 'Not a good thing in an Army wife, though,' she adds, smiling sweetly.

I am just thinking of a cool, smart reply, when she is called away by Mrs Bhandari.

'I told her a lot about you, Pia,' Mrs James gushes. 'She knows we are tight buddies, you and I. I told her you are the go-to girl in the whole station for fun and cheesy fries!'

She looks happily at me. I smile back. She might have talked me up a bit too much, but Mrs James is really sweet.

'So the mentoring has already begun, huh?' I tease her.

'Oh yes,' she nods. 'I've told her that she has got to take the whole Army wife thing seriously so that she doesn't suffer later.'

'Like us,' I sigh.

'Like me,' she says. 'Not you. You've fared pretty well, Pia. In fact, I told her to watch you and learn. You will set a good example for the newbie.'

Ha ha, I am about to laugh hysterically, when Mrs Sengupta and Mrs Singh join us. Very soon, I find myself telling them about the drama between Naina and Mrs Sahdeva. Both of them know Mrs Sahdeva socially.

'The woman has become a raging maniac since her husband became full colonel. This was waiting to happen. She's practically been begging for a confrontation. If not Naina, then someone else would have done it,' Mrs Sengupta says.

Mrs Singh nods, but adds, 'This is bad, though, for Naina. Really, really bad. Mrs Sahdeva is a colonel's wife, and there will be consequences.'

'I know,' I say sadly. Poor Naina.

'Whatever happens, at least she stood up for herself,' Mrs Sengupta says.

'True, but this is a little extreme,' Mrs Singh says. 'I hope this doesn't have any adverse effect on Naina's husband's ACR.'

An ACR—the Annual Confidential Report—is basically an officer's performance report. Would a CO actually ruin an officer's ACR because of what his wife says, I wonder. Seems petty, and shouldn't a person who the Indian Army thinks worthy enough to command an entire Unit be better than that?

Mrs Sengupta sees my worried expression and says, 'Chill. I bet Colonel Sahdeva will ask his wife to shut up about the entire matter because, if they take it forward and involve more people, she'll be found to be in the wrong. Come on, everyone knows she's vindictive, right? Senior people like the commander and his wife will also know the truth; they weren't born yesterday.'

She has a point and I'm hoping she's right, for Naina's sake.

'Plus, it's quite a loss of face for them too, so maybe they'll just hush it up,' Mrs Singh adds.

'This Mrs Sahdeva interests me,' Mrs Sengupta says out of the blue. 'People say she's the actual CO of the Unit, not her husband.'

'Yes, he is a good man I've heard,' Mrs Singh says. 'Drinks too much and abuses a lot, but he's good natured and generous. The wife, though, is power hungry. She influences him, they say.'

'But it's so strange. I mean, your husband is employed by the Army, not you,' I protest.

'Golden words, sweetie,' Mrs Sengupta says sweetly. 'Remember that when Captain Arjun becomes a commanding officer.'

'Of course I will,' I say seriously. 'It is his job, his rank. In any case, I could never be rude to people.'

'We can't,' Mrs Singh agrees with me, 'but some ladies can. And if the husband of that lady becomes a full colonel and commands a unit, God save the world!'

chapter thirteen

A Sudden Blast and Some Other Stuff

A week after the Ladies' Meet, all the Unit ladies are invited to Mrs Nair's house for coffee. See? There is never a dull moment in the Army. You are always attending something or the other, and I absolutely love all this socializing. I have even stopped trolling Facebook. For the first time in years, my real life is so much more happening than anything I could ever make up on Facebook.

Since I'm going to the CO's residence, I pick a sensible yet chic outfit—skinny-fit jeans and a long pink top paired with a dark pink shrug. Stylish, but fully covered!

I go over to Naina's house to get her opinion and she happily tells me that Colonel Sahdeva did not even discuss the quarrel with her husband. Perhaps Mrs Singh and Mrs Sengupta were right after all: the Sahdevas are trying to hush up the incident, pretending it never happened, to save their own reputation. What a relief!

After Naina approves my outfit and informs me excitedly that Kareena Kapoor was photographed in the same colour combination at a recent movie premier (holding me back a full ten minutes because she insisted on looking for and showing me the latest copy of *Stardust* where a glowing Kareena Kapoor is photographed wearing blue jeans and a loose pink tee and a shrug), I confidently head to the CO's house.

How does Kareena's skin glow so damn much? I mean, she's hardly wearing any makeup in the picture, just some lip gloss perhaps, and she looks fab. And what is up with her cheekbones? Naina says she 'got them done', but I don't quite get how you can get your cheekbones done. She's just lucky, I decide. Winner of the genetic lottery. Lacks miserably in the acting department though, which sucks. For her, I mean. I don't like her anyway. And I don't know why Arjun does. I've noticed him watching her with great interest several times. He even gets ready to watch her movies, which is a bit ridiculous to say the least. Arjun has no taste, really.

I reach the CO's residence and catch Mrs Sengupta who is just about to ring the doorbell. She's wearing a lovely long yellow skirt with a short kurta and a scarf.

'Good evening!' I wish her.

'Oh hello, Miss Pathankot Cantt!' she looks at me appreciatively and makes a hooting sound.

Once inside the huge, highly-decorated living room, Mrs Nair greets us. She is wearing a pretty kutra and jeans herself and she looks almost ten years younger. Everyone eventually settles down on the comfortable couches and with the smell of hot snacks wafting from the kitchen, we start dissecting the Ladies' Meet and the guests. Sarees, the response to the games, the décor and food are discussed. Tea/coffee and snacks are being 'shown' when Mrs Sengupta turns to me.

'Pia, tell us about your quality time with H. I'm sure it was enlightening.'

'Ah, time with H,' says Mrs Singh and flinches. 'One barely survives that! She sat next to me at some meet and those were the longest two hours in my entire Army life.'

'You are an Army daughter, Mrs Singh!' exclaims Mrs James.

'Yes, I am an Army daughter, so saying it was the longest two hours is really something,' Mrs Singh says with exaggerated horror in her voice. Everyone laughs.

'She is . . . well . . . strange,' I say. 'I thought she had excellent chemistry with her CO's wife, and then she tells me that—' I air-quote the words and try to imitate H's voice, '—"the woman is crazy, she bitches about me, is a buddhi, I'd rather be in your Unit", etc.'

Everyone laughs loudly, even Mrs Nair. Oh, she's there too, I suddenly realize. Maybe I should have skipped the buddhi part.

'Harassment, I told you!' Mrs Sengupta says to me. 'This H creature is *so* annoying, with all her "new mommy" and backslapping stupidity. Forget her CO's wife, even I'd pull her up any chance I got just for the heck of it,' she says, looking like something has left a bad taste in her mouth. I almost giggle and catch myself in time to change it into a sophisticated laugh.

'Her marriage and that entire *Ajab Prem Ki Ghazab Kahani* charade is a bit too much, if you ask me,' Mrs Singh says in true Army daughter-Army wife fashion, her tone severely disapproving.

'True,' Mrs Nair replies. 'It must have been difficult for her CO to control the situation.'

'Yes. This is the Army,' Mrs James speaks, looking only at me. 'Here, you don't stand out, you don't fade in, and you don't do anything that ruffles any feathers. Just be.' She then looks at Mrs Nair and smiles sweetly as if expecting her to draw a star on her homework for good work.

I suppress a smile at Mrs James' feeble attempt to get into Mrs Nair's good books. Unfortunately for Mrs James, Mrs Nair seems to have taken that dinner-hosting fiasco to heart, as if Mrs James meant to personally offend her that evening. Even now, she continues to sit there, expressionless, totally ignoring Mrs James.

Mrs James' smile freezes, but there's still hope in her eyes.

Nothing from Mrs Nair. She doesn't even look at her.

Mrs Sengupta, though, is glancing from one to the other with supreme interest. She catches my eye and I have a hysterical desire to giggle again, so I quickly grab a piece of chocolate brownie and stuff it into my mouth. Nose Hair looks at me with narrowed eyes and then gives Mrs James a look which I fail to comprehend.

'But hats off to the husband, no? He married the girl he loved, in spite of all the hoopla,' Mrs Singh breaks the awkward silence, and all of us nod. Except Mrs Sengupta.

'No big deal,' she says. 'What is an Army Officer, if not committed?'

I have to say, I'm impressed.

And though my heart must have known it for quite some time now, my consciousness just realizes it, at that very moment, among all these wonderful yet different women, that this is what Army instils in you—strength of character and fortitude, spunk and resilience. And it must be an Army association thing, because it's not just the officers and men, but the Army wives too who have this huge capacity to go on despite obstacles, to see a mission through to its completion. It reflects in every aspect of their lives, our lives. Really, *what is an Army officer if not committed?* I pull my shrug closer as I feel goose bumps rise on my arms.

Army is really overwhelming, I think on my way back home. Also, I have so much to learn. Like, not giggling like a ditz all the time. I decide I will also avoid looking at or listening to Mrs Sengupta during such gatherings. She just gives me the giggles somehow! Avoiding her will instantly solve more than half my issues. It will be tough since I'm really fond of her, but I have to be determined.

And I will practice keeping a straight face in the mirror every day. That will surely help, right? What a nice idea! I already feel mature. Nothing can affect my poise now, I tell myself with an Army-strong determination.

While having dinner that evening—aloo paranthas and mint chutney made by yours truly—Arjun says, 'Do you want to go to your mom's place for some time?'

'Nooo!' I say at once. I mean, I do miss my home and everything, but I think inviting them here and showing them my new life and my outstanding domestic skills will be a lot more fun. Imagine my mom's proud face when I carry a perfectly baked three-layer cake to her, all cool and composed in my 'Head Chef' apron! Or, scratch that. I can't bake or cook in front of my mother; she'd probably have a coronary. Anyway, I should probably talk to my parents first . . . . But—wait a minute . . . 'Why?' I ask Arjun.

'I'll be going to practice camp for a month, so I was thinking—'

'*What?*' I shriek. One bloody month? What the hell is this? I didn't sign up for this. 'Where?'

'Practice camp, away from Pathankot,' he says, as if it's the most obvious thing in the world. 'Don't worry, the phones will work there,' he adds quickly when he sees my expression.

I think I might cry now. To hell with poise, this is a total crisis situation!

One full month?

And didn't he go for a practice camp just before our wedding? He'd been away for a month then as well, and every time we spoke on the phone I would hear strong winds in the background.

What the hell is a practice camp anyway? I stare at him incredulously.

He quickly begins explaining how the entire Unit—officers and men—will be gone for a month to a certain location away from town, where they will practise their war skills.

'The more you sweat in peace, the less you bleed in war,' he says happily, and then, seeing the I'm-going-to-punch-you look on my face, quickly sobers up. 'We need to be ready and the weapons need to be used regularly too,' he tells me.

'What kind of stupid weapons are these, that they get bad if they're not used regularly?' I say. Clearly the government is not paying enough attention to the country's defence, giving the Army low-quality equipment that causes issues like this.

'It is lot more than just using the weapons,' Arjun says, suddenly an expert on practice camps. 'This is more about war tactics, about skill and performance.'

Whatever.

I am crying now. He's going away for a month, and if that's not enough, he is trying to make it sound all right. He attempts to hug me but I punch him in the gut and walk away.

Maybe he should have prepared me for this, instead of springing it on me at the last minute. 'I knew you'd react like a child,' he tells me, following me into the kitchen. 'And it's a regular thing, baby, I'll go at least twice a year.'

Did I say I was crying? Well, now I'm sobbing loudly, wiping my tears and my runny nose on his white tee-shirt.

Okay. I've finally come to terms with the fact that Arjun will be leaving for one month. Practice camps happen every year (*twice!*) and the sooner I get used to/get over it, the better. There are three weeks for him to leave, so we decide to make the most of it. Actually, this is his suggestion—as a truce; I was pretty mad after all.

We've been going out for dinner almost every day. I've even managed to blackmail him into shopping with me at the local market. Long drives at night, sometimes even till Jammu, are common now.

Needless to say, I've cut down on my evening walks and coffee sessions with Naina or anyone else, and I quickly finish household work so I have time when he gets home.

Some would say we're overdoing it, but come on! One whole month?

With one week to go for the practice camp, Mrs James calls me on the fauji phone.

'I can't believe he's going for a month!' she says.

'I know, right? I was in major shock when I heard about it,' I tell her. 'I've been trying to spend as much time with him as possible, these last couple of weeks—'

'Weeks? When did you find out?' she asks.

'Um. Arjun told me two weeks back.'

'I don't believe this!' she wails. 'James told me today!'

I don't know what to say. I feel awful for her.

'He doesn't tell me anything!' she continues, sounding really upset. 'He doesn't think it's necessary to keep his wife informed about such important things! Pia . . . I think he is regretting this marriage.'

'What? Where did that come from?' I say immediately. 'He must have been busy, they've all been busy. There's apparently a lot to be done before they leave.'

'No,' she says, in a voice that feels tinny and distant. 'It's not work, it's him. He couldn't be less bothered about me. He still thinks he's single and doesn't want to make any changes. Even Kanika says so, Pia. He isn't making any effort towards this marriage and it's breaking my heart.'

'Come on Mrs James!' I say cautiously. 'You know it isn't true. Don't go imagining the worst just because he forgot to tell you about a stupid practice camp.'

'You don't understand, Pia,' she says. 'You don't know. I think this wedding was a mistake.'

Her voice resonates with sadness and I feel bad. I don't know what to say or do to cheer her up.

chapter fourteen

Learning to Live Alone, and Liking It, Somewhat

It's here.

Despite all the positive thinking and visualization that the practice camp would miraculously be cancelled (so much for the 'if you want something with all your heart, blah blah' rule), the day Arjun is to leave for a month (*one full month!*) is here.

VH1 is playing *Leaving on a Jet Plane* as if on cue, and I am so emotional that I'm tempted to fake a heart attack to stop him from going. I don't, though. I'm a responsible person that way.

Yes.

Also, last night it suddenly dawned on me that there is indeed a bright side to the situation—being away from me for a month will definitely make Arjun love me more, realize my importance in his life and it will rekindle our fire!

Right? *Right?*

Not that our fire needs any rekindling or anything, if you know what I mean—but distance will make his heart grow fonder, I'm sure.

Feeling slightly optimistic, I lay down the breakfast on the table—a pitcher of iced tea and Arjun's favourite cheesy fries with salsa dip. Halfway through breakfast, however, emotions overtake me. 'What am I going to do?' I say helplessly.

'Miss me,' Arjun takes my hand and weaves his fingers through mine.

I nod and miserably stuff a spoonful of dip in my mouth. Oh God. I'm going to miss him so much.

'I'll call every hour, baby,' he hugs me warmly. 'And at night, we'll talk until we fall asleep. Every day.' Just like when we were dating. It cheers me up a little.

'Take care, okay?' I say to him and mentally check all the love notes I have hidden in his luggage. Just one more to go, so I hug him tight when the vehicle arrives to pick him up, and surreptitiously slip a neatly folded piece of paper in his pocket.

I'm so smooth, really. Imagine his delight when he finds it and reads a heart-wrenching love poem by Pablo Neruda, written out by me in pink glitter. He'll probably find it today, considering it's sitting in his pocket right now, and I bet he'll call me right away!

I wave at him till the vehicle disappears. Then, I run inside and cry. VH1 plays *Better Together* by Jack Johnson.

The shrill ring of the fauji phone wakes me up with a start. I was so upset after Arjun left that, in typical Bollywood fashion, I drew all the curtains and went to sleep at noon. The clock on the wall says it is two in the afternoon.

'Hello?' I mumble into the phone.

'I'm lonely!' Yes, it is indeed Mrs James, who I guess, has been crying since Major James left.

'I know,' I say rubbing my eyes. 'It's horrible.'

'I can't eat, I can't sleep. I'm going mad all alone in this house!' she says.

'Why don't you come over?' I offer. 'We can spend the evening together.'

'Okay-dokey!' she says at once.

And I regret it already. It's eight-freaking-o'clock, and she is still here! On my couch!

Don't get me wrong; I'm fond of Mrs James and, well, I feel a little lonely too. Plus, she brought a cigarette along. So in the beginning, all was good. We talked, gossiped and eventually even laughed a little about things. The mood lightened by about ten shades, with both of us feeling a tad better in each other's company. After all, we're both recently married, and this is our first separation from our husbands—we understand each other.

Or so I think.

It's kind of hard to tell with Mrs James. Perhaps it's because I'm in such a foul mood myself, but her absorption in her own (real or imagined) misery is particularly annoying this evening. She's warm and good fun, but she is not really sensitive to what the other person might be going through, you know? I blame her short attention span for it, really. I am obviously behaving myself though, in Army wife fashion—polite and good-natured. But inside, I'm worried I might burst a vein.

And, it is eight already, and she is in the middle of her I-want-kids-right-away-but-my-husband-doesn't-and-how-can-he-not-want-children-right-away?-He's-so-insensitive monologue, and I am getting a little irritated. I know I probably seem selfish here, happily sharing her one cigarette and then wanting her out of the way, but seriously, you try sitting through even one of these gloomy sessions and then tell me. You just try!

By eight-thirty I'm so aggravated that I even give her a few subtle hints—like holding my head in my hands when she talks about her art gallery and how art can save the world (from what, I don't know; I stopped listening about an hour ago), but she is too upset to notice anything. If only you would stop complaining for once, I want to scream in her ear.

Okay. Perhaps I'm overreacting, I tell myself as she starts talking about how she hates money. Or hates asking her husband for money. Something like that. Perhaps I am getting unnecessarily irritated because I am quite sad myself, you know, with Arjun leaving for a month and all. I should take it easy, really.

I breathe in and out slowly to calm myself, and I can't even get that right at the moment because I end up yawning twice.

'Oh, you're tired!' she says, looking guilty.

I'm a horrible person. Now I feel guilty.

'Oh,' I wave a hand and smile brightly. 'I'm just lazy all the time. No big deal.'

'Oh god, it's *so* late!' she exclaims looking at the clock. 'I've bored you with my problems, and see, it's almost dinner time. I'll make a move now.'

'Mmm,' I say, afraid she might interpret anything else as an invitation to stay longer.

'Okay, see you tomorrow then?' she gets up slowly.

'Mmm.'

'Back to my lonely dungeon, I go!' she sighs. 'A night of sleeping on the couch.'

'Huh?' It slips out before I can stop myself.

'Can't sleep on the bed, I get scared. These fauji houses with their high ceilings and creaking doors, too scary! I'll just switch the TV on and sleep in front of it.'

She looks so depressed and I wonder what to say or do to make her feel better. Maybe I should—

NO!

But she is lonely and heartbreakingly sad—

Nooooooooo!

Just for one night—

'Why don't you stay back tonight?' I hear myself saying. Am I schizophrenic?

Mrs James' face lights up instantly.

After a few minutes, though, I feel good about my decision. If she's in my house, I don't have to worry about her crying her eyes out on her couch the entire night.

We make some fried rice together and watch back-to-back seasons of *Desperate Housewives*.

We are at the episode where Julie asks Susan when she last had sex. Susan stops what she is doing and stands still.

Julie: Are you mad that I asked?

Susan: No. I'm just trying to remember.

Mrs James looks at me meaningfully and says, 'When was the last time for you?'

'This morning. Before he left,' I say, and feel my cheeks getting hot. It was awesome. It was unplanned and delicious and well, really, really passionate. I cautiously look down the neck of my T-shirt to see if a love bite is visible. 'And you?' I ask, still inspecting my neckline.

She remains quiet for a while and I think, Oh god, please don't let her say she doesn't remember!

'First thing in the morning today,' she says at last. 'And then after breakfast.'

Then she winks at me and we giggle. See? Hanging out with girls is so therapeutic.

'Are Army wives supposed to talk about sex?' I ask her with a straight face, after the giggles subside.

'It wasn't covered in the Etiquette Class, so I'm guessing it's okay,' she replies in an equally deadpan tone. 'But I'll confirm it with Mrs Nair for you.'

And we burst into a hysterical fit of laughter.

One whole week has gone by without Arjun.

I managed to find a few fridge magnets which I've put up to cheer myself up. My favourites are:

- Military Wives—Sacrificing Months of Sex for the Country
- God found some of the strongest women and made their match a soldier
- The Army may have my soldier, but I have his heart
- She who waits, also serves. Army Wives Rock!

And my absolute favourite:

- There is strong. There is Army Strong. And then there is Army Wife Strong

Pretty cool, right? Except, they've stopped making me feel good for more than five minutes in the past week.

To be honest, there are times when I mentally kick myself. I am an independent girl! I have moved to and studied in a new city, stayed in a hostel, lived alone, worked at a very stressful job and I never felt lonely.

It is strange how being with Arjun seems to have altered my basic composition in so little time. Now it's as if I need him physically close to even breathe.

And I'm afraid to admit it, but Ganga bhaiya's absence somehow adds to the gloom. His being around is somehow a reminder of Arjun's presence. And he's luckier than I am. He is with Arjun in the practice camp, obviously. I think I might be a little jealous of Ganga Bhaiya.

But all in all I think I'm holding it together; I'm actually doing better than I thought I would. All the other wives seem to be coping well too—most of them have experienced the practice camp several times by now. They even kindly call Mrs James, Nose Hair and me several times to make sure that we—the relatively newbie wives—are not hanging ourselves from our shower rods.

Mrs James has been my constant companion all week long. She told me once that she invited Nose Hair as well, but she refused, saying she was doing fine. Anyway, with Nose Hair declining to join in, the two of us are having fun. We often cook together at her house or mine, and spend most of our days together, browsing magazines or surfing TV channels. We are two extremely lazy girls with zero motivation.

A suggestion from Mrs James that we try out a new cake recipe is met with my lazy 'Meh.'

When I say, 'Let's go to the gym and check out the people

who work out there,' she rolls over in the bed and says, 'People are stupid.'

We often find ourselves with too much time and no way to spend it.

'That's why I want kids,' she tells me one evening. I look at her to see if she's joking. She's not. In fact she is so serious I think she might cry because she doesn't have any yet. Children, I mean.

'With children, you have no time to even think about anything else. Plus, motherhood is so fulfilling,' she says with that misty far-away look in her eyes. Like conjunctivitis. I bury my head in the *Stardust* I borrowed from Naina. Mrs James gets really bizarre at times, I think.

As much as I like her company during the day, it is getting difficult to have her around in the night. This entire week, Mrs James has been sleeping over at my place—in my bedroom, with me.

First, her husband isn't calling her as frequently as Arjun calls me. And when he does call, it's only to say that he's busy and that he can't talk. Every time Arjun calls me, her face becomes long and, later, she complains nonstop about Major James and how insensitive he is.

'They are together, doing the same thing! Then how come Captain Arjun finds time to call you and he doesn't? He always says he is busy! How can someone be too busy to call his wife of less than a year, Pia?'

I tell her that since Major James is senior to Arjun, maybe he does have more responsibilities.

'Bullshit,' she replies angrily.

And second, with her sleeping next to me on my bed, I cannot talk to Arjun properly. Forget phone sex or any naughty conversation, I can't even kiss him good night without the fear of her listening.

What's annoying is that she makes no effort to give me space—at times, she even joins in on the conversation, adding a point or two or suggesting things to say. The situation is just too awkward and neither Arjun nor I know how to handle it.

Sigh.

chapter fifteen

We're Gonna Be All Right

I'm sitting cross-legged on Mrs James's carpet, painting my toes a deep blue, when her doorbell rings.

'Rejoice! It's a Welfare meeting,' Mrs James announces and hands me a notice to sign.

'Welfare' is a term given to the interaction between officer wives and the OR/jawan families that are living in the station—to communicate with, to listen to and resolve their issues if any, to talk to them about their children's education and health, encouraging their participation in the various vocational courses that the Army organizes for the families and much more. At least this is what I know so far. This will be my first Welfare meeting, and I'm excited.

A few days go by, and then we're all off to the OR family residence block. On our way, Mrs Sengupta tells me, 'Their husbands are away for the practice camp as well, so we need to talk to the wives and find out if they are facing any trouble.'

'What kind of trouble could they be facing?' I ask.

'Any kind. Like the vegetables they are getting are not fresh, or their children are not going for tuitions because the father is not home. Domestic, mainly.'

'Um. What am I supposed to tell them?'

'Talk about how important education is. Tell them that the children must study hard. Bring up hygiene and health and tell them to keep their houses clean.'

I frown. No matter how my domestic skills have improved, I just don't see myself lecturing some woman about her own child's education and hygiene. Mrs Sengupta looks at me and shrugs.

'It's a tradition in the Army, Pia. They look up to us,' she says without a touch of irony. 'For them, we are mentors. But our Unit has really good and well-educated jawan wives. Don't worry, you'll be fine.'

On reaching the main gate of the block, we find a whole group of ladies gathered in the compound, waiting for us. One by one, all the officer wives reach, and finally Mrs Nair—after meeting a lot of ladies personally and hugging a few—introduces Nose Hair and me to the lot.

'This is Pia memsaab,' she says putting an arm around my shoulder, addressing them all in Hindi. 'She is Captain Arjun's wife, and as you know, they recently got married.' Several nod in excitement and I smile nervously.

'She wanted to meet you all. If someone hasn't received wedding sweets from her, this is your chance,' Mrs Nair jokes and laughter follows.

I am promptly left to my own devices after that, as every other officer wife starts talking to a different group of ladies. Mrs James, and even Nose Hair, seem to know what to do, whom to talk to and I feel somewhat inadequate.

I am fidgeting in my heels when a group forms in front of me. One lady, who seems to be guiding the others in this group, tells me that they are wives of all the soldiers in Arjun's Battery.

'Oh!' I say confidently, as if I know exactly what a Battery is.

They are all looking at me now, so I clear my throat and say timidly 'You're all fine?'

They nod and smile widely. The lady who came up first says, 'Memsaab, we're happy to meet you. My husband works with Arjun Saab, he's the head clerk.'

Another woman invites me to her house; she's made paani-puri she says; so we all walk toward her home with her and I learn that she is a JCO's wife and her name is Anita.

'Anita,' I say, remembering my mentor-duty suddenly, 'is everyone okay here, with the husbands not around and everything? There's no problem, is there?'

'Aaall izz well, Memsaab!' she recites the famous line from a song and giggles. 'But a few houses have leaking roofs. We've complained to the MES, but no action only.'

'Oh. Anything else?'

'No, Memsaab; just, when the menfolk aren't here, we feel a little empty-empty, that's all,' she says, and a few others nod.

Aww, I think, look at us! A bunch of girls, missing our soldiers! I sigh loudly.

Once inside Anita's house, I talk to the three ladies whose roofs are leaking and take down their husbands' names in my cell phone. Another lady says her husband has been given the patrolling duty to Sambha every month and she is alone a lot, so could I tell some officer to please put someone else on patrolling duty? This, I know nothing about. The Unit does patrolling as well? Wow, this is like the movies! I had no idea. I'll find out, I tell her anyway and make another note in my cell phone.

Then I ask everyone their names, about their children and themselves. They are a delightful lot. And extremely talented—they know how to knit complicated patterns that my mother would love to learn, how to make adorable stuffed toys that you could sell in a mall, how to make amazing candles, how to paint bed sheets and a hundred other things that I didn't know people could do in their houses.

Each and every one of these women has completed school, about eleven of them have completed or are doing their graduation, and one is an LLB.

We talk about everything under the sun. Anita shows me a soft toy she made (a frog! adorable!) and Chimmi, another young wife from the Battery, asks me if I am on Facebook. Lata, the candle expert, hands me a bag full of scented handmade candles with glossy wax crystals in them and I hand it back politely, with all the persuasive power I have in me. Who knows whether accepting gifts is allowed in the Army or not! But on the whole, I am having a great time, chatting and laughing with them.

It dawns on me that there is so much they can teach me about Army life, and life in general. They are strong women, living alone every once in a while, bringing up their children with good values, and the camaraderie amongst them is commendable. I wonder what 'welfare' *I* can possibly do for this group.

In Anita's drawing room, my newness in the Army becomes a topic of conversation, and stories about the Army—funny and educational—start to unfurl. Postings to stations I lost count of, and to places that I've never even heard of, are being discussed as Anita serves us delicious paani-puri. Suddenly, I notice one young lady—Anita had introduced her as Chitra—who has remained quiet through the evening. She looks a bit sullen.

'Why is Chitra looking so dull?' I ask.

She just smiles and averts her eyes. Suspicious! I look at Anita, who sighs and says, 'Memsaab, this poor girl was told that her husband was a soldier in the Army. She married him and stayed with her in-laws in Haryana for a year. She came here this year because her in-laws were treating her badly. Only after coming here she came to know that he is not really a soldier, but is in the housekeeping staff, the safai wala.'

'She is a BA pass, Memsaab!' Chimmi says, and pats Chitra on her back.

The other ladies look sympathetically towards her, while she looks like she might start crying any moment. I don't know how to react to this. She was lied to, was tricked into marrying someone who wasn't what he said he was, and now she must feel trapped in this marriage.

'How long have you been here?' I ask her.

'One year,' she replies.

'No children?'

She shakes her head, and Anita gives me a look which I am supposed to understand but I don't.

'Did you meet your husband before the wedding?' I ask her.

'No, Memsaab,' she says in a low voice. 'We met only after the wedding. We saw each other at a function, that's it.'

'And who told you about his job?'

'His parents told mine.'

'So Chitra, your husband didn't lie to you, right?' I ask her.

She doesn't reply, just continues to stare at the floor. 'You can't keep punishing him or yourself for something his parents did, right?'

She nods and Anita immediately supports me. 'See, Memsaab is also telling you now. Go easy on the poor man. Not talking to him or crying all the time will not solve anything.'

'She cries all the time? It's been a year!' I say in surprise.

'Yes, she cries and curses him. Poor fellow has been very patient but till when will a man bear all the drama, Memsaab?' Anita says philosophically.

'This is bad, Chitra,' I say, shaking my head. I am already feeling very mentor-like. 'Don't treat him like that. If he's put up with all this for a year, I can tell you that he loves you, hai na? Make the most of life. And he is a soldier after all! Not just everyone can get into the Army. If the Army recruited him, it means he is better than the rest!'

Everyone nods and Chitra nods faintly too. I feel pleased about the way I handled this. Also, I have a feeling she'll think about what I just said, because I meant every word. Anita smiles brightly and whispers, 'Thank you Memsaab', in my ears.

I like Welfare! Who knew I had mentoring skills!

My smooth mentor skills seem to have zero affect on Mrs James though; she gets more and more miserable as the days go by. She misses her husband, which is a bit strange, if you ask me. I mean, she is so pissed at Major James all the time, and her complaining about his insensitive behaviour never stops, so missing him this much seems a bit queer. But that's just me.

Naina thinks that absence has made her heart grow fonder, like the saying goes, and that if she stays away from him for a few more weeks, she might even be ready to overlook all their problems.

I doubt it though.

Anyway, she doesn't have a few more weeks—the practice camp gets over in about ten days, and I am already making plans for when Arjun returns. I want to make it super special.

The good news is, Mrs James is finally sleeping in her house. Yes! I guess she got the hint when I started going to the living room each time Arjun called, and once I even slept on the couch there. She woke me up early in the morning. 'Why didn't you come back to the bedroom to sleep?' she asked.

'Um. I guess I fell asleep while talking on the phone,' I told her, bleary-eyed.

She made some breakfast for me in my kitchen that day, and after we had dinner that night at her place, she said she would try and sleep in her own home. 'I have to get used to it, after all,' she said. 'You're not going to be with me on every posting, right?'

I immediately felt a little guilty.

'Ma'am is right; she has to learn to be on her own,' Arjun said to me on the phone that night. 'This is the Army, Pia. Women have to be strong.'

'Good riddance no, Pia?' Mrs Sengupta says when I tell her on the phone. 'And she has Kanika next door to bunk with if she gets lonely or scared.'

Oh yeah. Nose Hair, her neighbour, could help. If she's willing to, that is. She hasn't seemed particularly interested in socializing with either of us so far.

Anyway, I finally I have my entire room to myself and I can talk as trashy as I want on the phone with Arjun, ha!

Only, it's not possible when one of you is sleeping in a tent. Talking trashy, I mean. But who's complaining? I get to talk to him without someone peering over my shoulder, and it's all I want for now.

Tonight we talked for a long time. I feel warm inside and I hope Mrs James is sleeping peacefully, or better still, talking happily on the phone with Major James.

She is right; I am not going to be with her on every posting. Arjun is right too, she is an Army wife—she has to be strong.

Strength is so much more than just living alone, and now I'm totally questioning if *I* have what it takes, because Arjun will be back in a few days and all I have to do right now is just deal with the 'meanwhile', and yet it seems pretty daunting.

'Meanwhile is the worst time,' Mrs Sengupta says to me on the fauji phone. She is calling to see how I am doing.

She is right, meanwhile is the toughest.

I often find myself wondering if I am cut out for the unusual Army-wife life. This month-long practice camp has certainly tested my mettle, and there are still about nine days to go.

Sure, I have fun; I have Naina and we go on evening walks around the park together. She and her husband invite me over to their house a lot. I experiment in the kitchen with Mrs James (who comes over for dinner and cooks lunch when I go to her house—my suggestion). I also talk to Arjun for hours in the night, till either of us falls asleep.

But there's a teeny-tiny part inside of me that feels lonely. Night after night, when an exhausted Arjun goes to sleep and I lie awake on my side of the huge bed, I find myself thinking about all the real-life stories I've heard so far about Army wives who are clearly braver than I am.

An Army wife is a single mother even when she is married, she is the saree-clad maverick who manages the show single-handedly with family and house when the husband is busy saving the country, and she is the stylish woman who smiles and winks through a heap of problems that her civilian friends would *never* understand.

An Army wife is probably the only woman in the world who knows and readily accepts that she is the mistress, because, let's face it, the Army is the wife and the wife gets all the damn attention!

It does not matter if the husband wears a brigadier's cross swords, a captain's three stars or a jawan's stripes, because they all have wives who worry about them equally.

And like I said, this entire week I wondered if I am strong enough.

'I am lonely for the first time in my life,' I complain to Arjun on the phone.

'Our mind plays tricks on us in situations like this, but it's how we find our true courage and strength to deal with things,' he says. His words echo in my mind a million times.

Will I find my strength soon? I hope I do.

chapter sixteen

Overestimating and Underestimating

The day I thought I wouldn't survive to see is here at last.

Yes, Arjun (and the entire Unit) will be returning home today!

I've been so jumpy and restless since the morning that Naina says it's hard to believe I managed not to kill myself in the last month. I ignored her because, frankly, people who are not first-time-practice-camp-survivor-wives should not be allowed to comment on those who are.

And she's not as cucumber-cool as she's pretending to be right now: both times her husband went away for practice camp, she ran off to her parents' house, returning a month later with shopping bags full of stuff she claims she bought because she was depressed. For instance, a fluorescent green birdhouse that hangs on a tree in her garden. Honestly, I have never seen one single bird go near that thing. In fact, I'm sure it works somewhat like a scarecrow.

'Stupid birds,' she says, sounding casual whenever I bring up the subject. 'Can't stand all that chirping anyway.'

So anyway, Arjun is going to be back today! Eeeeeeee!

I could dance around with joy all day. In the morning, Arjun had said playfully, 'It's a date, baby!' and I blushed.

That's another thing about Army: no matter how long you've been married, there will always be stretches of time when you live alone, so coming home is always special.

For days I have planned this evening in my head. I will cook Chinese food, put on a nice (but not skimpy) outfit and—my grand plan—light candles all over the house. Sounds clichéd, but it will make the house look romantic, right? *Right?*

Between preparing for dinner and reading an amazing book that Naina gave me, *Lovers Reunite: Stories to Melt Your Heart*, I call Arjun a lot, monitoring where he is.

The Unit is moving in a convoy, all vehicles together in a line. All the guns, all the 2.5 tons, all the jeeps—everything moves at a synchronized pace. I am thrilled when he tells me about this: it is incredible how the Army never ceases to amaze you with its love for order. Maybe it's my civil-background, but I'm awestruck.

'It's not all that organized,' Arjun laughs at my excitement, his voice weak against the loud noise of the moving vehicle. 'Tires get punctured, engines get heated up and, sometimes, part of the convoy gets left behind or even takes a wrong turn.'

Whatever. It still sounds great.

The convoy stops somewhere for lunch and urging Arjun to eat something, I disconnect the call. I continue to read the extremely spellbinding story that I'm in the middle of in *Lovers Reunite*: a couple from different religions are forced to give in to social

pressure and marry other people; years later they discover that their children are now in love! The story is at that dramatic point where each is going through much turmoil, the heavy burden of a decision that will affect their children's lives in their hands. Gripping, right?

Arjun told me he will be home by seven, and it's only three in the afternoon now, so I decide to finish the story before I begin cooking dinner.

Just then *Get the Party Started* starts on my cell phone. What? That's my ringtone and I like it.

It's Mrs Bhandari and I'm impressed that she's calling me on my personal phone, instead of the fauji phone like Mrs James always does. Mrs Bhandari asks if I think it's a good idea to have a Unit dinner party in the Mess, to welcome the officers and celebrate their return.

'*No way*!' I want to wail. I do *not* want to spend my first evening with Arjun after a month in the freaking Mess! And why is she asking me just hours before they arrive? Aren't they, we, supposed to be more organized? And, excuse me, aren't all the good cooks with the officers in their convoy? So, no thank you, I don't think the dinner-tonight-in-the-Mess idea is a good one.

'Um . . . well, do we really have time to cook for a party? The Officers' Mess cooks are coming back with them. Isn't it better to give them a break tonight?' I tell her desperately. Please God, I pray, please don't let them have this dinner tonight.

'You're right,' she says. 'I'll talk to Mrs Nair. We can do it tomorrow, maybe.'

'Tomorrow is good,' I reply, happy with my brilliance. The cooks really need a break, right?

She hangs up and, still a bit shocked by the close shave with crushed plans and enforced boredom, I decide to call Mrs James to tell her about the outrageous idea I managed to successfully nip in the bud. I bet it was Mrs Nair's idea! Why can't she hang out with her own husband and let the others be with theirs? Doesn't she have better things to do with her gone-for-a-month husband than to tire him out at a dull dinner!

I dial Mrs James' extension and wait for the fauji phone to connect the call. Why did I pick the fauji phone today? God, I'm turning into one of them!

After just one ring there's a quick, 'Yes?' Very proper for Mrs James, I must say. I want to giggle but I have news to share.

'They were arranging a dinner tonight in the Mess! Imagine!' I say.

'Who?'

'They, who else? But no worries, I managed to convince her out of it,' I say inspecting my new nail polish. God, my nails look fab.

'You did?'

'Yes, and you're welcome,' I say with pride. 'We want to spend the evening with our husbands *alone*! Not at the Mess, sitting separately and talking about stupid things for God's sake!'

'Um, Pia?'

'Yeah?'

'What number did you dial?'

Oh. My. God.

This is not Mrs James, is it?

'264?' I say in a faint voice.

'This is 246.'

I recognize the voice now. It's Mrs Nair.

Does she sound mad? Insulted? Outraged? Oh god.

I am so dead. Good Lord, why did I have to say 'Yeah?' when she asked if it was me? I could have pretended to be someone else! Oh but in any case, she could have called the exchange and known exactly who called her—me.

Did I mention any names?—I quickly try to remember. No, I didn't, so maybe I can say something like the OR wives wanted to have a dinner with us. But that would be ridiculous, and it never happens anyway. Maybe I can say something about H inviting me over . . . .

'I'm sorry, Mrs Nair. I didn't realize it was you. I was trying to call Mrs James and must have dialled the wrong number. Oh, and good afternoon, Mrs Nair. Actually I was just talking about—'

'Don't worry,' she says calmly. 'The numbers are confusing, 4-6 and 6-4. I know.'

'Yeah. I, er . . .' She doesn't sound mad, but that's not possible, is it?

'So? All excited about Captain Arjun's homecoming tonight?' she asks pleasantly.

'Oh yes,' I say, still stiff and panicky, but I manage to chat for a couple of minutes before hanging up. Maybe she didn't understand what I was talking about, after all.

'Maybe she understood but is saving the lecture for another Etiquette Class,' says Mrs James when I call her from my cell phone. I am not going near the fauji phone for a few thousand years.

By five-thirty in the evening, after confirming with Arjun that they are right on schedule—no detour, no flat tires and no delay whatsoever—I am busy in the kitchen, cooking.

I'm quite excited about the menu, actually.

I've never made Chinese food before and yet it all seems to be coming together nicely. I've clearly underestimated my cooking skills because everything is under control. Um, except for the Manchurian balls, which are not the nice round shape I can see in the cookbook. They're more like doughy lumps, and they taste like corn flour and cabbage. Maybe I'll just ditch the balls altogether and drop some paneer cubes into the Manchurian sauce instead.

Other than that, everything else looks great, and the smell of ginger-garlic is making me hungry. Just as I am stir-frying some veggies, the fauji phone breaks into its shrill ringtone, and with a start, I knock the pan down.

More than half the vegetables fall out and I bang the spatula on my head in frustration. Whoever the fuck is calling me right now better have something super urgent to talk about or be ready to get brutally murdered, I think. Now I'll have to cut some more bloody vegetables and God knows how long it takes me to cut broccoli into perfect bite-sized florets. I run towards the phone, cursing loudly.

Of course it is Mrs James.

'What happened?' I ask impatiently.

'Nothing. Just wanted to check if everything is on track,' she says, music blaring in the background.

'No, nothing is on track. I just dropped my stir-fry vegetables and my Manchurian balls are a failure,' I say, feeling depressed all of a sudden.

'Haww,' she says and clicks her tongue. 'Anyway, James hasn't called yet and I've zero idea if they are on time.'

'Yes, they are,' I say weakly. 'How's the tandoori chicken coming along?'

'I burnt it. Plus the spice mixture I made with so much effort tastes revolting. So I sent my bhaiya to get two plates of tandoori chicken from the dhaba outside the Cantt,' she says coolly.

In fact, she sounds unusually relaxed. I bet she's helping herself to a glass of wine along with that music. Maybe I should have ordered Chinese food too and been done with it. I'm such a fool! Now I have no time to dress up.

'Pia, listen,' she says, and then pauses.

'Yes?'

'Did you tell Mrs Bhandari that James and I are fighting because I want kids and he doesn't?'

What? She can't be serious.

'What? You can't be serious!' I say.

'Actually, I am,' she says in an odd voice. 'She called me ten minutes ago, explaining that marriage is much more than food and shopping and generally just having a good time. And she mentioned that kids are a mutual decision and a wife or a husband shouldn't force the other on this issue.'

I think I might pass out. Mrs Bhandari actually talked to her about such a personal issue? She seemed more sensible than that.

'Really?' I say. 'That's *so* unlike her.'

'Yeah. It is,' she says, sounding cross. 'And that's why we think you told her about it.'

What is she talking about? And who's 'we'?

'Look Pia,' she continues, 'I told you about the kid thing because I trusted you. I'd hung out with you for some time and I felt close to you. I have been in a bad place, marriage-wise, and

I confided in you. Does that give you the right to go around discussing my problems with other people?'

It sounds like she's written the speech down on a piece of paper and is reciting it to me. And why is she talking in the past tense—trusted me, felt close to me? What in God's name is happening here?

'Mrs James, I did not discuss—'

'Save it, Pia,' she sounds almost rude now. 'I mean, everyone knows you are a bit childish and immature—'

What? Immature? Me?

'—but I didn't think you could be so . . . so insensitive.'

'Mrs James, I swear—'

'Anyway,' she cuts me. 'It's my fault, trying to make friends with a junior wife.'

For a moment, I'm too stunned to respond. She cannot be saying this.

After all our time together and my putting up with her eccentricity for so long and even feeling guilty about her being miserable all the time. . . .

I don't know what to do. Shout? Disconnect the call? Apologize? Instead, tears of humiliation and hurt start flowing down my cheeks. With enormous effort I try to silence a sob.

'Are you okay?' comes Mrs James' voice over the phone, still sounding cross. There's a faint sound in the background that sounds like Nose Hair. Is she doing this in front of Nose Hair?

'I'm fine!' I say, trying to get a hold of myself. It is silly, I tell myself, to be crying like a baby over something so ridiculous. My perfect response should have been to laugh and hang up the phone after saying something clever. Like, 'Get a grip, Mrs James', Or 'Whatever, Mrs James'. I shouldn't let her subject me to nonsense like this. Maybe I should just say, 'Fuck you', and bang the receiver down.

But I don't. Hang up on her, I mean, or say fuck you. Her words have got to me. Despite all her complaining and clinginess, I am fond of her. I always tried to make her feel better and I genuinely felt bad for her when she was troubled. And it suddenly dawns on me that perhaps she never felt the same way.

She didn't hang out with me because she saw me as a friend. No. She spent time with me because I was probably the only one who listened to her non-stop complaining. And now she is sitting with Nose Hair, blaming me for something I would never do, for something that I am incapable of doing—a friend would have known that.

And I thought . . . all this while . . . I clearly overestimated our friendship. Oh, it's all gone wrong, hasn't it?

A loud sob escapes my throat and she sighs loudly.

'I'm sorry if I upset you. But you should know it's the Army and malicious backbiting is not appreciated here.'

With this, she hangs up and I am left clutching the heavy receiver of the fauji phone.

chapter seventeen

Running To Stand Still

I sit on the uncomfortable MES sofa, the dark green receiver of the fauji phone lying in my lap. I'm still reeling from Mrs James' accusations.

How could she think I would do something so petty? Doesn't she know that I'm her friend, and I would never do anything like that, ever?

And, what was it about everyone knowing I'm childish and immature?

I haven't had a showdown with a friend—or any girl for that matter—in ages. I mean, the last time I was part of a girlie fight was in college when a total bitch (fat ass, *huge* ass) tagged me as Miss Goody Two Shoes in a cartoon image on Facebook, which I thought was kind of offensive. I totally took her down on that one, as did my group of friends, who strongly felt that I deserved the tag of Drama Queen, not some shady Miss Goody Two Shoes.

But that was it, nothing after that. And now this accusation. I feel dejected. She was so rude! She didn't let me speak at all, did she?

And what was all that gyan about Army wives? Imagine taking Army wife lessons from Mrs James, who is in fact the epitome of what an Army wife should *not* be. I sniff loudly and drag myself to the kitchen.

I clear up the mess, start cutting up vegetables mechanically and try hard not to think about what happened. To think that I wasted so many nights with her in my house, when I could easily have talked with Arjun for hours! Does she even realize— oh no, think about something else, quick, I tell myself.

Anything but this.

Because the moment I start thinking about it, hurt and anger that are waiting vigilantly at the back of my mind, will troop in and take over.

And I have a lot of work to do, haven't I? I will deal with this later, I tell myself.

By six forty-five, I have got my act together, and I am fairly certain I've left the conversation with Mrs James behind me. It's all in the past, as far as I'm concerned. It is her loss anyway, I tell myself. I'm not going to humiliate myself by denying ridiculous accusations to people who don't care *and* who don't matter anyway.

What is she, really?

Just a posting away from fading from my memory. Bah.

So, with rejuvenated spirit, I am back to work. Cooking is all done, ta da! I have placed several FWO candles in the house and I've put on my white linen shirt that Arjun loves and which I was wearing when he proposed to me (though I doubt he will remember, he's kind of slow in that department), with ripped jeans. A touch of barely-there makeup, and I'm all ready to receive my man.

I feel *so* good as I fidget with a packet of matchsticks, and I'm blushing a little. Which is quite uncharacteristic, I have to say. I mean, Arjun is my husband and I never blush when he is about to come home. But today it feels like I am meeting him for the first time and the anticipation is almost tangible. Silly, I know.

After ten minutes, I start to light the candles. They are so many of them all over the place that I begin to think that perhaps I overdid it a bit. Good thing I cut out and placed cardboard underneath all the candles, otherwise the wax would have spoiled every surface. I really am shaping up to be some sort of domestic genius.

Arjun will be here any moment now. I know he is every bit as excited as I am, but his phone battery died two hours back while talking to me. I could call Ganga bhaiya, who is in Arjun's vehicle, but I think that might come across as desperate.

So I wait and admire the way the bedroom looks, all washed in candlelight. I quickly chew a fruity-minty gum, for fresh breath you know, and pray that Arjun comes home before the wax drips too much. Who likes candle stubs?

It's seven-fifteen, and I hear a vehicle stop in front of my house. Giddy with excitement, I run outside.

Mrs Nair and Mrs Bhandari are getting out of one of the CO's vehicles.

'Pia!' Mrs Bhandari exclaims, as if she didn't expect to find me in my house. Her forehead is beady with sweat, though she looks nice in a fancy kurta and leggings. Mrs Nair is wearing a— gasp!—short kurta with a Patiala salwar, and she looks different. I take a step forward and wish them both a good evening.

Why are they here, though?

My mind at once leaps to horrendous possibilities: maybe the welcome dinner at the Mess is happening after all and they are here to drag me to it. Or, oh no, maybe they are here to talk about Mrs James' accusation and to give me a quick at-home Etiquette Class. Which I absolutely cannot take right now.

I mean, I'm on the verge of snapping at people after that phone call, the kitchen debacle and the entire past one month in general. I might punch someone in the face or I might break down right here. No, I instruct myself, I will not be subjected to anything that I don't want. Not now.

I will firmly decline to go to the Mess or talk about malicious Mrs James, whichever of the two it is. Or maybe I will just fake a stomach ache. In preparation, I clutch my stomach.

Mrs Nair reaches me and puts a hand on my shoulder. 'Pia, there has been an accident.'

The next hour is a blur to me.

I am now sitting in a fauji vehicle, on my way to the Military Hospital in Jammu.

There has been an accident.

Arjun is unconscious.

Someone is saying something to me but my mind isn't registering it.

I am perched on the edge of the seat, tears rolling down my face.

Mrs Nair told me that a truck hit the vehicle Arjun was in; that he is in a hospital in Jammu; that we need to go there. I kind of went blank after that. I think she took my hand and we went inside my house where she brought me a glass of water. Or was it lemonade? Did she make lemonade in my kitchen? I don't think I said anything for a while, until Mrs Bhandari held me, took me out again and we sat in the vehicle to start for Jammu.

Before going out, I'd stopped at the door and looked at my pretty, candlelit living room. Arjun would have loved it, I thought. I think that is when the tears kicked in. Mrs Nair said something like she'd take care of the candles. Or the house . . . keys, something, and I slumped in the vehicle.

It didn't occur to me to lock the house, or to take some cash.

All I could think of was, 'Don't let this happen, God', and I am still repeating it under my breath, over and over again.

Mrs Bhandari, who is going with me to Jammu, is holding my hand and asking me to beat Tron.

Beat Tron?

As in Tron Legacy?

I look at her and she is out of focus because my eyes are prickling with tears.

'Be strong,' she says.

Oh. Be strong. Okay.

I recite the Hanuman Chalisa. It takes us three hours to reach MH, Jammu.

Not too long back, I was asking for a little courage, a little strength.

Now, I am asking for more.

I am asking for the kind of strength that will let me face whatever is inside that hospital. Or just enough power to not collapse on the floor and die right now.

I don't know how bad it is.

I don't know what injuries Arjun has suffered from.

I don't know because I wasn't listening and because I haven't asked. I couldn't bear to ask.

I am not sure what to do, how to react. We are at the depressing white building of MH, Jammu Cantt, and Mrs Bhandari is holding my elbow as we walk through long corridors full of strange people.

Then, suddenly, a lot of familiar looking bhaiyas seem to gather around us. Colonel Nair, along with all the officers of the Unit, also materializes from nowhere.

Everyone is looking at me and suddenly I can't breathe.

Maybe it's the crowd, maybe it's the huge sign board on the door that we seem to be approaching.

It doesn't make any sense, I tell myself, and stare at the sign.

God no, I think, Arjun can't be in the Intensive Care Unit. It is just a small accident, right? He doesn't need to be in the ICU. I start to cry again. Colonel Nair walks me to a plastic chair next to the huge glass doors of the ICU and I sink into it. Another man in combat uniform approaches me, along with Colonel Bhandari. He's the doctor, I'm told.

'SCI,' he says and my brain becomes alert with a jerk.

SCI?

Spinal cord injury?

A fresh wave of panic washes my disorientation away and now I sit up, listening.

'We're going ahead with a radiographic evaluation to determine if there is any damage to the spinal cord and if there is, then the location of that damage,' he says with an expressionless face.

'Radiographic evaluation,' I repeat his words.

'Yes Ma'am, a radiographic evaluation using an X-ray, MRI or CT scan is the general procedure in such cases,' he says helpfully.

I nod. 'Can I meet him?' I manage to ask.

'No, Ma'am, that won't be possible right now.'

'Is he conscious?'

'No, Ma'am.'

'Since when has he—'

'He is under anaesthesia, Ma'am, and his condition is stable,' he says and gives me an awkward nod before turning away.

'Wait!' I say. And I finally ask the question I have been avoiding till now. I have to know. 'Is the injury—is it . . . bad?'

He turns to face me again and looks into my eyes. I feel a shiver go through me and I wrap my arms around myself.

'So far, we are not sure, Ma'am,' he says, his face is devoid of any expression again and I wonder if he is telling me the truth. 'Surgery may be necessary to remove any bone fragments from the spinal canal and to stabilize the spine, but we will know about that only after the scans.' With another nod he turns and walks away.

The entire night, with my Arjun trapped behind the glass doors of the ICU, and Mrs Bhandari constantly by my side, I speak to several people—doctors, nursing assistants and officers, trying to figure out the exact picture and get some sort of answers.

Turns out, there are no answers.

With an injury to the most vital part of the body, it isn't easy to predict the future just now. Unlike a fractured limb or a wound, where a doctor can easily tell the recovery time, a spinal cord injury is tricky.

I did manage to see Arjun for a few minutes when his hospital-bed was being wheeled into the ICU, back from a set of scans. There was thick glass separating us and I was barefoot because you're supposed to leave your shoes outside the ICU. I saw him and my blood froze.

He was under anaesthesia, and his face showed no signs of the nasty, nasty accident that he faced just a few hours back. If you ignored the tubes and various contraptions strapped to his body, you would think he was sleeping peacefully.

My Arjun, I thought; I started to cry again. Nothing will happen to you, I say to him in my heart.

We'll get through this, I say to myself. We have to.

Standing on the brutally cold floor inside the ICU, my hands on the glass wall, I incongruously remember various scenes from movies about people in the same situation. Nothing could have prepared me for this. Nothing could be worse than this, I think.

God please, please let Arjun be all right again, and I will be a good human being, I think desperately. I will pray regularly, and I never do anything bad again. I must have started praying out loud, because I was escorted out at that point.

The driver bhaiya and a jawan were also injured in the accident, but they are out of danger and are in the general ward.

I now know that Arjun only has a couple of minor bruises on his arms, no other external wound—thank god. But he was sitting next to the driver when the collision happened, and it was difficult to pull him out of the crushed vehicle.

He was conscious though, until the bhaiyas managed to pull him out of the wreckage, and he must have sensed something about his body because just before he lost consciousness, he told Ganga bhaiya that his back hurts and that he should not be moved too much. And he wasn't, which is extremely important in SCI cases. A lot of movement could have done further damage.

But there can be horrible results from this kind of injury, including paralysis.

Paralysis. Yes.

Determining the exact type of injury is critical in making accurate predictions about the specific parts of the body that may be affected by paralysis and loss of function. The doctors will do this in the morning, which seems so, so far away right now.

There is a morbid silence outside the ICU, where I am sitting on the same plastic chair, clutching a cup of coffee that went cold long ago, lines of dry tears streaking my face.

I'm praying for strength.

chapter eighteen

Knockdown

The creaking of metal wheels wakes me up in the morning. With effort I open my eyes and see a bright red light. Ouch. I shut my eyes quickly and rest my head against the hard wall. Bright red makes no sense. Where am I? What happened? A hollow feeling starts to grow inside me as last night starts coming back to me in bits and pieces.

Mrs Nair came to my house to take me to the Mess for dinner.

No, that wasn't it.

Oh god.

Arjun is in the ICU.

My candles were burning.

Spinal cord injury.

Military Hospital Jammu.

Arjun.

My Arjun!

I keep my eyes closed. Maybe this is a bad dream, I tell myself, without sounding one bit convincing. Maybe, if I remain asleep for long enough, it will all go away? So, like an unrealistic fool, I continue to sit stiffly in the chair for a few more minutes, counting my heartbeats. It's not working, of course. Plus my neck is hurting like I was up all night trying to stare at my own face. Ouch, ouch. Slowly I open my eyes again and find Ganga bhaiya looking at me, a cup of hot tea in his hands.

'Memsaab,' he says softly and offers it to me. He looks like he didn't sleep the entire night, and I feel a rush of emotions. I look away.

'You didn't sleep, bhaiya?' I ask him finally, staring at the tea.

'No, Memsaab,' he says, his voice low. Then he adds, 'They've caught the man who was driving that truck, Memsaab.'

The truck driver who rammed into their vehicle and then ran away has been caught. Strangely, it doesn't cheer me up even one bit. I nod mechanically though, because he sounds glad. His Saab is hurt and I can see that he is as devastated as I am. Does he feel guilty that he couldn't do more to help, I wonder. He was in the same vehicle, after all.

He then tells me that 2IC Memsaab, Mrs Bhandari, has called twice since the morning. She left late last night, after trying hard (and failing) to take me to the guest room that was booked for me.

I haven't got my phone with me; I didn't remember to pick it up when leaving for Jammu. I have to call our parents now as well, I realize wearily, and instantly feel sorry for them. Spinal cord injury is something that would scare anyone, let alone parents. I am not allowed inside the ICU yet, so I let Ganga bhaiya lead me to the guest room.

Once inside, I use the fauji phone to call Mrs Bhandari. She is taking a shower, so I leave a message with the bhaiya who receives the call, telling her not to worry and that I will call again later in the day.

Then I call Naina and tell her. To my astonishment, she

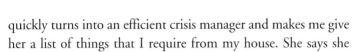

quickly turns into an efficient crisis manager and makes me give her a list of things that I require from my house. She says she will get in touch with Mrs Nair and get my house keys from her.

'I'll start for Jammu ASAP,' she tells me. 'Be strong.'

I call Arjun's parents and then mine and all four of them take the news pretty badly, with my mother-in-law breaking out in sobs on the phone, making me cry as well. Arjun's father regains his composure faster than the others and tells me that they will start from Delhi immediately. My parents are also looking for the fastest transportation to Jammu.

Meanwhile, I sit alone in the guest room, waiting for the doctor to check Arjun's reports and tell me the next course of action. Also, I want to hide under the bed.

I mean, it is pretty hard to deal with the unexpected turn my life has taken—from cooking Chinese food and lighting pretty candles to welcome Arjun, to sitting in this depressing guest room, surrounded by that hospital smell mixed with the reek of strong disinfectant. *Depressing*!

Okay, I know it's a hospital guest room. It's not supposed to be a riot. But they might have tried to make it look a little less dreary; maybe add a bright rug instead of this sad, dull brown carpet, no? It is *so* not fair. I hug my knees tight to my chest and try hard to stop the tears from building. Nothing like this happened in any story in *Lovers Reunite: Stories to Melt Your Heart*. Not even one. Every couple reunited merrily, without any calamity making an appearance.

Maybe I *should* hide under the bed until this is all over.

When you are in the kind of trance induced by misery, time passes by quickly.

Or slowly, I'm not sure, actually.

I have been sitting in this guest room, thinking about the different turns life could take from here—the doctor did mention paralysis as a possibility, didn't he?

Even as I think of 'paralysis' as a word, minus the meaning it could cast on lives, just as a stand-alone, impartial word, a chill runs down my spine.

Arjun is my hero, my superman.

To see him suffer from—okay Pia, you need to stop, I tell myself strictly. Be positive. Nothing is going to happen anyway, right? I mean, Arjun is strong. He can come through anything, he is a fauji, he is a fighter. I jerk my heavy head and shake away my depressing thoughts.

Arjun has to be all right, he has to—I repeat in my mind and check the time. It has been an hour. Did it feel like a complete hour? Did it feel like an entire day? I don't know. Like I said, my sense of time isn't very accurate right now.

Also, I have no idea how long I sat on that plastic chair outside the ICU last night. I can't seem to recall when it was that I sat in the vehicle for Jammu. Logically it must have been last evening, but it feels like last week. Or like I just got here. I can't tell anymore. Time is playing tricks with my mind and I feel utterly lost.

Ganga bhaiya informs me after another fifteen minutes (or five, who knows?) that the doctor wants to speak to me. Finally, I think, some answers. We rush towards the ICU.

'Ma'am, we have to give it around six months. Recovery is typically quickest during the first six months of the injury . . .' the expressionless doctor is saying.

Six bloody months? That's long, isn't it? Which means the injury is serious, right? Oh god. I think I might faint. Really? Six months? He can't be serious.

I hold on to the glass wall for support; we are inside the ICU—the doctor, a nursing assistant and Colonel Bhandari (who must have stayed back the night, bless him and his wife). Ganga bhaiya is lurking outside the ICU doors, and I think it's his ear pressed against the glass door.

The doctor goes on, unaffected by my display of weakness, '. . . but like I said, it's what we call a low-level SPI. We are glad that any major consequences can be ruled out, like loss of function, muscle control or paralysis.'

My heart performs a cheerful somersault. On the basis of the MRI and other scans, the doctor tells me, Arjun is diagnosed with a low-level SCI, and there's no need for a surgery either. Yippie! But . . .

Why would a low-level injury need six months of recovery time?

'The recovery requires six months?' asks Colonel Bhandari. He must be thinking the same thing.

'Bhandari, the officer is lucky . . .' the doctor says, and I realize he is senior to Colonel Bhandari. He certainly doesn't look like his senior though. But perhaps that's because Colonel Bhandari looks a bit haggard right now. Maybe the doctor's years of experience, exposure to injuries and accidents have made him numb. I suddenly feel sorry for him, being surrounded by death and illness all the time.

And with zero warning, I feel tremendously sorry for myself, being caught in the most awful situation one can imagine.

How am I going to cope? How is Arjun going to cope? He gets super irritated if he catches that one rare round of seasonal cold that is practically mandatory for everyone.

'. . . spinal cord injuries can have grave consequences,' the doctor is saying. 'The level is assigned according to the location of the injury by the vertebra of the spinal column. But the prognosis of complete injuries is generally predictable since recovery is rare. In this case, however, the injury is incomplete, or low-level, and determining the exact recovery pattern or time is almost impossible.'

'But there will be no long-term effects?' I'm happy that Colonel Bhandari is there to ask all the right questions. I just stand there like a dumb fool, tongue tied in knots.

'No long-term effects,' the doctor assures. 'He might need a wheelchair for a month or so, and—' he looks directly at me and says, '—he might experience insufficient motor control, numbness or loss of sensation in his feet or fingers at times. Short term, of course. It will eventually go, the body will recover.'

I nod. Be strong, I plead with myself, at least there is full recovery in the end. I wipe my forehead which is sweaty even inside the unpleasantly cold ICU.

Six months will go quickly and we won't even notice.

I mean, it's been almost six months since our wedding and do I think it has been a painfully long time? Nooooo, not at all.

See?

I feel a lot better after this pep talk with myself. Six months will have to go by quickly.

Colonel Bhandari walks with me to the guest room, talking about my stay here and the arrangements that will be required. He tells me that Ganga bhaiya will stay here with Arjun and me, and the Unit's nursing assistant will travel from Pathankot to Jammu every other day.

Arjun is to be kept under observation for a few more days, and Colonel Bhandari has booked another guest room in Jammu Cantt, not far from MH, for our parents.

He then leaves, wishing me softly, and asking Ganga bhaiya to bring some food for me. They are such a helpful couple, Colonel and Mrs Bhandari. She's been so warm and supportive the entire time. I really appreciate her for letting me be when I was in total shock. She just held my hand and sat there with me. Bless her.

But then I am alone again, and fresh despair starts to circle around in my head.

What if the diagnosis is wrong?

I mean, Arjun is always saying that fauji doctors are not to be trusted, isn't he? Shouldn't we be heading straight to Delhi now, consulting well-known doctors from those palatial, five-star-type hospitals?

What if we can't handle the pressures the six months of recovery require?

What if I fall short, and fail Arjun?

What if both of us aren't strong enough to see this through? What if—

'Home delivery!' Naina's voice breaks through the cloud of doom I'm creating for myself, and I am delighted to see her face peeking from behind the curtain.

'You!' I say happily. She must have started from Pathankot soon after my call! She enters the room, carrying a huge duffle bag and a crisp paper bag smelling of freshly-baked goodies.

My stomach rumbles in response to the aroma. I haven't eaten since last evening, but my body hadn't seemed to notice till now.

'Hi to you too,' she says and dumps the things on the couch. She then hugs me tight. 'How're you holding up?' she asks as we sit on the couch, side by side.

Just about to walk towards the river with stones in my pockets, ready to see the dark waters close over my head, I want to say. 'Okay, I guess.'

'Let's eat something first. I made my driver bhaiya go mad searching for Pahalwan Di Hatti in Jammu market, to get good food for us.' She starts to open the paper bags, laying out disposable plates and paper napkins and hot chole bhature. There is also a fresh fruit cake, a few muffins, mushroom pies and paneer puffs. She did go all out, I think, a smile reappearing on my face.

Just then, Ganga bhaiya also brings breakfast—bread and cutlets along with an entire pot of hot coffee. There is an array of food in the room now, and I feel nauseated.

All I need is coffee, the restlessness of caffeine in my blood that will keep me on my toes and ready for whenever Arjun is up and I'm allowed to meet him.

I do manage to eat half a bhatura though, to make Naina happy, and then gulp down two cups of coffee. I tell her what the doctor told me and she listens intently.

'It's a blessing, Pia,' she says. 'I got totally scared when I heard spinal cord injury.'

'Me too,' I admit.

'With God's grace there will be no long-term effects, and that is something to be thankful about. And don't worry about category, it hardly makes a difference,' she says.

'Category?'

'Medical category?' She sees my blank expression and continues, 'It is what they do in the Army, put injured or unwell officers under this medical category. No big deal. Officers with high BP are also put into it.'

'What are the implications of a medical category?'

'Oh, nothing too big. In fact, some of it is good, like they won't be sent to high altitude postings. Which is great. Who wants to go on those postings anyway, right?'

'Right.'

'Also, medical category has some sort of degrees. Or levels, I'm not sure. But there's a high category and there's a low category which gets removed on full recovery. So, there,' she says helpfully.

'Oh,' I say. As long as it is not something awful like being forced to quit the Army or something.

'And Pia . . .' she says solemnly, 'don't be too hard on yourself. You're coping well. Just hang in there. It will be over soon, you know?'

If only, I think, that were true. If only she knew that I am not 'coping well', nowhere close to acceptable even, and I can't do anything about it. But I nod and smile weakly.

Naina stays with me for a couple of hours and I feel much better. Her visit has lifted my spirits a bit, and I'm thankful for not being alone with myself and my thoughts. I also now have a few clothes, my cell phone and charger and other things that I need. As she is leaving, I am told that I can meet Arjun.

chapter nineteen

It's All Right. Or Is It?

Okay, I tell myself—out loud apparently, because Ganga bhaiya looks at me like I'm about to throw stones at him—okay Pia, breathe.

We are standing outside the ICU, where I've come running, and now all of a sudden I can't seem to find the strength to push open those glass doors and meet Arjun.

He is waiting for me, I'm told.

I have been waiting for him.

But now, I'm not sure if I can face him.

It's Arjun, I tell myself, my Arjun! But I'm shaking a little bit.

What am I going to say to him that will make it all right? How am I supposed to behave? Broken? Rock strong? Casual, like nothing's wrong? How am I supposed to look him in the eye and not cry? God, I am so nervous. Which is ridiculous, because it's just him. Just him!

And I've been waiting, counting the seconds to be able to go inside those doors and meet him, haven't I? Then why, I wonder miserably, have my feet turned to rocks? I feel beads of sweat on my forehead.

I place a weak hand on the glass door, but don't attempt to push it. I'm half hoping someone will shout out and stop me from entering; it's the ICU after all, not a general ward. One part of my brain is appalled at how I would prefer being stopped from seeing Arjun. I can sense Ganga bhaiya standing just two steps behind me, fidgeting. He must think I'm crazy. I must find strength, I plead with myself.

I close my eyes.

Strength, obviously, is eluding me when I want it the most.

I can feel weakness oozing out of my body like black ink, engulfing me, suffocating me.

And just then, what Arjun said to me just a few days back comes to me like a flash of bright light. Our mind plays tricks on us at times like this, because this is how we find our true courage and strength to deal with situations.

Okay, I think to myself as the dark cloud of weakness begins to lift and I can breathe again. I am here, in this situation. There's no going back, no undoing possible. Either I move forward from here and face reality, or I keep denying it until it squeezes the last drop of courage from my body. One has to move forward and face life, because that's the way it is. Forward is the only place one can go, right?

I push open the door with all the goddamn strength in me and step inside the cold, cold ICU.

'Hey,' Arjun says in a hoarse voice as soon as he sees me. He has been waiting, I realize, and a shooting pain finds its way to my heart.

'Hey sleepyhead,' I say, and take in all the machines and contraptions attached to him, like aliens trying to take over his body. I flinch.

'Half of them will go by tomorrow,' he says casually, following my gaze. 'Just monitoring me, most of them.'

I nod and look at Ganga bhaiya who is standing at attention just behind me. His face is contorted and I think he might burst that nerve on his forehead.

'Ganga, you're fine, no?' Arjun asks him and he steps forward.

'Haan Saab,' he says in a choked voice. 'Saab . . . Saab . . . you . . .' He breaks off and I turn away. He deserves his personal time with his Saab. He has been equally worried all this while.

'I'll get coffee,' I say and walk off before either of them can stop me.

This is the human condition, I think. All of us have our personal hell to go through, our own private miseries to deal with.

I return quickly, after walking a lap outside the ICU. Ganga bhaiya leaves as soon as I reach Arjun's bedside, looking devastated. I sit by Arjun's side and hold his right hand. His skin is deliciously warm in spite of the low temperature here. Why the hell do they lower the temperature so much anyway?

Arjun is looking at me with a smile that is almost apologetic. I smile back nervously. It is so good to finally see him, touch him.

'So . . .' I say, trying to sound casual. 'How are you?'

'I've been better,' he smiles and it breaks my heart. I look away quickly.

'I'm sorry,' he says softly.

'For getting into an accident?' I tease him.

'Yeah,' he says sincerely, and I have to physically clench my entire body to stop the tears.

'It's okay. No biggie,' I say, my voice heavy with emotion, warning us of the impending flood.

'Pia, I'm okay.' He tightens his grip on my hand and looks into my eyes. He knows me too well. 'Okay?'

I nod weakly.

'You know what the doctors have said, right? I'll be fine in no time,' he says.

Look at him, I think, making sure I am okay when I'm the one who should be his pillar of strength right now. His dark eyes are full of concern, and looking into them, I feel my vision getting blurred.

Oh great, now I'm crying! God, I'm the worst wife ever.

'Oh, Pia,' he pulls me gently towards him. 'Come here baby, don't cry. I'm okay. Oh Pia, I'm going to be fine.' My silent tears turn into loud sobs and I bury my face in his disinfectant-smelling shirt.

I'm not crying because you are not okay—I want to tell him. I'm crying because you are so positive and strong and I am just a pathetic, selfish person who is terrified to the extent that she almost didn't want to face you. But words don't find their way as I cry my heart out against the warm skin of his neck.

Everything else can wait.

While walking out of the ICU, I turn back to look at Arjun once again. He is talking to the doctor (who has just made me leave, the expressionless creature from hell). As I look at Arjun's face, my feet feel heavy again. I'm still oscillating between the pathetic—shocked denial—and the wretched—resigned acceptance. In fact, I feel numb because of the heavy assault of emotions.

I need to get my act together, I tell myself. Very soon we will go home and things will be even more challenging then, right? I mean, the doctors did mention the possibility of a wheelchair. And regular exercise. I will have to be supportive and strong throughout Arjun's recovery and I have to start now.

As I'm lecturing myself for the zillionth time, my phone rings. It's Arjun's father. He informs me that they will be arriving tomorrow morning along with my parents.

Arjun looks at me through the glass wall and for a second he looks as fragile as I feel. Rush of emotions again. Then, it is quickly replaced with a reassuring smile and I wave back energetically, trying to look upbeat. He gives me a thumbs-up sign. Yeah, right.

I turn away and drag myself out of the ICU.

Such a simple question, how are you? Who gives much thought to it, especially when things are hunky-dory? No one, that's who. But when faced with a tough situation, a girl tends to question everything. How are you—people have been asking me all my life. 'I'm *great*, how about you?' I would reply mechanically. People are still posing the 'How are you' question in a casual manner or just out of habit, but now I don't know how to respond. Suddenly it seems like such a loaded question. How are you?

How *am* I? What do I tell them?

I am fine, I suppose.

It is a little over a week since Arjun's accident. We are back in Pathankot—Arjun and I along with the two sets of parents.

The Unit ladies have been amazing. Delicious food is sent to us every day—fish curry from Mrs Sengupta's house, pasta from Mrs Nair's house, chicken curry from Mrs Singh's house and awesome Rajasthani food from Anita, the OR wife. I think I have gained an entire inch around my waist.

We are struggling to get our life back on track, dealing with a lot of visitors along with numerous medicines and stressful exercise routines for Arjun. On the surface, and for a good number of layers under that, I am okay. I mean I'm not hiding in the abandoned (and probably haunted, by the looks of it) outhouse behind my house, am I? Its Arjun's wheelchair, which creaks like a constant background score of our current life, that sometimes fills me with misery, but I recover quickly.

Arjun is also taking it in good spirits, my fighter. We meet people, listen to their stream of sure-fire home remedies, and laugh at them later. Arjun is perfectly composed in front of family and friends, but when we're lying down in our bed at night, I can tell that a massive anxiety is weighing him down. Full recovery is a long way to go from here, we both know it. It's tough, but we're taking it one day at a time.

Our parents are leaving today.

Fifteen days have gone by since . . . er, the day, and it was nice to have our parents around for a while. My sister Anya, who came along with my parents, was my stress-buster.

Our parents did try to talk us into shifting to Delhi, citing better medical facilities and family support, but Arjun cannot travel right now: his backbone cannot be put to test so soon, the expressionless doctor from Jammu had dictated. So we're going to stay in Pathankot for some time and figure out our next step later.

Arjun is on medical leave for two months. This entire period is going to be crucial for his recovery, and will involve a rigorous exercise routine. I know it sounds quite demanding, but the ultra-positive side of me has already figured out the bright side to this. It is a month-and-a-half with Arjun! No practice camps, no office, no bloody games in the evening! Just him and me.

Maybe I can get him to watch a few seasons of *Gossip Girls* with me! Who knows, maybe he will get hooked to it and we'll never have a tussle over the remote control ever again.

Perfect married life.

I smile at the idea and tune in to what my mother is saying to me—something about making Arjun eat sprouts for energy and drink milk for calcium.

'Like he will ever drink milk!' Anya rolls her eyes, and I giggle. Arjun claims he is lactose intolerant, but I have a feeling he says that only to escape drinking milk because he eats cheese cubes directly from the fridge and drinks cold coffee whenever he gets the chance.

'Well, he has to,' Arjun's mother interrupts. 'Milk is necessary to make those bones stronger. Force him to drink it, Pia. And call me if he doesn't.'

'Deal,' I say to her and give Arjun an all-business look. He rolls his eyes and moves his wheelchair back and forth to irritate me with its squeak. Anya laughs.

chapter twenty

Eh, Eh (Nothing Else I Can Say)

Top Five Things That Suck In My Life Right Now:

1. Seeing Arjun in a wheelchair. He's my hero. My Super-Duper man. How can the sight of him in a wheelchair not shatter my heart? I know it is only temporary, and that Rest and Recoup is all he needs, but still.
2. Arjun losing sensation in his toes at times and sometimes even in his fingers. Million-piece heartbreak, really.
3. Watching him go through rigorous physiotherapy sessions in the morning for an hour, followed by other exercises that he does on his own.
4. Not being able to share this with Arjun because he might get upset too. Or worse, he might think I am not a strong, capable and supportive wife. Which I totally am.
5. Not being able to share this with anyone else because they might think I am not a strong, capable and supportive wife. Or worse, they might tell Arjun.

Top Five Things That Are Awesome In My Life Right Now:

1. Unlimited and uninterrupted time with Arjun. We still have one full month of medical leave remaining, yaay!

2. Arjun's improving taste in television and movies. He sat through *Bridesmaids* with me and—I can hardly believe it—we have finished Season 1 of *Modern Family* already! I've seen it before of course, as well as Seasons 2 *and* 3. But Arjun has never been interested before. This is huge progress for someone who watches only war movies. Or *Dexter*. Yaay, again!

3. I haven't been attending any Ladies' Meets etc. because a) Arjun is injured and I need to be with him *all the time*, and b) Officially we are on leave, and just because we are in the station doesn't mean I can leave my unwell husband behind and attend parties. I'm not that shallow.

4. Believe it or not, Arjun has turned into a totally different person from the man I married. In a positive way, of course. One month of no-work-only-staying-at-home-with-Pia, and the former formal, never-experiments-with-clothes fauji Arjun has been replaced with this cool guy who has longer hair and glowing skin, thanks to the herbal bleach (all right, I forced him) and the weekly facial (which he likes now) given by yours truly. He is even wearing his colourful Nirvana tee-shirt: I gave it to him ages before our wedding, and he thought it was a joke.

5. Because Arjun is more or less dependent on me for a lot of personal things now, Ganga bhaiya's hold over him is slackening a bit. I mean, he can't be inside our bathroom everyday at six in the morning to hand a toothbrush with toothpaste on it to Arjun, can he? Neither can he sort out Arjun's underwear drawer now that he's married, shares a cupboard with me and can't do it himself. I don't mean to be cruel, but it feels like a battle won. Score one to me.

Okay, there is one other thing that sucks in my life. It's actually just a little thing that I'm sad about but that I'm totally ready to overlook because of all the quality time I'm spending with Arjun. Before the accident, Arjun had been selected to represent his Unit at a three-day conference-cum-training session in Delhi. I was supposed to go along with him. *To Delhi*!

It would have been a weekend getaway and I was really looking forward to it, having sent Let's-Meeeeet-Bitches! emails to all my friends and making a list of street food I want to gorge on. But now we can't go, obviously, and it would have been fine by me, really, if only we weren't being replaced by the evil Mrs James and her insensitive husband. Yes. The CO has asked them to attend the conference instead.

A paid trip with her husband! She's probably dancing around with glee, thanking God for Arjun's accident. She must be planning to go to all the shady bars that have Happy Hours all day long. I haven't spoken to her since she basically called me a gossipmonger and accused me of backstabbing her, and the fact that she hasn't called even after Arjun's accident—as Army etiquette demands, let me add—is making me even more angry at her. No phone call, imagine! She's unbelievable, really.

But who needs people like her anyway? Good fucking riddance. I hope she gets super drunk at the conference after-party and throws up on some major general. That will serve her right!

How cool is *Devil Wears Prada*? And how awesome is Meryl Streep? The woman can play any character. Like Cam says— Meryl Streep can play Batman and still be the right choice for the role. I totally agree with him. You know, Cam? Cameron from *Modern Family*?

Anyway, we are watching *The Devil Wears Prada*, my all-time favourite movie. Arjun is rubbing his head and frowning a bit, but as I recite Miranda's one-liners to him, word for word, he looks amused.

So, another relationship milestone achieved easily. This month's *Vogue* had an article on how important it is for a couple to appreciate each other's taste in art and theatre. Movies and television count, right?

Then I make the mistake of casually mentioning how, in a parallel universe where accidents don't happen and everything goes according to plan, we would be getting ready to leave for the conference cocktail party in Delhi.

'It was going to be hectic anyway,' Arjun shrugs. 'And I told you that your shopping, catching up with friends and eating out plans wouldn't have worked out. Too little time.' He looks relieved.

'I know,' I say in a small voice. I want to tell him that I'm upset because Mrs James is getting to go instead, but I don't, because then he will ask why we aren't best friends anymore and I will have to tell him about the humiliating phone call. About how she accused me of being a bad friend; how I couldn't even defend myself. I just listened to everything she said like a dimwit, and let her get away with it. Arjun is looking at me, perhaps surprised at my easy surrender, so I beam at him brightly.

'I'm more excited about *Sex and the City,* Season 1,' I say with a wicked grin.

'Oh well,' he says. 'I hope it's as charrrrming as "Evil in Heels". Bring it on.'

'It's *Devil Wears Prada*. And SATC is even better,' I inform him and we snuggle down to watch episode one.

In the evening, when both of us are having a nice cup of coffee with yummy yet healthy homemade snacks courtesy our mothers who took over the kitchen while they were here, the doorbell rings. It's a circular for a Ladies' Meet at the Brigade level.

Why are they sending these circulars to me? We are on leave and everyone in the Unit knows I will not be attending these things for some time. With the last two circulars, I'd called Mrs Bhandari and informed her about my inability to come, diplomatically mentioning that we are on medical leave anyway and I should be considered as a not-in-station member for the time being. She said she'd escalate the concern to Mrs Nair. Obviously she didn't escalate it enough, or she did and Mrs Nair decided to ignore her.

This is *so* annoying.

I sign angrily against my name and write 'ON LEAVE!!' in capital letters.

'Are you sure you'll be okay in the garden?' Arjun asks with concern.

'Oh yes. Don't worry about it,' I say.

'But these mosquitoes?' He looks a bit unsure. Promptly, a mosquito hums loudly around his nose.

'And this is where kachua chaaps come handy,' I say, waving

two mosquito coils. When I was buying them at Big Bazaar a few months back, he'd asked when we would ever need these ancient coils. Now he knows how foresighted I am. (Actually, I wanted to bring the bill to a certain amount because they were giving away a set of two tinted glass jars; I ran to the nearest aisle and grabbed whatever came in my hands—the coils. But Arjun doesn't need to know that.) I give him a look that says, *See how resourceful I am.*

He looks unconvinced but decides not to say anything. He's hoping I won't change the plan.

You see, Mrs Sengupta and Mrs Singh are coming over for a cup of coffee, and Arjun gets super uncomfortable with these kind of social encounters with women. He'd rather not have anything to do or make any conversation. Or be present, even. He usually just mumbles some polite greetings, wishes them, and then hides in the bedroom till they've gone. He's even worse with these things since the accident, because he hates having to answer the same health-related questions.

So, like the thoughtful wife that I am, I have arranged for the three of us to sit in the garden, leaving Arjun to his own sweet devices in the house. I light the coils and place them strategically around our garden chairs.

'Who are you planning to suffocate?' comes Naina's voice. I turn to find her standing in her garden, behind the hedge that encloses all the gardens in the Cantt. From the corner of my eye, I see Arjun slowly wheel backwards, trying to blend into the wall. What an antisocial husband I've got!

'They might suffocate us, but at least we won't get malaria,' I say to Naina.

'You'll spend the evening coughing! Hey bhagwan, look at that smoke!' she scrunches her nose. 'Wait,' she says and runs inside her house.

Arjun quickly wheels himself inside the doors, mock salutes me and disappears behind the curtains before Naina or the two Unit ladies arrive. As if they are dying to have long, in-depth conversations with him, Jesus!

Naina returns with a mosquito killer racquet and hands it over the hedge.

'Just switch it on and kill any flying bastard that comes your way,' she says.

'Cool,' I say. I switch it on and move it around experimentally toward her like a sword. 'Hiyaaa!' I do my best karate imitation. A mosquito that is around at the time instantly burns into nothingness with a faint pop.

'There you go. Enjoy,' Naina smiles happily.

When Mrs Sengupta and Mrs Singh arrive, we settle down on the garden chairs and while I am serving coffee and 'showing' snacks to the two of them, they inquire after Arjun's recovery.

'He's doing really well,' I tell them with pride. 'The physiotherapist is pleased with his progress.'

'How long till the wheelchair is no longer required?' Mrs Sengupta asks.

'In about two weeks. It's hard to tell exactly when, but he is spending more and more time out of it now.'

'And the lack of sensation?' Mrs Singh whispers and then immediately looks towards the door, checking if Arjun is eavesdropping.

'He's watching TV,' I tell her. 'It's getting better. The numbness comes and goes, but it has reduced a lot over the past two weeks,'

They both nod. I notice a pile of books in a bag that they've brought.

'We went to the station library,' Mrs Singh explains. 'I

wanted to get the *Twilight* series. I read the first one recently. Have you?'

'Yes, I've read the first two.'

'And . . .?' she leans forward with interest.

Before I can say anything, Mrs Sengupta interjects. 'They're rubbish. I mean, an entire series of books and movies with a central character who is a fool!' she shakes her head in disgust.

Mrs Singh looks hurt and by the way she's glaring at Mrs Sengupta, you'd think she's Stephenie Meyer's PR manager.

'Listen, I *loved* the first book. Why do you dislike Bella anyway?' she asks Mrs Sengupta.

'Let's see,' Mrs Sengupta put a finger on her lips as if thinking hard. 'Maybe because she's weak, and she's the central character. Maybe because she ditched her family and friends and stared out of a window because a guy she had just met relocated . . . . God!'

'She was in love. L.O.V.E,' Mrs Singh says with an air of solemn drama. 'People do crazy things in love all the time.'

'Oh come on! He didn't even treat her right, always fussing over her like she's five and can't take care of herself,' Mrs Sengupta retorts.

'Perspective,' says Mrs Singh. 'Some might say it's adorable. Some girls want to be taken care of.'

'Yeah, foolish girls like Bella,' Mrs Sengupta says. 'And then she ran to some other guy while she was still hung up on the first one. Even jumped over a cliff for the sparkly fellow!'

I glance at Mrs Singh. She looks so speechless with shock, I almost burst into giggles.

'If you hated it so much, why did you read it Soma?' Mrs Singh finally asks.

'I was curious. Everyone was talking about it. Also, I wanted an answer to the question once and for all—Team Edward or Team Jacob?' Mrs Sengupta says sweetly and even Mrs Singh can't help but smile.

'Well, I think they're good to kill time with, if not literary masterpieces,' I offer, as a truce.

'Speaking of killing time, there's a Ladies' Meet day after,' Mrs Sengupta says, and pretends to yawn to show what she thinks of that.

'I know!' I exclaim. 'I got the circular even though I made it clear to Mrs Bhandari that I won't be attending these things for now.'

They both exchange a look and I ask—'What?'

'We heard,' Mrs Singh says.

'Heard what?'

'That you are not attending any meets,' she replies, avoiding my eyes.

'Of course I'm not!' I say with indignation. 'Everyone knows my situation.'

They both hmmm in unison, but they look unconvinced. This is crazy! Even they think I should be waltzing in and out of useless Ladies' Meets. The look on their faces makes me feel defensive.

'My husband is injured and we are on leave. On *leave*! What if we were away in Delhi? What if I had broken my leg? I would have been forced to perform a dance number for a Ladies' Meet then as well I suppose!'

'Pia—' Mrs Singh places a hand on my knee to calm me down. But this is cathartic. Now I've started, I can't seem to stop.

'But no one can force me. No. One. I even signed on that damn circular and wrote . . .'

'On leave,' Mrs Sengupta finishes my sentence.

'With two exclamation points,' Mrs Singh says.

'In caps,' Mrs Sengupta adds.

'How do you . . .' I start, and with a jolt I realize—I am being talked about for not attending these functions. They are gossiping about me. I can feel my cheeks growing bright red.

'Oh my god. I don't fucking believe this,' I say.

'What? It's nothing Pia,' Mrs Singh rushes to explain, confirming my suspicion. 'We just came to know, you know, casually.'

'Kanika noticed what you wrote in the circular and she told Mrs Bhandari yesterday. At the badminton court. Mrs Bhandari was a bit annoyed about it,' Mrs Sengupta says.

At the badminton court? Have they ever played a game in that court, I wonder. All they seem to do there is dress up in outdated gym wear and gossip about people.

'Kanika . . .' I repeat. She really is annoyingly nosy, isn't she? And why was Mrs Bhandari upset? Didn't I tell her that I wouldn't be attending anything? If she had a problem with that, why didn't she say anything to me directly? I am now suddenly angry. Nose Hair is a bitch. Mrs Bhandari is awful too, and to think that I liked her!

'I thought Mrs Bhandari was nice,' I say.

'Of course she is not,' Mrs Sengupta says in a reassuring manner. 'She only *seems* nice.'

'Of course she's nice.' Mrs Singh interjects, giving a not-again look to Mrs Sengupta. 'But I think Kanika exaggerated a bit and that got Mrs Bhandari worried. She has to answer to the CO wife for all this, you know.'

Nose Hair exaggerated. She is so manipulative.

'Well, what exactly did she say to Mrs Bhandari?' I ask.

'Nothing, really,' Mrs Singh says with a bright smile. She is

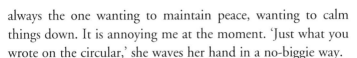

always the one wanting to maintain peace, wanting to calm things down. It is annoying me at the moment. 'Just what you wrote on the circular,' she waves her hand in a no-biggie way.

Mrs Sengupta shakes her head.

'We were talking about the Ladies' Meet. Discussing what to wear, you know? When Kanika jumped in and said, "Oh my god Pia is so funny, she wrote 'on leave' on the circular in *huge* letters, ha ha ha." Then she pretended to laugh like it's the funniest thing ever. She's wicked, I tell you. Then she sweetly asked Mrs Bhandari how she explains to the CO's wife about Unit ladies not attending formal functions. Imagine,' Mrs Sengupta says.

'What did Mrs Bhandari say?' I ask nervously.

'She said that Mrs Nair was indeed inquiring about who won't be attending this meet and she'd told her that you won't because of your situation,' Mrs Singh tells me. Then she exchanges a look with Mrs Sengupta and continues. 'But Kanika clicked her tongue and said, "But Pia is in station! And she goes for evening walks and stuff, no? I heard ladies try to escape responsibilities in the Army, but using your husband's injury as an excuse is horrible." I wanted to tell her to shut up; she is quite malicious, no?'

'And why does she call you by your name anyway?' Mrs Sengupta asks me. 'Captain Arjun is senior to her husband. You are Mrs Mehra to her.'

It has never even occurred to me that she must address me like a senior's wife. Now I feel even more angry.

'I guess I didn't notice. Did Mrs Bhandari react to it?' I ask them.

'No. But you should notice such things, Pia,' Mrs Sengupta says. 'It is equally your fault if you don't correct wrong behaviour.

Army is all about hierarchy.' Correcting behaviour is the last thing on my mind right now, but I nod.

'It's okay, Pia, don't worry about it,' Mrs Singh says genuinely. 'Things like this happen all the time.'

'But they don't, do they?' I say in a bleak voice, hurt replacing anger. 'I mean, people don't go around saying mean things like this in civil life. It's not like I'm staying home for nothing! Arjun spends half his time in a wheelchair. And they think I am using his injury as an excuse? That's awful.'

'Yes, we agree,' Mrs Singh says softly. 'But you are in the station, people see you around and they wonder why you aren't socializing. I know it's not fair, but that is how it is.'

'But I have a situation going on right now, in case Mrs Bhandari didn't notice,' I say acidly. 'You know what, Army really sucks. If this had been civil life, I would not have to deal with people like her. In fact, I would be surrounded by comforting friends and relatives, even helpful neighbours for that matter!'

'Don't be so negative now, Pia,' Mrs Singh says in a soft voice.' You have us, don't you? And your neighbour Naina is so concerned about you that she is right now hiding behind that hedge listening to every word of this conversation.' She jerks her head towards the common hedge and after a few seconds Naina's head pops up.

'Hey there, good evening,' she says in a sheepish tone and I find myself smiling. I gesture for her to come join us and she walks toward us with a guilt-ridden face.

Mrs Sengupta pats her on the back and says, 'This is the Army, Pia. Everyone has a role to play, rules to follow. The Army expects discipline and perfection not only from their soldiers, but also wives and children. Here, perception often overrides reality.'

'And malicious people are everywhere Pia, not just here!' Mrs Singh says. 'You know that, you've worked in media.'

She's right, I know. And I do have awesome, supportive people around me. But right now I feel like there are just too many expectations, and I clearly don't fit the bill. I am trying my best, though. It's not like I'm trampling all over the rules in pink stilettos just for fun. I'm dealing with a damn lot more than I ever imagined I would. I blink several times, trying to stop tears from making an embarrassing appearance.

'Aww, Pia. It is not your fault, you know? This is life, honey, things like this will happen. People will talk about you, you will be judged and your behaviour will be questioned. But it is just one of those lows that come with all the great highs, right? You are part of the Army now, and we army wives don't let anything get to us,' Mrs Singh says, so kindly that I feel ridiculous tears welling up again.

'A girl like you, I thought you would laugh it off. Or better still, abuse those old farts,' Mrs Sengupta says thoughtfully. 'Sheesh. You disappoint me,' she slumps back in her chair dramatically and I can't help but laugh.

chapter twenty-one

Rumour Has It

It's been almost a week since that evening in the garden, and I am happy to report that I've recovered from the shock and hurt. In fact, in retrospect, I think I overreacted a bit. After all, it's just some bored women bitching about someone awesome who they secretly envy because their own lives are so un-happening and un-exciting. It's their problem, not mine. In Army and outside, there are people who want you to behave in a certain way, to make certain choices because it fortifies their own notion of the world and of what is right. And who is to say what is right for someone else? I mean, hot pink with orange might be a right combination for you but a complete no-no for me! But you have to do what is right for you.

Plus, where's the time to get upset about such a petty issue when better things are happening—Arjun is recovering fast and is spending more and more time out of the wheelchair. Even the expressionless doctor seemed impressed with Arjun's recovery at the last check-up we went for in Jammu MH.

Arjun is sitting on the couch in the living room reading Military Law Something-or-the-Other, looking happy. He hasn't touched the wheelchair for two days now, and both of us are full of a renewed energy. I feel a surge of pure, unadulterated joy.

It is soon going to be over.

As I settle down next to him with my laptop, I feel like I'm floating on air. Our medical leave is about to get over in ten days and things are looking up already. Then I log on to my Facebook account and accept Chimmi's friend request. Chimmi? The OR wife from Arjun's Battery? She is obviously very active on Facebook. Her wall is full of status updates (mostly lyrics and Urdu poetry) and she seems to have taken every possible quiz and poll on Facebook. Amused, I click on my own timeline and my mood is instantly ruined.

Jincy James: *Awesome party at Delhi Cantt, shopping in CP, late night drive at India Gate and romantic time with my darling husband. Life is good!*

She has also put up about sixty pictures of herself—taken from very unflattering angles, I think—at each of these places: Sitting in a chair in a dark conference room, standing by a pillar in CP, licking an ice cream at India Gate and hugging her uncomfortable-looking husband in what looks like the inside of an auto rickshaw. Show off. Maybe I should unfriend her on Facebook.

Arjun makes me mad sometimes, really. I mean, I love him and he is my soul mate and all that, but sometimes I wish he were a girl. He just doesn't see things the way I do (and my way is great, let me tell you). His reaction to certain things is the complete opposite of mine. For instance, he's just got a call from the CO, Colonel Nair, post which he's been pacing the living room in this angry fashion. Over what? Over the extremely good news that the CO delivered personally—that he (both of us actually) will be going for a two-month long course in Deolali, School of Artillery, this month! Two months! Eeeeeeee! I want to shout with glee, punch the air with a loud YESSS! and dance around to Beyonce's *Naughty Girls*, and he is walking around, fuming. Why?

'He's sending me away because he thinks I am not fit for an office job at the moment,' he says crossly.

'It's okay, baby! Sitting for long hours in an uncomfortable office chair isn't good for you anyway. Didn't the doctor tell you that just last week?' I try to talk some sense into him.

'The doctor said it's not ideal with this kind of injury, but that I could try it and see if I am comfortable. I thought I would figure out some kind of a schedule, you know? Like, working from home for a couple of hours or something?' he says.

Stupid doctor.

'But you don't *have* to work!' I say in a firm voice. 'It's a superb chance, Arjun! We'll be away from the Unit and it'll be lovely in Deolali!' I already know these courses are super duper fun, and I don't see why he's not rejoicing. Men and their silly ideas.

'You don't understand, Pia,' he says. 'This course is not easy. It's important for my career that I do well and score good grades. How can I do well if I have trouble sitting for long hours?'

'Oh shut up and just be happy,' I tell him. 'Two months of being away from all this! I already feel good from inside,' I clutch my heart and close my eyes, smiling.

'Yeah, being away from the Unit—definitely a bright side. Okay, we leave in two weeks,' he says with a smile.

For some reason Naina also seems to think that Arjun's CO is being unfair, but she agrees that being sent to a course is a blessing in disguise because we'll get to be in Deolali which everyone knows is *the* fun posting! Plus, I'll be leaving behind all the Unit drama, Mrs James, Mrs Bhandari and Nose Hair. I am so excited that I'm considering on calling Colonel Nair and thanking him personally.

I won't, obviously.

But this is super cool, isn't it? Mrs Singh has already called me to congratulate us about the trip, and Mrs Sengupta has made me promise to bring back a bottle of her favourite Sula wine from Nashik.

Arjun is also coming around, however grudgingly. He isn't using the wheelchair anymore and is feeling better, so I keep telling him that he'll do fine in the course. Right now, I'm using the wheelchair as a trolley to bring breakfast-in-bed for him, to lift his spirits, you know.

I've begun packing for our two-month stay in Deolali. (Can you believe it? Two months!) So today, during Arjun's physiotherapy session, I decide to check out the station FWO (Family Welfare Organization) shop called Tohfa to see if there is anything that might be useful for our time in Deolali. Naina visited it last week and raved about the little purses and cell phone pouches that have just arrived, and I want to see those too.

Naina was right, the coin purses are awesome! They are bright, covered in shiny tissue material and the clasps are tiny metal hands. They are really small though, and will probably fit only four or five coins at a time, but maybe that's the point—who wants to carry too many coins around anyway? I decide to buy two in different colours.

I float happily towards a rack of newly-arrived woollen kurtas and immediately plummet to earth. Mrs James is standing by the other side of the rack. My first impulse is to duck behind the clothes, but she has already seen me.

'Hi,' she says in a flat voice and Nose Hair steps into my vision from behind a display rack. She is now looking at me with interest. My gaze falls, as if by habit, on her nose hair. Yuck.

'Good evening,' I say quickly, forcing my eyes away from Nose Hair. There is an awkward silence for a minute and then Nose Hair coughs.

'I hear you are going to Deolali? Must say you're having all the fun, Pia!' she says in a sugary voice. And she's calling me Pia. The nerve of the woman!

'Well, yes, if you think your husband meeting with a serious accident is fun,' I say in my best casual tone, pretending to be interested in an olive green woollen kurta.

'Oh, but he has recovered, hasn't he?' God, she is relentless! 'And Deolali will do the rest, trust me. It's *the* destination for someone who wants to relax and escape work, if you know what I mean,' she says, and then openly winks at Mrs James, who attempts a nervous laugh.

What is going on here?

And, excuse me, isn't Nose Hair new and everything? How does she even know about Deolali and the course? Mrs James is unbelievable, gossiping with her so much. I stare at Mrs James.

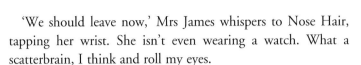

'We should leave now,' Mrs James whispers to Nose Hair, tapping her wrist. She isn't even wearing a watch. What a scatterbrain, I think and roll my eyes.

'Yeah, let's go,' Nose Hair says. 'See you around!' she says to me sweetly. I think of giving a nonchalant shrug but end up nodding instead. She flicks her finger at Mrs James. 'Come.' They hold hands and start to walk away, leaving me there, awestruck by the display of camaraderie.

New BFF alert!—A small voice in my head begins to chant.

Then, Nose Hair stops abruptly and turns to face me.

'I hope Mrs Bhandari wasn't too hard on you,' she says innocently. 'About the Ladies Meet. I got the impression she was quite angry.'

I cannot believe she actually has the nerve to bring it up!

'No . . .' I mumble. 'We didn't . . . she hasn't . . .'

'Awesome!' she smiles brightly, turns quickly and leaves with Mrs James in tow, both gleaming like they've just emerged victorious in MTV Splitsvilla.

'She is such a bitch,' I say to Naina, who nods furiously. We are standing in my garden in the heat; both our husbands are taking their afternoon naps.

'That James woman is very clever, haan? She's telling Nose Hair all nasty things about you.'

'I know! So insulting,' I say, fanning myself with the copy of *Good Homes* that Naina has just returned. 'And, oh my god, the cheek! *"I hope Mrs Bhandari wasn't too hard on you",*' I say with disgust.

'Nose Hair seems to be very anti-you, Pia. Why is that?' Naina says seriously.

'She hates me.' I say in a flat tone. She obviously must hate me for something, that's the only reason for such malevolence.

'But why?' Naina is talking to herself now. 'Maybe Nose Hair is a lesbian and has fallen in love with the James woman?'

'Ha-fucking-ha' I say. 'In love with Mrs James? Please.'

'Maybe Nose Hair is in love with Captain Arjun?' Naina offers thoughtfully.

I roll my eyes.

'Then Nose Hair is just evil and wants to have fun at your expense. Sadist, you know.' Naina concludes.

'It's so weird Naina,' I say tugging at my hair. 'Mrs James was my friend. And that Nose Hair has some nerve, trying to make me feel guilty about not attending Ladies' Meets! She thinks she's an expert on Unit matters, on the Deolali course, on Arjun's health and recovery even. But she doesn't know the protocol—I'm a senior officer's wife, and she didn't show any respect, called me by my first name and didn't even wish me. They just walked off! No half-hearted goodbye, no I'll-see-you-around.'

'Losers!' Naina says. 'One of a kind, those two. You know I never approved of that James bitch anyway. She reminds me of the evil queen of Narnia.'

'Or the awful red queen from *Alice in Wonderland*,' I suggest.

'Or Rita Skeeter from *Harry Potter*!' she offers.

'Or Alicia Bitch Longlegs, from *Shopaholic*!' I exclaim.

'Oh—oh, I know!' Naina says excitedly. 'Or the female version of Shahrukh Khan from *Kuch Kuch Hota Hai*!'

'Um. But he was the hero and a positive character . . .' I say doubtfully.

'He wasn't a positive character! Throughout the movie he kept up that innocent I-didn't-notice-two-women-falling-in-love-with-me act, kept saying, *"Hum jeetey ek baar hain, martey ek baar hain, pyaar ek baar hota hai aur shaadi bhi ek baar hee hoti hai"*. And then suddenly he has no qualms whatsoever about chasing an already-engaged girl, whom he snubbed years ago for a sexy bombshell. He doesn't even care that his eight-year-old daughter is playing cupid for him at such a young age. And then he seems pretty pleased to get married at a venue that is supposed to be someone else's *shaadi ka mandap*. Salman Khan's wedding for crying out loud!' She is panting a bit now. 'So no, he wasn't a hero at all. He was a negative character, and your Genius James is like him.'

I have to say, I'm a bit awed by her critical analysis.

Time really does fly. Arjun's medical leave is over today and he has gone to office, dressed smartly in combats and looking as handsome as ever.

This is the thing about Arjun: he always manages to look handsome and elegant, even if he's in boxers and a crumpled tee-shirt.

Following the instructions of both our mothers, I managed to put a *kaala tika* behind his right ear to protect him from the evil eye. Of course I had to do it stealthily—I pretended to pat his hair down and then held him by the ears to check if his face looked okay. Tough one to pull off, I know!

He has to finish some paperwork over the next week before we leave for Deolali, and though I can't say he's deliriously happy about going for the course, I've managed to make him look forward to it. And me? I'm ecstatic, obviously.

Mrs Singh and Mrs Sengupta come over in the evening, when Arjun is in office. They're on their way back from one of their irregular evening walks. Mrs Singh has brought a couple of freshly-made doughnuts for me.

'Yummy . . . so . . . soft . . .' I manage between mouthfuls.

'Thanks!' Mrs Singh says happily. 'Mrs Bhandari's recipe.'

'Speaking of Mrs Bhandari—' Mrs Sengupta says. 'Have you spoken to her since, you know . . .'

'Yes . . . she calls regularly,' I tell her, wiping my chocolate-covered mouth with a tissue. 'She didn't say anything though, so I didn't either.'

'Yes, it's best to just let it be,' Mrs Singh says.

I nod. 'She's seems sensible, you know? She knows the extent of Arjun's injury. She might have reacted in the heat of the moment, but I think she thought about it later and sees I'm not at fault.'

Mrs Sengupta makes a face and says, 'Yeah maybe. But all these senior ladies are always evil, so who knows what she's up to.'

'You're just cynical Soma.' Mrs Singh shakes her head. 'Pia is right. Mrs Bhandari is rational enough to know better.'

'Yeah; but I'm always on my guard with her now, making sure I don't say anything that will make people think I'm a tattletale.' I tell them.

'What do you mean?' they sing in harmony.

Ah. What the hell.

I tell them about Mrs James' accusations the day of Arjun's accident, and then about my encounter with her and Nose Hair and the sly comments about Mrs Bhandari and my escaping work.

'I can't freaking believe it!' Mrs Singh looks shocked.

'Why didn't you tell us before, Pia?' Mrs Sengupta asks me. She looks a bit offended, I think.

'I don't know,' I say evasively. 'It never came up I guess.'

Both of them shake their heads in disappointment.

'It never came up?' Mrs Sengupta echoes incredulously. 'It never came up, Pia? You've got to be kidding me! Last time we met I told you about the gossip doing the rounds in the Unit and the Brigade, and even then you forgot to mention such an important thing?'

'I didn't think it was important. I mean, she's just a sad person who doesn't know better . . .' I trail off, not believing myself. The truth is, I feel ashamed. It hurts to even think that someone is accusing me of something so petty. No one except Naina knows, not even Arjun.

'It *is* important Pia,' Mrs Singh sounds slightly outraged. 'The Unit is a family and such bullying is not acceptable. Not at all!'

'You should have told one of the senior ladies and she would have been sorted out immediately. She can't just call and abuse people,' Mrs Sengupta frowns.

'Er, she didn't exactly abuse me . . .' I mutter.

'But she accused you!' Mrs Singh thumps the table, looking agitated and a bit accusatory herself.

'Wrongly,' Mrs Sengupta says darkly.

'Didn't let you explain!' chimes in Mrs Singh.

'And now she's spreading more rumours about you along with Kanika,' Mrs Sengupta adopts an inscrutable tone.

'Nose Hair,' Mrs Singh corrects her. 'Nose Hair suits her,' she nods towards me.

'Yeah, nice dig Pia,' Mrs Sengupta approves. 'What is with

her nose hair? It's so disturbing. I lost my appetite for a day after meeting her.'

'Hasn't anyone told her?' Mrs Singh inquires.

'Don't worry. I will.' I say forthrightly.

'You do that!' Mrs Singh pats my back.

'And I will tell the CO's wife. She needs to know what rubbish is going on right under her nose.' Mrs Sengupta smiles sweetly.

Mrs Singh giggles. '*Nose*!' she says and laughs loudly.

'Strange that she has not smelled trouble yet.' Mrs Sengupta comes up with another one.

'*Smelled!*' Mrs Singh says and laughs.

I laugh as well, and then what Mrs Sengupta said clicks. 'What rumours is she spreading now?'

'What else yaar? That you are trying to escape from your responsibilities using Captain Arjun's injuries as an excuse. And that you are immature, childish, shallow—' Mrs Sengupta says in a matter-of-fact way.

'That's enough Soma,' Mrs Singh stops laughing and shoots her a warning glance.

'What? She should know!' She looks at me. 'Pia, be verrrry careful in Army, not everyone is your friend. People are complicated and situations within the closed Army circle can bring out the worst in people.'

I nod.

'And this Jincy is crazy. Mrs Bhandari trying to counsel her is her own fault anyway. She is always telling everyone about everything—wanting kids, cooking disasters, adventures in bed. If I cared to listen, I could even tell you the date she last had her period,' Mrs Sengupta says. 'So chill, everyone knows that Jincy is a mad cow.'

'Yes. And if anyone is shallow, it is her,' Mrs Singh says thoughtfully. 'I mean, imagine saying things like "Pia just tries to please everyone" and "Fashion and clothes is all Pia cares about".'

Mrs James said that? I want to strangle her! I bet Nose Hair contributed to this poisonous outpour.

I sit there staring into nothing, trying to process all that I've just heard about myself. Malicious gossip about me is circulating in the Unit and the Brigade. Everyone probably thinks I'm unfit to be an Army wife. I really don't know what you're supposed to do with this information. Feel good that you are aware of what's going on? Or, feel miserable that you're being targeted for no reason? Or maybe just sulk it out till you feel all right.

I choose the last option.

I'm getting the hell out of here next week anyway.

I force myself to focus on Deolali and all the fun I'll have there.

But really, shallow? Immature? My head feels thick and heavy. I know Mrs James and I aren't friends anymore, but we were at one point of time! It is just a stupid misunderstanding and I thought . . . I honestly thought it was temporary, and that sooner or later she would come around because I really didn't do anything. But she . . . Oh god. Whatever. I don't even care anymore.

Mrs James can kiss my ass.

chapter twenty-two

God, That's Good!

Deolali. Lovely, welcoming, lush Deolali, oh how much I love this place! It's like a nonstop party here, and life inside the grand, awe-inspiring School of Artillery is FAB.

For me, I mean.

Arjun, unfortunately, is here to study, and has to read up on dull sounding subjects like Military Law and Surveillance and Something-Or-The-Other. But he has weekends free and there's no pressure of work, no office, no men to manage and hence—no big deal, right? In our free time we can explore Nashik, the nearby hill stations and check out the eating joints. There's even a mall in Nashik, and I'm already excited about it.

Arjun, however, doesn't seem to feel the same way. We've been here for five days, his classes have begun and he keeps saying things like, 'The course is *huge*', or 'I'm screwed, I'm not prepared for this', or—the most irritating one—'I'll have to study all the damn time'.

I mean, how hard can War Tactics be? Or Military History? Come on! I'm sure he must have studied this in the Academy anyway. But he is totally freaking out and even refused to eat breakfast today saying he feels sleepy in the morning class when his stomach is full. Imagine.

Anyway, I've decided to let him be for the moment. Soon enough he'll realize it's not all that big a deal and will relax.

Meanwhile, I am setting up the cute two-room set allotted to us for the duration of the course. We're on the ground floor of a block comprising similar accommodation for thirty families. Most of the officers are of the same seniority as Arjun, a few are his juniors and about ten are his seniors. The senior-most officer in a course is referred to as the course senior and, in this one, it's Major Chandok, senior to Arjun by almost seven years. He is here with his wife and lovely four-year-old daughter, and they stay in the quarter (that is, the apartment; look at me, so clued into Army-lingo already!) on our right. Next door to us on the left are Captain Madhavan and his wife Manpreet. He is Arjun's course mate from the Academy and they are good friends. She is an awesome Punjabi girl with an obsession for nail art and we are friends already.

He's from Karnataka and she's from Chandigarh.

He's reserved, like Arjun.

She is, well, like me.

See? This is what I love about the Army—you get to meet people from all over! Five days and I've found a friend who has done my nails already (dull orange with a delicate silver pattern— adorable!), has borrowed a book from my newly set up shelf (*Boy Next Door* by Meg Cabot—totally recommended!) and has synced my iPod with hers so it is now loaded with the latest music.

There are other wives in the block and I have met quite a few already. Everyone is about the same age, there's no senior-junior rigidity and I think everyone is breathing easy in the relaxed setting away from the Units.

Each one of us has a horror story that we're escaping—a vindictive CO's wife from hell, a senior's wife who thinks she wears the rank along with her husband, alienation by the entire Unit for standing up for oneself (imagine!), being made to sing at every Ladies' Meet despite zero vocal skills, etc.

Me too, obviously. In fact, for me, it's like my life has rebooted without saving the changes. Bliss!

Every morning, as soon as our husbands leave for their classes, all the girls gather around in the corridor and a long session of sharing breakfast and conversation starts. Fun-fun-fun!

I have a feeling that these two months are going to be super awesome.

Days are quickly becoming weeks. Arjun continues to be obsessed with his books and studies till late night, but we still manage to go out a lot and have eaten at all the recommended restaurants in town. When he is studying for a test, I team up with the girls and we hire a cab and go camp in the City Mall at Nashik. Life is *good*. All the ground floor wives are a tight group by now. We spend so much time together in the corridor talking every day, that it feels like we've known each other for ages. There's no formality, we call each other by our first names, except for Mrs Chandok, the Course Senior's wife, but she is nowhere close to a scary senior wife. She is more like a big sister to all us ground-floor girls and she cooks amazing stuff for us when the husbands are out for an entire day.

Manpreet and I are in the grocery store, buying some fancy instant coffee and candy when we meet Isha.

Isha lives on the first floor of our block and I have seen her couple of times, driving around in a red Getz. She is really pretty, but for some reason has had her hair coloured blonde. It's very disturbing. I mean, why would a deliciously dusky girl get her hair coloured *blonde*? It's such a pity, really. She would have looked awesome otherwise.

Anyway. Not my business.

Isha compliments me on my engagement ring within ten seconds of our introduction.

'It's awesome,' she says, yanking my hand towards her. And before I can even open my mouth to say thank you, she says: 'I've got a similar one. But with bigger diamonds. And it's platinum.'

'Er, great . . .' I say. Manpreet gives me a what-is-*wrong*-with-her look, raising her eyebrows.

Once we have paid for our shopping, we wait for Isha to finish her billing (out of courtesy) and I notice that she has, among other things, two jars of mayonnaise. Two jars for two months?

'One is eggless and the other one is regular,' she explains. 'You know, sometimes some vegetarian people drop by for grub. Eggless is for them.'

'What people?' Manpreet asks.

'My husband's course mates, you know?' she says. 'Bachelors? From our husbands' course? The ones that live in P-12?'

Neither Manpreet nor I have any idea about the bachelors or about P-12, but we nod nonetheless.

We walk back to our block together, with Isha showing her tattoos to us—she has three: an angry-looking dragon on her left shoulder, a colourful butterfly on her left ankle and a Sanskrit *shloka* on her right wrist. Each tattoo has an oh-so-interesting story behind it, obviously, and in order to tell us those stories, she enters my house when I unlock it. The last story ends with how the Sanskrit *shloka* etched on her wrist has given her peace of mind and a mission in life.

'What mission would that be?' asks Manpreet, but she's totally ignored by Isha who is now looking around the room with interest. Her eyes fall on the shelf full of my books and magazines.

'These are all your books?' she asks, and before I can nod, or say yes, she waves her Sanskrit *shloka* hand dismissively and says, 'I've read all of them!'

'Good for you,' Manpreet says, clearly annoyed.

In fact, Manpreet looks so irritated that I want to giggle.

'You know,' Isha starts again, ignoring Manpreet, 'my husband bought me a cake last night. You should come over and taste it. It's huge!'

'Was it your birthday? Or anniversary?' I ask.

'No. We had a fight and didn't speak for a day,' she shrugs. 'Then he bought the I-am-sorry cake. Massive, it was!'

'The cake?' I ask.

'No, the fight.'

'What did you fight about?' Manpreet asks.

'Um. I don't remember,' she shrugs.

'You don't remember?' Manpreet echoes, traces of sarcasm in her voice.

'Nope. It's not important anyway. But I got angry when he pushed me and I fell over our new printer. Smash! All gone. Irreparable. Five grand.' She holds up the *shloka* hand to show five fingers, and then waves it. 'All gone.'

Manpreet looks at me in confusion. I raise my eyebrows.

'He got the cake at eleven in the night! It's so expensive,

chocolate truffle!' Isha's eyes twinkle and she smiles. 'He is crazy about me.'

Standing in the corridor with a bunch of wives later that day, we find out that everyone on the first floor, especially Isha's next door neighbours, suspect that the couple has plenty of brawls and even gets into physical fights.

Why am I the last one to know everything, always?

'Domestic violence,' says Mrs Chandok with a serious look. 'They are a volatile couple. Very Oh-Tee-Tee.' Mrs Chandok tends to intersperse her sentences with sms-speak. It took me some time to catch on.

'She gets beaten up regularly,' Rohini says.

'Then he buys her expensive gifts,' Arti says.

'And all is well in lover-land,' Geetha says.

'That can't be true,' I say. 'She's modern, strong and educated. Why would she put up with something like this?'

'Phuleez! She's not "putting up" with anything,' Mrs Chandok says making quotes in the air. 'They both hit each other and throw things around.'

'And what has modern or educated got to do with it?' Geetha says. 'She has a mental disorder, that one.'

'That might be true!' Rohini says. 'She's always singing the annoying "My husband loves me so much, my husband buys me such expensive shit" song. What is with her?'

'Has anyone seen anything actually happen?' Manpreet asks, coming back to the main topic.

'No, but people have heard them arguing. She often has

unexplained bruises. And last week she was spotted running out of the house crying loudly,' Mrs Chandok says in a matter-of-fact way.

Manpreet and I nod, but I'm not convinced. This doesn't have to automatically mean domestic violence at all. We all have arguments, and these houses are so small even the slightest sound is audible outside. And I cut myself all the time with a knife because I'm clumsy and I suck in the kitchen. Maybe she is too, right?

I tell Arjun about the domestic violence rumour that evening and he says he doesn't think it's true. The officer in question, Isha's husband, is Arjun's junior and is a good officer, according to Arjun. I ask what I think are piercing questions, aimed at figuring out whether Isha's husband is good at hiding his streak of violence, but Arjun just says, 'Why don't you watch some TV, baby?'

He is really working hard at this course and a major test is coming up next week. He has done really well in the past few tests and I'm sure he will cruise through this one as well, but since he cannot sit on a chair for long durations (his back starts to ache) and his fingers become numb sometimes (though it only lasts for a few minutes now), he is anxious.

So instead of watching TV (nothing good is on air these days anyway), I walk over to the corridor hoping someone or the other is loitering outside, also letting their husbands study in peace. And, no surprise, I find Manpreet leaning against the railing, staring at my door. She breaks into a smile worthy of an Olympic winner when she sees me emerge.

'I willed you to come outside,' she says.

'My husband willed me to go outside,' I correct her.

'So did mine,' she says and we giggle.

'It's like dating paranoid school kids, man!' she says. 'I wasn't this worried about my board exams for God's sake!'

'Me neither,' I admit. In fact, when I was in twelfth grade and taking those crucial board exams, all my late nights 'studying' were actually spent going through the stash of Jeffery Archer novels I'd discovered in my mom's room.

Seeing that we'd been made redundant for a couple of hours by our hardworking husbands, we decide to go for a walk. Around P-12. The alleged Bachelor block for our course.

'Let's see if it really exists or if it just exists in Isha's imagination,' Manpreet says. She has concluded that Isha is delusional; that she makes things up, tells these grand stories and then promptly believes them herself. To get away from her real life with an abusive husband, apparently.

We walk past the other blocks, reading the numbers on every building, and sure enough, P-12 does exist.

It's an old block, quite similar to ours except that there are no clothes hanging in the corridors, no fancy name-plates on the doors and no local maids running from one house to another trying to finish work. The block looks almost bare actually—closed doors, no lights, no noise even. We casually stroll by, looking up sneakily, and just as we are about to pass it, my eyes focus on the first floor.

A girl.

A girl in tiny shorts and a super tight black top! She has emerged out of one of the doors to hang a towel in the corridor and her back is towards us.

A girl in the Bachelor's block!

Manpreet has also spotted her by now, because she is clutching my hand tightly, digging her sea-blue nails into my flesh.

'Ouchh!'

'Did you see . . .?' she whispers.

'Yeah . . .' I whisper back.

'Girls aren't allowed in Bachelor quarters,' she says.

'I know . . .' I say.

'Those are the tiniest shorts I've ever seen,' she breathes.

'Might as well be undies,' I say.

And the girl, as if feeling two sets of eyes on her butt, slowly turns to look at us. We, the ogling idiots, quicken our pace, flick our hair, wave our hands and pretend to talk to each other to look like we're just regular evening-walkers instead of a couple of bored gals looking for some drama. Obviously we don't fool her at all. She looks alarmed and almost breaks into a run. The door closes loudly as she disappears behind it.

'We overdid it,' I sigh, and start to walk away.

'Noooo . . .' Manpreet whispers excitedly. 'Let's lurk. Let's spy!'

Good idea. We won't be welcomed back in our houses anyway, I think.

So we lurk.

'Note the quarter number!' Manpreet hisses.

'What? Why?'

'Oho! To find out which officer stays there, of course,' she says impatiently.

Good point, I think, and squint at the black paint above the door that has just banged shut. We have stopped walking altogether now, and both of us are standing in the middle of the road, staring up at the Bachelor's block.

'Fourteen,' I say, reading the flaking black paint.

'Yup! P-12/14,' Manpreet says happily. She then flips out her cell phone and starts jabbing the keys. 'Writing it down. You shouldn't just rely on memory in such cases,' she tells me with an air of drama. I roll my eyes.

'What are we, detectives now?' I say as I drag her from the road and we turn towards our own block.

'Why not?' she says and saves the note with a faint ping on her phone.

We reach our block and, while passing my apartment, I peek through the mesh door and see that Arjun is at his study table, chewing the end of a Reynolds pen and frowning in concentration.

Just then, Mrs Chandok comes out with her daughter in her arms; she looks livid. Mrs Chandok, I mean.

'He wants to study in peace,' she says, gesturing towards her husband who is also at the study table, his head bowed over a thick book. 'In. Peace. What a joke, Ell-Oh-Ell.'

Manpreet clicks her tongue in sympathy.

'You cannot have peace with children,' Mrs Chandok says. 'You can have fun, love, excitement, anger, and frustration. But no peace.' She looks at the two of us, like she's warning us in advance.

'Chill, Mrs Chandok,' Manpreet says. 'Guess what we just saw.'

chapter twenty-three

Honey We've Come Far . . .

We recite the entire girl-in-undies-spotted-in-Bachelor-block incident to her. Manpreet and I smile smugly, feeling like we're an accomplished undercover-agent duo, till Mrs Chandok says she knows about it already. (Again, everyone knows everything but me! And also Manpreet.) She doesn't even wait for Manpreet to check her cell phone note; she waves her hand and says, 'That will be Captain Anand.'

'What—how do you know?' I say in a deflated tone.

'Everyone knows,' she says. 'The girl's name is Priya. At least the last one was Priya. Wouldn't be surprised if it's a new one this time,'

'Who is Captain Anand?' Manpreet asks.

'Someone from the course. He has several Gee-Efs in Mumbai and Pune and they keep coming over to spend the weekend,' Mrs Chandok explains.

'GFs? Girlfriends?' I echo. 'Plural?'

'Well, yeah,' she nods. 'But not girlfriend-girlfriend, you know? He says he isn't serious about anyone.'

'And they stay over for the weekend?' I ask. 'No one notices?'

She shrugs.

'But it isn't allowed, right?' Manpreet says.

'Who cares enough to report him?' Mrs Chandok says. 'Army is conservative only when it comes to wives. In our Unit in Ambala, there was this officer who went around for a long time with this local girl. She came over to his room all the time, accompanied him to many formal parties and he introduced her to everyone. We thought he was going to marry her. And Eff-Why-Aye, we even gave her a prize she didn't deserve in one of the raffles. You know, to be welcoming and all that? But then he went and married someone else.'

'Poor girl,' I say.

'What poor, yaar? She started seeing another officer from the same Unit. In less than a month,' Mrs Chandok says. 'And even he didn't marry her. They broke up after a few weekend holidays, if you know what I mean,' she gives us both a conspiratorial look. We nod.

'But no sympathies for her. She was a horribly smug woman. No embarrassment about attending parties with the second officer, like everything is hunky-dory,' Mrs Chandok wrinkles her nose. 'At the last party she attended, she told me that she loves the Army. I said to her that, Look, Kanika, Army is good and all that, but you need to be careful, not everyone's intentions are good and you are a woman, put your dignity before anything else. And she looked at me like I'd come straight from an ancient excavation site.'

Manpreet shakes her head like she can't believe the audacity of the girl.

'Yeah. Imagine. I was like, Whiskey-Tango-Foxtrot. I was only trying to be nice to her. Bee-Tee-Doubleyou, I heard she got married to another Army officer.' She shakes her head and her daughter, still in her arms, imitates her. 'Arranged marriage.

Poor guy, to be married to such a—' she spells out the word 'slut' softly, and then gestures towards her daughter who has been listening to the entire conversation with rapt attention. We nod in understanding.

And then, like a bolt of lightning, something comes to me.

Kanika?

And isn't Nose Hair from Ambala too?

I remember Mrs Singh mentioning something . . . And boy, she sure is smug.

I feel almost dizzy at the possibilities.

Could it be?

Oh-Em-Gee.

'Mrs Chandok,' I say, trying my best to keep my voice from quivering in excitement. 'What did this Kanika look like?'

'Like a—' she spells 'slut' again and Manpreet giggles.

'Tell me! I think I know her!' I demand.

'Okay, well,' Mrs Chandok says. 'I'll show you. I've got pictures, somewhere. Bee-Aar-Bee, hang on,' she says, and with her daughter in her arms, she heads inside her house.

'You know the S.L.U.T.?' Manpreet asks me.

'I think so,' I say, trying not to get too excited.

'Here you go,' Mrs Chandok reappears with a camera, leaving her daughter inside this time, and massaging her arm. 'She's getting too big to carry,' she explains.

I snatch the silver Sony Cybershot from her hand and stare at the picture—Mrs Chandok sitting next to the McDonald's mascot, smiling widely at the camera.

'Browse!' she rolls her eyes. 'Go back. There must be some party pictures and she's there in one of them. In the background of course,' she explains to Manpreet. 'Who would take her picture?'

I press the back arrow, scanning each picture quickly and in about two minutes, there it is.

Draped in a bright hurts-your-eye red saree, a wine goblet in her hand and a tacky diamanté hair-clip on her head, there is Nose Hair smiling cheerfully, her claw-like pale white hands on a man's shoulder.

In the background, of course. The picture is meant to be of Mrs Chandok and another lady eating chicken tikka. Nose Hair is behind them and the man she's with is hardly visible, but she is clearly noticeable, in all her pale fake-brilliance. I am delirious. I am overjoyed. About two hundred million scenarios of my thrilling victory over her through cheap insults are doing the rounds in my mind, all at once.

'Found her?' Mrs Chandok asks and I nod.

Mrs Chandok and Manpreet huddle around me to look at the picture.

'This one,' Mrs Chandok points to Nose Hair and tells Manpreet.

'She's . . . white,' Manpreet says.

'As a ghost,' Mrs Chandok confirms. 'You know her?' she asks me.

I nod and swallow hard.

'She recently married an officer in Arjun's Unit.'

'Oh-Em-Gee!' Mrs Chandok says.

'Wow,' Manpreet says, leaning in to take a look at the picture again. 'She looks . . . weird.'

'She has nose hair,' I inform her. 'Peeking out of her nostrils.'

'Yuck!' both of them exclaim in disgust.

'I never noticed!' Mrs Chandok says to Manpreet. 'But then we only met at night. And, I usually ignored her.'

'Is she a friend?' Manpreet asks me.

'No way!' I say. 'Not even a month in the Unit and she's been trying to act smart with me. Bitched about me to the 2IC wife and has been particularly mean to me whenever we've spoken.'

'What about her husband?' Mrs Chandok asks. 'Drunkard? Old? Divorced? Man whore?' Now that her daughter is inside the house, she's saying the words out loud. Her husband coughs from inside. She claps her hand over her mouth.

'Good chap,' I tell her. 'As far as I know. Very shy.'

'Well,' Mrs Chandok says. 'I'm impressed.'

'I'm speechless,' I say.

'I'm amazed,' Manpreet says, zooming in on Nose Hair's nose and screwing up her own in distaste. 'How did she manage to get not one, not two, but *three* Army officers in such a short time?'

'I told you,' Mrs Chandok says. 'She was determined to get into the Army. With such resolve, she would have passed the freaking SSB with flying colours; tricking officers is nothing.'

'No wonder she's so clued-in to all the Army-related nonsense,' I say. 'Trying to make me feel bad, hah! Wait till she knows that I know,' I say brightly.

'Oooh, revenge!' Manpreet is excited. 'Sweet!'

'You can take this picture as evidence!' Mrs Chandok offers.

'Blackmaaaaail her,' Manpreet whispers like we are in some sort of suspense movie.

'Put this picture up on FB and tag her poor husband!'

'Write her an anonymous mail and ask her to confess everything to her unsuspecting husband!'

The ideas keep flowing for another ten minutes or so, until Mrs Chandok's husband—after fake-coughing several times without any response from her—calls out her name.

'Tee-Tee-Why-Ell,' she says to the two of us. 'My soldier needs me. Keep me updated!'

Manpreet and I also head to our respective homes—she is excited, like she's been a victim of Nose Hair's cruel remarks herself, and I am giddy with joy. I'll show her and the spiteful Mrs James. Yes. I'm going to do it.

'You're not going to do anything,' Arjun says.

We are in our bedroom; I'm resting on his chest after a steamy lovemaking session. There really is something special in Deolali's air; we've become even more romantic and we can't seem to keep our hands off each other. It's the lack of stress, I think. Everything is so laidback and relaxed here. Except for the pressure of studies, that is. But Arjun scored more than eighty per cent in that big test; he's in the top five in his class, and it proves what I always said—it's no big deal.

Anyway, I've just told him everything: Mrs James' phone call, the gossip she's spreading about me along with her her new best friend Nose Hair and also Nose Hair's unpleasant comments. Also about Nose Hair's background, the picture (that I now have on my laptop) and my plans to deal with both of them as soon as we go back to Pathankot.

After his initial shock at their 'impolite and unacceptable behaviour' (his words, not mine), this is what he has to say—that I'm not going to do anything.

Is he warning me? Telling me not to do anything? How dare he?

'How dare you?' I say crossly.

'I mean, you will not do anything,' he rephrases. 'I know you.'

'Huh?' What is that supposed to mean? 'Of course I will!' I say.

He just shrugs and keeps stroking my hair.

'Well?' I demand. No response. I raise my head from his chest to look at him, and give him my nastiest glare.

'Well,' he says at last, 'you can't handle confrontation.'

'Excuse me?' Sometimes it's hard to tell if he's joking.

'Confrontations are just not your thing,' he says.

'What?' I laugh with surprise. 'Confrontations are totally my thing.'

'When have you ever confronted anybody?' Arjun asks.

'Loads of times!'

'Name one.'

God, he is relentless.

'That time in college? When that girl tagged me on Facebook as Miss Goody Two Shoes?'

'Come on,' he says. 'You just removed the tag and stopped talking to her. Tanya and Ruchi cornered her to "confront" her and you ran to the loo saying that you "just have to pee".' He is smiling. Tanya and Ruchi used to be my besties, my soul sisters before Arjun came into my life. Now they are his best friends apparently. And by the way, this is not how I remember the incident. I was totally there when they summoned the girl to the canteen. I had to rush to the washroom a bit later, granted, but it's not my fault I have a teeny-tiny bladder!

'Please,' I say indignantly. 'I don't have to prove myself to you.'

He laughs and kisses me on my head.

'Why are you getting so worked up anyway?' he asks. 'It's not like you're going to have them around forever.'

'Yeah, I know. The Army, always moving, new people, blah blah,' I say. 'But I keep thinking about it. Until I do something about it, it's not going to go away.' Which is true. No matter how deep I try and bury it, it always comes up unexpectedly, making me feel low.

'Your call,' Arjun says. 'I'd be proud of you if you do it. But even if you don't, it doesn't really matter. People are stupid. Who cares?'

'Those two are definitely stupid,' I agree.

'Yes. Come here, now,' he smiles lazily and I forget about it for the next hour or so. Oh, the romantic city of Deolali! Like an aphrodisiac. Mmmm . . .

Two months are over? Who would have thought two months could be this short? I am so depressed that I have thrown a shrill tantrum over a missing pad of sticky notes. I don't even use sticky notes. Manpreet is suffering from an extreme case of denial. She hasn't even started packing yet (we have to vacate the quarters in two days) and sticks her fingers in her ears and loudly says na-na-na-na-na-na every time her husband tries to reason with her.

There is one thing to be happy about. Arjun has scored an Alpha in the course—A-grade in Army lingo. Only six out of the forty-one officers attending the course have scored an Alpha. So much for all his 'I screwed up the test' (head hung low), 'I didn't finish the paper on time' (punching the wall) and 'I'm not in the right state for this course' (loud sigh). He worked really hard and he is sharp, so it was a piece of cake for him. Hate to say it, but I told you so, didn't I? No big deal.

We go out for a lavish lunch to Mainland China the day before leaving. Manpreet and Captain Madhavan accompany us, and we have a good time. Just when Arjun is finishing his dessert, his spoon falls on the tiled floor with a loud clink. After twenty-three days, his fingers have gone numb again. I hold his hands and massage his fingertips, while Manpreet and her husband continue talking—politely ignoring what happened. Captain Madhavan knows Arjun gets frustrated with his injury, that he faces a lack of sensation sometimes and that talking about it embarrasses him a lot. I feel a familiar gush of emotions run through me like an electric shock. It has been almost five months since that dreadful day. Visions flood my mind like a tsunami—Arjun unconscious in the ICU, Arjun in a wheelchair, Arjun rubbing his toes frantically when he lost sensation for the first time . . .

Stop it, a voice at the back of my head warns me.

Arjun has made an amazing recovery. We have crossed that bridge. We have gone through the worst and have emerged successfully. Who would have imagined that in such a short time span we'd be here, celebrating Arjun's brilliant performance in the course? And the expressionless doctor did say it would take at least six months, right? We'll be all right. I look up at Arjun and smile at him. We'll be all right, baby, I say to him in my head. He nods and squeezes my hand. We get back to the dessert.

We're driving back to the School of Artillery when my phone sings *My Milkshake Brings All The Boys To The Yard*.

It's Naina.

'Ello!' I say happily into the phone.

'Hey. All set to leave Fun-City?' she says.

'Yeah. Have you called to rub it in?'

'Um. Actually I called to tell you that—' she hesitates for a minute and I begin to imagine all the possible scenarios. Is she pregnant? Is Kareena Kapoor pregnant? Oh god, is Salman Khan getting married?

'What is it?' I ask.

'Our posting has come, Pia,' she says. 'To the Northeast.'

This is worse than Salman Khan getting married. I mean, Naina is my BFF. How am I supposed to survive Army life without her? She is equally miserable. First, she is moving away from me, and second, to the Northeast. She says she isn't even sure if she'll get to stay with her husband or not.

'I might have to stay in SF in whichever Cantt. is nearest to his post,' she informs me sadly. SF being Separate Family, the saddest term I've heard in my life. My heart sinks. In two days I'll be back at the Unit: to the unpredictable Mrs Bhandari, crazy Mrs James and Nose Hair, and now Naina is abandoning me.

My only consolation is that Naina will be around for one more month.

chapter twenty-four

As You Were!

We're back at Pathankot.

As we were.

Super sad, I know.

It's my first morning here after two months of total bliss. I sigh loudly as I get up from the bed. The whole Deolali episode already feels like a dream.

In an hour, I'm sitting at our dining table, eating breakfast, sipping coffee and staring down at the photographs we took at Sula Vineyard in Nashik.

Were the past two months even real?

What a sad weekend this is going to be!

Arjun also looks a little gloomy, only he refuses to admit it. He says he is looking forward to joining office on Monday. He gets busy with his files and arranging papers and stuff, and according to expected Army behaviour, I call all the Unit ladies to inform them of my arrival in the station.

Except the evil Mrs James, of course. And Nose Hair, who I suppose should be calling me according to protocol. I'm the senior's wife, after all.

Mrs Nair asks in detail about Arjun's health and compliments me on taking good care of him. Mrs Bhandari welcomes me warmly and also sends fresh cherry tomatoes from her kitchen garden. Mrs Singh sends chicken biryani for lunch as a welcome gesture. Mrs Sengupta eagerly fixes a time we can meet so she can pick up the wine that I've brought her from Nashik.

I spend a lot of time with Naina and tell her how lonely I'm going to be once she's gone. She says she'll be far more miserable because by now it is almost certain that the place her husband has been posted to is not a family station. She will have to live in SF. It's either SF, or live with either of the parents for two years. She chose SF.

'We knew our field posting was due,' she tells me. 'But I was hoping that we'd at least be able to stay together. This is so unfair,' she sulks.

I wonder if I will ever be able to stay in SF, all by myself, and shudder at the thought.

Mrs Singh and Mrs Sengupta come over the next day and it feels good to see their friendly faces. They are going to be my only solace here, now that Naina is about to leave. Without any delay, I hand over the wine to Mrs Sengupta who inspects each bottle and then gives me a thank-you shoulder squeeze.

'So Pia. Honeymoon over. Back to reality,' Mrs Singh says.

'Yeah,' I say in a low voice. 'Sad, sad reality.'

'Very sad indeed,' Mrs Sengupta says. 'There's a Welfare to be organized for the GOC's wife and I'm already dreading it.'

'Relax Soma,' Mrs Singh tells her. 'Mrs Nair just suggested

that you look over it. It's not final or anything.' She gives me a what-are-we-going-to-do-with-her look.

'She suggested it, so she might actually mean it!' Mrs Sengupta says accusingly.

'When is it?' I ask.

'*Next* month!' Mrs Singh says and rolls her eyes.

'I'm going to have viral fever next month,' Mrs Sengupta says and all of us laugh.

'I'll let Jincy handle it. She needs to get off that fat ass of hers anyway,' Mrs Sengupta finishes.

'Ooooh, Mrs James. How is my frenemy?' I ask with a bright smile.

'Joined to the hip with Nose Hair, that's how she is,' Mrs Singh replies.

'Friendship still going strong, eh?' I ask.

'I give it another month,' Mrs Sengupta says.

'That is, if Nose Hair doesn't put a leash on Jincy and put her in her backyard by then,' Mrs Singh says.

'Really?' I ask with interest.

'She bosses her around like Jincy is her personal maid or something,' Mrs Singh tells me. 'And boy, she's arrogant.'

'Arrogant she is,' Mrs Sengupta says. '*Na akal na shakal*, God knows what she is so proud of. Oh, by the way, I told Mrs Bhandari about Jincy's accusations and Nose Hair's behaviour with you. She was furious. You're welcome!' she says happily.

'Awesome Mrs Sengupta,' I sing happily too. 'You're a rock star!'

'But they are toxic people. You steer clear of them Pia,' Mrs Singh instructs me with concern. 'I don't want you to be bullied. Again.'

Why does everyone think I am easily bullied? God!

'Not in a million years,' I say dramatically. 'I know her dirty secret.'

Both of them look at each other and back at me. Their anticipation is palpable. I grin wickedly.

'Out with it!' both of them say.

I tell them the story, show them the picture on my laptop and declare war. They cheer me.

Arjun is back from office and extremely upset. The CO has relieved him of his responsibilities as Adjutant—a super-important role that he had entrusted Arjun with until the accident—and has given him some other trivial job.

'It's a physical injury goddammit! It's not like I'm mentally ill!' he says angrily.

'Maybe he wants you to take it easy right now,' I offer.

'Bullshit,' he says. 'He's overreacting.'

'Why don't you have a chat with him?' I suggest. 'Tell him that it's bothering you?'

He looks at me like I've just suggested he take the CO out on a date.

'Are you nuts? One such chat and he'll be filling Form No. 10 for me.'

Form No. 10 is for mental illness. Having an open and grown up conversation with your boss is apparently a sign of mental illness among the male species. I sigh.

The next evening I'm standing in front of my house, waiting for Naina to join me for an evening walk, when none other than the founding (and only) members of the Evil Sisterhood of the

Unit appear in front of me. They are deep in discussion and notice me only when they are right in front of me. Mrs James nudges Nose Hair in the ribs.

'You're back?' says Nose Hair, in such bright, artificial tones that I instantly know they were talking about me. Mrs James looks a bit constipated.

'Good evening to you too, Kanika,' I say equally brightly. 'I'm back, yes.'

Mrs James is totally ignoring me, choosing to bury her head in her phone. Fine, two can play that game, I say to her in my head. So I don't acknowledge her, don't even wish her. She can add 'rude' to her list of grievances against me, for all I care.

'Congratulations to Captain Arjun for the Alpha,' Nose Hair sings.

'Thanks. You sure keep tabs on everything,' I say.

'Can't help it,' she says. 'My husband is the Adjutant. Basically runs the entire Unit.'

'Wow,' I say. 'Good for him.'

'Yeah. He has streamlined a lot of work and processes for the Unit since taking over. The CO says he regrets not appointing him earlier.' Her eyes gleam with pleasure—pleasure at crushing my soul yet again, because Arjun was the Adjutant before being replaced by her oh-so-capable husband. God, she is Satan.

'Brilliant,' I reply, anger rising in me.

'Anyway, see ya!' she says with a wave and they walk off, Mrs James still pretending to be occupied with her phone. Oh come on, I want to tell her, what important thing could you be doing on that prehistoric phone that you have? It's a Nokia 7210. Loser. But like always, they are already half a kilometre away from me, leaving me standing there, seething.

Okay, perhaps Arjun is right about the confrontation thing—

me not being so into them, that is. You know, because people always seem to be walking away before I can start. Or maybe because I just ... can't. I just can't deal with unpleasant confrontations or the fact that there's a need for it in my life.

So I just hope the two catch herpes and do nothing about it. For now.

Arjun has been going to the office regularly for over a week now, and though he says he's fine, I know he is not. His long working hours leave him drained, but he refuses to slow down. I have tried to tell him to take it easy for a while but he doesn't listen.

'Oh Pia, I feel GOOD! Fully recovered!' he always says in a dazzling tone that tells everyone within a ten-kilometre radius that he's not.

But today, it's different. Something is wrong, I can sense it. I can tell by the way he is slouching; by the way he's trying to smile at me during lunch, like it's normal for him to not say a word through the entire meal, and like he always eats kaddu ki sabzi without any complaints. I know he's buying time to share some bad news. I am alarmed, to say the least, but I decide not to prod. He will tell me in his own time. So I just play along, sending silent prayers to God. Please, let it not be a field posting!

Finally, he tells me. And though it is not a field posting (thank God!), it is heartbreaking on a different level. Arjun is already frustrated by the jobs he's been given in the Unit and today he discovered that the CO is making regular calls to the

Artillery Posting and Transfer Department in Delhi about Arjun, trying to get him posted out of the Unit and bring in a 'better resource' in his place, as Arjun is a 'liability' to the Unit now.

Arjun is sitting on the side of our bed, head in hands, and in the dim light from the curtained window, he suddenly looks frail. My six-foot one fighter looks defeated.

Did I say heartbreaking? Change it to soul-crushing, gut-wrenching anguish that grips every cell in your body until you can't breathe and fall face first on the ground.

And seeing the despair in Arjun's eyes is just making it worse by a million degrees.

I feel a bone-deep weariness take over me. Like I am suddenly a million years old.

He has been so strong all through the long months of pain, working at recovering fast with such dedication. It was his strength that has kept us both from sinking into despair. And now, in his weakest moment, I can only tell him how his ability to hang on and not crumble has also fuelled my spirits, has kept me afloat through times when it was easy to give up.

'Arjun,' I say in a dark voice. 'We've gone through a lot recently. And I've learned a lot from the past few months . . . I've learned that things don't always happen the way we plan them, or they way we hope they would. I've learned that things will go wrong, no matter if we are ready or not. And what's worse, is that the things that go wrong don't always get fixed. There's no rule. We can go on being scared, or keep walking with hope. We can dream of disappearing, of hiding under the bed or even for a miraculous escape, like I did . . . But in the end, it's up to us to get up and face the music.'

Arjun is looking at me like I'm speaking Latin. But I can't

stop now. I have to try and tell him everything that went on in my head when he had the accident, and every single time when the event comes to my mind.

'Baby,' I say, 'we don't get to choose where we come from, what happens to us and the turns life takes. But we still get to choose where we go from here, right? We can still do things to make it right, or at least try. Life is unpredictable, and who knows? Maybe a posting will be good for us. Or not! Maybe it will be worse. But we owe it to each other and to all the people that love us, to try and feel okay about it . . .' I stop to take a breath.

Arjun is now sitting straight. Maybe he's about to laugh hysterically at what I said; maybe he'll credit me for changing the mood by making him laugh. But I don't care. Right now, I'm on a roll. I've avoided these overwhelming emotions till now, successfully avoiding a confrontation with myself. I've kept all this in a part of my brain where even I've been afraid to venture. But I can't seem to do it any longer. It's a 'speak my mind today or forever hold my peace' situation.

So even though my throat feels tight, I carry on.

'I was devastated when the accident happened. I was afraid to see you the next day. I didn't know what to say to you . . . how to make it better. I wanted to sleep endlessly, or to run away and pretend everything was normal. But I didn't. Because Arjun, sometimes the worst thing that happens to us, the thing that makes us wish we could disappear, is the thing that makes us better than we used to be.'

When I finish, I realize that I am shaking.

Arjun is looking at me strangely. His eyes look teary. Or maybe because I'm crying now, his eyes look wet too. He stands up and hugs me. I bury my head in the reassuring warmth of his chest and breathe in slowly. I hear him sniff as he kisses my forehead. I feel weightless, like a feather, like I've finally gotten rid of the invisible backpack full of stones that I've been carrying around all this while.

'I love you,' he whispers against my hair. 'You know that, right?'

Something tells me he won't be laughing hysterically at my speech, after all.

chapter twenty-five

Never Back Down, Don't Surrender

Well, well.

I don't mean to sound show-offish, but I'm a rock star.

My little outburst has worked magic. No, really. Arjun is optimism personified; he seems to have found a whole new level of self-confidence. And I feel motivated too. I mean, I did go through a lot recently and it didn't break me at all! No sir. In fact, I've emerged a much stronger version of the plain old me.

Arjun told me that the way I refused to back down and kept smiling (well, he said giggling), finding fun and humour in everything, gave him strength during those bleak days. 'You've been my positive force,' he said. And I had no idea I was his inspiration all this while. Ha!

Arjun has decided to prepare for a competitive exam called Advanced Artillery Senior Something-or-the-Other Course which, if successfully cleared, leads to—hold your breath, ladies and gentlemen—a year-long course in Deolali!

Ta da!

Arjun has told me that the exam is really tough and the course is extremely demanding, but that's Arjun for you. Remember how he used to worry nonstop before tests in Deolali and then got an Alpha?

Yeah.

He's going to get through easily.

But he hits panic mode whenever I sound so sure of it, so I'm just taking it easy and being a good wife by letting him study for long hours.

If he does well in the course, he might be retained in the School of Artillery as an instructor for another two years and, hand-on-heart, I really hope he does. Three years of fun-fun-fun in Deolali.

I'm already imagining our weekend holidays in Goa . . . .

Arjun's recovery is complete now, according to the expressionless doctor. He says one odd thing here and there might still happen, and that it is completely normal, but I'm happy to report that Arjun has not experienced any lack of sensation for the longest time ever.

So I'm in a great mood as I'm about to set out for a meeting with the Unit ladies at the Officers' Mess. The agenda: discussion and task allocation for the upcoming Welfare, the one Mrs Sengupta was dreading. This is going to be huge since the GOC's wife is the chief guest, and all the Units in the Brigade will be preparing for it together. Every OR family in every Unit in our Brigade will attend this function, and obviously all the officer wives will help put this event together. Events like this can bring out fierce competition between Units because every Unit wants to do better than the other. So much pressure, I know.

I haven't attended anything since Arjun's accident, and you know how that was blown out of proportion. I don't want to give the ladies more feed for gossip, so I figure I'll go and meet everyone, see what's up and maybe even confront Mrs James if I get a chance.

At exactly five in the evening, I'm seated inside the Officers' Mess, wearing a sea-green salwar kameez from Fab India and towering green jute wedges. I practiced a few, 'Good evening Mrs Blah', 'Ah, good to see you XYZ', in the mirror before leaving the house, and I have to say, I impress me. Very classy, very Army-wife like.

So here I am, sitting elegantly on a couch when the ladies begin to pour in.

Mrs Singh comes and immediately sits next to me. She tells me that Mrs Sengupta is 'not feeling well' and we giggle as quietly as possible.

Mrs Bhandari arrives a bit later and hugs me warmly.

'Glad to have you back, Pia. No Unit gathering is the same without you,' she says.

She puzzles me, this one. She seems so nice every time I meet her or talk to her, that I can't believe she said anything bad about me. Maybe she didn't, after all. Who can trust rumours, you know? I smile back brightly.

Then the Unit duo tumbles in, ten minutes late. Mrs James is wearing jeans and a shabby tee-shirt. Mrs Singh rolls her eyes.

'Typical,' she whispers in my ear.

Mrs Bhandari looks at the two of them and then at her watch.

'Was this the time conveyed to you?' Mrs Bhandari asks Mrs James.

'No,' Nose Hair replies instead. 'She forgot,' she says, pointing at Mrs James.

'I didn't forget! I just got the time wrong,' Mrs James says defensively and glares at Nose Hair.

'You said you forgot,' Nose Hair tells her. 'She didn't even bathe today. Came rushing as she was,' she informs the rest of us with a sweet smile.

Oh-oh, trouble in Sisterhood, I think with wicked pleasure and then mentally chastise myself for being so petty.

'Excuse me? I did bathe and I was—' Mrs James begins to say something, but Nose Hair cuts her off.

'Well, bathing is not anyone's concern, is it?' she says in a sugary tone. 'The point is you forgot and I reminded you.'

Sisterhood is really breaking up, I think. Mrs James looks like she's been hit over the head with a hammer. Her jaw has dropped by about a foot. Mrs Singh nudges me softly.

'Soma wins, goodbye hundred bucks,' she sighs. They had a bet going on?

Mrs Nair arrives that very second and as we all get up to wish her, I meet Mrs James' eyes. There's a flicker of . . . something, and then she looks away.

The discussion about Welfare begins and since everyone looks so grave and nervous, I gather this event is extremely important.

Apparently the new GOC's wife is a meticulous fourth-generation Army daughter and a very talented Army wife. She is known to take welfare activities very seriously and follows Army rules like the Bible. Those Army rules strictly say that no lady—officer wife or jawan wife—should be forced to do anything against her will, or asked to perform (dance or sing) for an audience if she is not comfortable with it.

That is where the problem lies.

You see, it is clearly stated by the high-and-mighty that ladies should not be forced into anything but it is a known fact that no lady does anything willingly in such events. I mean what grown up lady wants to sing or dance in front of a crowd? Officer wives or OR wives, both are either coaxed to perform or the fear of the outcome (What if I don't? Will my husband get the boot?) drives them to agree to perform for Ladies' Meets and / or Welfare.

But since the GOC's wife is strictly against it, no one knows how to fill in the hour between welcome and snacks without making it boring or without making it obvious that we have never followed the rules.

Nose Hair keeps coming up with ideas she thinks are brilliant, like, 'Let's have a cooking competition!' and Mrs Nair keeps ignoring her.

'I don't think that will work,' Mrs Nair finally says, in response to Nose Hair's, 'Let's have the OR wives play a game of hopscotch and the GOC's wife can experience the life of the poor' idea.

'Isn't it a fantastic idea?' Nose Hair appeals to the rest of us. 'Hopscotch? That's what poor people do!' she says triumphantly.

Such an overconfident fool, I want to giggle hysterically. Everyone obviously feels the same way, because the other ladies begin coughing or sip from their tea cups to camouflage smirks and giggles. Mrs Nair is looking at her with dry amusement. Mrs Singh nudges me and whispers, 'Hop-fucking-scotch? Really?' This is too funny. I snort.

Nose Hair jerks her head in my direction and her eyes narrow.

'Any ideas yet, Pia?' Nose Hair says in encouraging tones, as though I'm a subnormal child.

'Well, yes,' I say to her and then look at Mrs Nair. I actually do have an idea; it might not work with this group, but at least it's better than hopscotch.

'I think we should have the OR wives give short educational talks based on their educational backgrounds,' I say to Mrs Nair.

Mrs Nair nods thoughtfully. 'Do you have something specific in mind?'

'Not really,' I confess. The idea just came to me a few seconds back. 'But an education or information-based programme might be better than . . . the usual.'

'Hmm. Needs some thought,' Mrs Nair says, and then turns to Mrs Singh. 'What do you think we should do?'

Mrs Singh launches into her idea about enabling the OR wives to sell their arts and crafts, and having done my bit by offering an idea, I happily turn instead to stealthily observing the sorority-sisters' body language. There is an undercurrent between the two. Nose Hair is paler than usual, but otherwise she's totally unaffected and looks the same, with her nose hair claiming all the glory like before. Mrs James looks haggard and wounded, for obvious reasons, and she's pouting a little. She's also a bit jumpy and keeps looking at Mrs Nair and Nose Hair, as if expecting to be abused or slapped or something. I definitely sense tension in the air.

I'm busy imagining various wicked bitch-fight scenarios between the two when Mrs Nair suddenly addresses me.

'Pia, I like your idea, let's take it forward,' she says and Mrs Bhandari nods.

Um. What idea?

'How do you want to execute it? Tell me what you plan to do and everyone will pitch in,' Mrs Nair rests her chin against her hand and looks at me expectantly.

Oh god, my educational-information-driven blabber. Is she serious? Naina was right, give one idea and then they leave you to carry it out singlehandedly. No one is going to pitch in, obviously. Silence has descended in the huge hall and everyone is looking at me. What the hell, I think, and start giving random ideas. At most, they'll reject them.

'Let's see,' I say, forcing a confident tone. 'There's an OR wife from Arjun's Battery who has an LLB degree. She can give a short lecture on women's legal rights. You know, in an Army setting?'

'Women's rights,' Mrs Bhandari repeats and scribbles in her writing pad.

Mrs Nair nods seriously, as though everything I say is incredibly important to her. I must be making some sense, so I keep talking.

'And there are a few women who are quite active on Facebook. They can host an internet-demo for things like Google, emails, Facebook and stuff,' I say, remembering Chimmi and her Facebook updates that have been dominating my timeline since I accepted her friend request.

'Yeah, it's definitely helpful for the kids' homework and school projects,' Mrs Bhandari says to Mrs Nair. 'Most of the families are getting desktops for the children.'

Mrs Nair nods and smiles at me.

'Very nice,' she says. 'Unique. No other Unit will do anything even close.'

I must be dreaming, because the calm and poised Mrs Nair looks excited. I glance at Nose Hair who is frowning and her nostrils are flared. Ha-ha. Score! Then I quickly look at Mrs James, and to my surprise, she makes eye contact (for the second time in an evening!) and smiles at me—first encouragingly, then nervously. Then suddenly she looks exhausted, hangs her head and pretends to write something on her notepad. What is going on with her today? Is she trying to reconcile with me? And what the hell is she writing?

'Will you ask these two ladies if they are comfortable giving these short demos?' Mrs Nair asks Mrs Bhandari. 'Take their details from Pia. And of course we need to fix a timeframe, look over the content, etcetera.'

'I'll do it,' I say easily. I'm suddenly feeling good.

'Great,' Mrs Nair says. 'Let me know if you have any other ideas.'

'I do, actually,' I say. What Mrs Singh suggested earlier has given me an extraordinary idea! God, I'm super-creative!

'Like Mrs Singh suggested, we could help the women earn a little extra money. There are some really talented women who make unbelievable stuff at home—candles, soft toys, glass paintings, embroidered bed sheets . . . . We can help them set up an account on eBay and start selling their stuff. We can then showcase the entire process of e-commerce at the Welfare event.'

'Wow,' says Mrs Singh. 'That is so high-tech.'

'State of the art,' Mrs Bhandari says.

'Very modern,' Mrs Nair says. 'It might be a little difficult to do, but definitely worth a try. And we will definitely showcase it to the VIP ladies anyway.' I'm not imagining it, she really *is* excited. And she is smiling at me widely. I feel a glow of pride. Take that, Nose Hair!

We discuss things a little more and finally everyone agrees that New Age Education-Information-Awareness is a great theme for the event and Mrs Nair is sure that the GOC's wife will be extremely pleased with the Unit, if we manage to pull it off. Which we will. Pull it off, I mean. This is my vision, my baby, and I'll work on it even if I have to do it alone.

When the discussion is over and it is time to leave, Mrs Nair comes to me and says pleasantly, 'Good to have you back, Pia.'

As soon as she leaves, Mrs Bhandari summons Mrs James and lectures her about her timing and shabby attire. Nose Hair leaves while Mrs James is still inside. Mrs Singh and I are standing outside, discussing the fall of the Sisterhood. A few minutes later, a tearful Mrs James emerges out of the hall and looks around.

'Where's Kanika?' she asks us.

'Gone,' Mrs Singh says.

Mrs Bhandari steps out behind her.

'She left?' Mrs Bhandari says, with disbelief. It's not a written rule, but out of respect, we generally wait for the senior ladies to leave before stomping off ourselves.

'Yes. Almost with the CO's wife,' puts in Mrs Singh.

Mrs Bhandari looks livid.

'Well, please call her, Jyoti,' she says to Mrs Singh. 'Ask her to come back immediately. This is unacceptable!'

Mrs Singh is already dialling away.

We wait in anticipation till Nose Hair's vehicle comes back towards the Mess and she gets out, looking extremely bothered.

'What's the emergency?' she says walking up to Mrs Singh and glaring daggers at her. Mrs Singh points towards Mrs Bhandari without flinching. Nose Hair notices Mrs Bhandari and her rude demeanour changes in a split second.

'Yes, Mrs Bhandari?' she says, her bright tone back in place. 'You wanted to talk to me?'

'Yes. Let's step inside,' Mrs Bhandari says in an odd voice, and then adds, 'Everyone.' Mrs Singh and I rush inside, our blood pressure increasing with excitement. Mrs James comes in after us.

Once inside the hall, Mrs Bhandari turns to Nose Hair. Without any pretext, she starts. 'Kanika, I've been wanting to have this chat with you for some time now and your deteriorating manners just makes it all the more urgent. You are not new anymore and your behaviour has been unacceptable so far, to say the least.'

Mrs Singh grabs my hand and holds it tightly. Nose Hair looks shocked. Mrs James stares at her notepad. Mrs Bhandari continues.

'Talking about senior ladies, spreading gossip in the Unit and interfering in your husband's work—these are things that are strictly prohibited.'

'But I did not—' Nose Hair starts but Mrs Bhandari cuts her short.

'You interfere in your husband's official affairs regularly and then talk about it openly. You don't wish anyone other than Mrs Nair and me. You even call Jincy by her first name even though she is a senior officer's wife. You two are friends and she might be okay with it, but you also call Pia by her first name and as far as I know, Pia isn't . . .' she gestures towards Nose Hair and Mrs James with a dismissive wave of hand '—one of you. Stop calling Mrs Nair to complain about everyone else. Stop telling me things about Jincy that she tells you in confidence. Stop treating your husband's sahayak like your personal servant. Just—stop! Stop whatever you think you are doing Kanika. You are a part of the Indian Army now, and you need to follow protocol. Trust me—this is for your own good.' With this, Mrs Bhandari gets up, says goodbye to the rest of us and leaves.

'So it was Nose Hair who told Mrs Bhandari about Jincy's marriage problems and then blamed it on you. How convenient!' Mrs Singh whispers in my ear.

Nose Hair looks like she has just been slapped. She glances at Mrs James, who stares back at her. Perhaps she's realized what Nose Hair did.

Nose Hair looks at me, and seeing my smile (seriously, I can't do anything to stop smiling), she says, 'If you have a problem with me, you should have the balls to say it to me directly—*Mrs Mehra.*'

'What?' I am taken aback by this.

'Don't pretend. I know you complained about me to the 2IC's wife. Grow up!' she says angrily.

'Look,' I say feeling a bit rattled at her tone. 'This is the theme you keep coming back to and I honestly don't understand it.' I turn towards Mrs James who looks like she'd give anything to be anywhere but here at the moment.

'You know what? I'm tired of you and her. I have never talked about you to anyone. *Never,*' I say to Mrs James' sweating face. 'Mrs Bhandari just told you that your new best friend is the one who spills your secrets, not me. I am not your problem, Mrs James. I was the one friend you had, and lost. Stop acting like I'm the one to be blame for your issues, stop spreading gossip and calling me names! My only fault was thinking that we were friends and now I know better.'

Then I point at Nose Hair who is huffing and puffing in background. 'She's catty, vicious and she's a bad influence on you. She's turned you into a bitch which I hope you are not.' Mrs James' eyes widen at this and Mrs Singh snorts loudly. I am not done yet.

'And you,' I turn to Nose Hair. 'I know all about you and

your prestigious past in Ambala. I even have a few pictures, in case you want to reminiscence about the good old days.'

It takes her less than a second to realize what I'm referring to. She stares at me, her eyes like daggers. Her hands are on her hips, her nostrils are flaring and thick dark hair is peeking out. She juts her chin high in the air like a bull ready to fight and I shake my head in amusement.

She's not worth it, says a little voice in my head.

And I think the little voice is right. I'm better than her, and getting into a fight with her is like wrestling with a pig in the mud—both get dirty but the pig likes it. She is also pouting now, as if on cue, resembling a fat white pig. Suddenly, I feel a giggle building up.

She looks so pathetic, so funny and the entire situation seems like a pointless exercise to me. As the sides of my mouth twitch, I decide that she's really not worth one second of my attention or the tiniest bit of my energy.

'So. What are you going to do?' she hisses.

'I'm going to give you some advice,' I say to her. 'Trim your nose hair. It's gross.'

She looks at me dumbfounded and her hand flies to her nose. Mrs Singh is now laughing uncontrollably and Mrs James giggles through her tears. I hold Mrs Singh's hand tight and walk out.

On our way back, with Mrs Singh still laughing loudly and recounting the entire episode, sentence by sentence, to Mrs Sengupta on the phone, I get a text from Mrs James.

I'm sorry Pia. I've been mad, insensitive and can I please blame it on bad influence? Coffee session soon?

I smile. I've just had the first successful confrontation of my life. Let's see what Captain Arjun has to say about that.

chapter twenty-six

Growing Up. Somewhat

'I'm impressed,' Arjun says.

We are sitting on the couch in our living room, eating ice cream, and I have just finished recounting the details of my grand confrontation with Mrs James and Nose Hair.

It feels so good that I wonder what the hell has been keeping me away from confronting people all the time.

It's healthy, you know.

No bottled-up feelings, no long-term effects in the form of stress. All upfront and honest!

And the look on their faces? Ha! That should teach them not to mess with me ever again.

I feel like I've evolved as a person, like my higher self has taken over. It's funny how one incident can have such an intense effect on your life. Oh, the tranquillity. . . . It is like a spiritual awakening or something . . . and honesty really is the best policy, even if it means unpleasant conversations with nasty people once in a while. And I realized today that I love, no, I adore confrontation! I can do it. No problem.

I am so elated that I'm not all miffed about the fact that Arjun is going for patrolling around the Sambha district. He told me about it in the morning and I was alarmed. You have to agree that going with a 'patrol party' does sound a bit dangerous. All the movies teach us that patrolling an area can only mean trouble. Sambha is a relatively peaceful region, he has assured me; but there have been the odd incidents of blasts and terrorist intrusions around it and I was scared.

But not anymore: I believe in him and I believe in the positive power of the universe. See? The radiance of my inner enlightenment is already making me a stronger, better person!

But . . .

Oh my god. Oh my god!

Tomorrow is also Naina's last day in Pathankot.

Her last day! And Arjun goes on patrol after lunch.

Today sucks.

Arjun had a light lunch and left for Sambha. I'm terrified. He said he would be back shortly after midnight and I wonder what kind of patrol party works till after midnight . . . the one that goes on a dangerous mission, that's what.

Naina has finished packing and is now sitting in my living room.

'Today sucks,' I say, my face contorted with anxiety.

'Yeah,' she says, looking equally morose. 'Sucks big time.'

'You are going for, like, forever! Arjun is being sent away for some dangerous mission! I'm miserable!'

'For the millionth time, Pia, It's *not* dangerous!' she says. 'It's not like the patrol from the movie *LOC Kargil*. You know, the

one where all the soldiers were killed? It's just a routine thing. That area is far from any danger,' she says impatiently.

'Killed?' Oh god.

'And I am going, but we will keep in touch,' she says, ignoring the look on my face. 'If that godforsaken place has internet or a phone line, that is.' She sighs.

'I can't deal with it! I can't deal with it!' I say throwing my hands in the air in defeat.

'Me neither,' Naina says.

'All because of our husbands' profession, imagine!' I say in exasperation. 'Would we be going through all this turmoil in our lives if our husbands had chosen to be normal engineers or doctors instead of being in the Army?'

'I know!' Naina says. 'Honestly, we wives serve the Army along with our husbands.'

'We wear no ranks, get no medals or even acknowledgement for our years of service,' I say, feeling a ball of emotion in my throat.

'Yeah, we are the silent ranks—we are the backbone of the fighting set. The one that sacrifices the most. Just look what the two of us have gone through in such a short time already!' Naina says with a tired smile.

'True.' I rest my head against the MES sofa and say, 'Are we strong, efficient and seasoned Army Wives yet?'

Naina smiles warmly and squeezes my hand. I smile back at her and it dawns on me that we might not be the ideal military spouses yet, but the two of us have definitely come a long way from being clueless outsiders.

Sitting cross-legged on the floor, I stare hard at the vegetable drawer of my fridge, hoping that some bright idea for dinner will jump at me, when the doorbell rings.

It is Nose Hair.

At my doorstep.

'Can I come in?' she says.

I nod and step aside to let her enter. She's alone. Mrs James is not tagging along with her this time.

She walks towards the couch in my living room, turns around and just stands there, checking out the room with a smug look on her pale face.

What the hell is she doing here?

I bet she wants to even the score from last evening, or to beg me not to tell anyone about her past.

Personally, I'd prefer it to be the latter.

Then I can tell her in a superior tone that I am way better than her; that I would never stoop so low for some meaningless game that's only in her head; and could she please now leave. Yeah, that would be nice, ha! I might even gesture towards the door and jerk my head towards it, for effect. I'm not feeling too chatty anyway.

'What brings you here?' I say.

'I'm here about the thing you mentioned last evening,' she says without missing a beat.

'What about it?' I ask.

'I hope you haven't told anyone about it,' she says aggressively.

I'm confused; is this how it's supposed to go? Isn't she supposed to fall on her knees and beg me not to tell anyone?

'Look, I know you hate me,' she says. 'And last night you had your chance. But it was in bad taste! And it shows your poor upbringing, Mrs Mehra.'

'What—'

'Don't play dumb,' she puts a hand up. 'You dragged in my past in front of all those ladies because you didn't have the guts to fight me fairly.'

This is outrageous and I am not taking this shit anymore.

'Hold on, Nose Hair,' I say. 'I won't deny hating you. At all. I hate you and your stupid face. And yes, I do know about your past and I did bring it up last night because—and get this straight in that thick head of yours—you started it.'

She is still looking at me with narrowed eyes and I want to punch her.

'Everyone has a past and I don't care how murky yours was, but there's a difference between you and me. I wouldn't stoop as low as you just for an ego trip or to claim superiority. And why would I want to fight with you anyway? Who are you to me? Just get over yourself and go get a life.'

She is fidgeting a little now. And when she speaks, there's a faint tremble in her voice.

'So . . . you won't tell?' she speaks slowly, her voice unsteady. 'My husband can't know . . .'

Is she nervous?

She looks almost . . . vulnerable.

Oh god, who would have thought Nose Hair could ever look vulnerable?

'Kanika, I will not lie to you—Mrs Singh and Mrs Sengupta already know,' I say. 'But I wasn't going to say anything to anyone anyway, and neither will they.'

'Really?' Her voice is low now. I nod.

'We are Army wives, this is our code. We protect each other, even if it's . . . well, someone undeserving like you. So if that is what's bothering you, you can relax and go away,' I sigh and slump down on the sofa opposite her. Confrontations are exhausting.

'Thanks,' she says awkwardly.

I shrug.

She leaves.

Um. Why exactly am I finding myself in awkward situations so frequently? To what sudden bad karma do I owe the pleasure? Somebody just tell me so that I can rectify it immediately, because I hate it. I totally loathe it!

There. I said it. I hate confrontations. They wear me out.

Why can't people just be nice? I mean, how hard is it to be polite? It definitely is less demanding and a lot less strenuous than being mean all the time and trying to outsmart people for no real reason. Living the life of a bitch sure has its challenges, and I clearly am not up for it.

I'm nursing a slight headache with a mug of hot chocolate and going over the details of the Welfare. I have had a talk with the concerned OR wives and, thankfully, they seem enthusiastic about my idea.

'I can teach Facebook as long as you want. Thank god it is not a dance that you want me to perform!' Chimmi had said earnestly.

I have given them their respective topics and asked them to prepare a ten-minute talk on it, which Mrs Bhandari and I will listen to next week. Mrs Nair has made it clear that the final call will be mine, and that the programme will be according to my vision. I feel so powerful! I'm the commander of this troop, ha!

Planning an event is no child's play, let me tell you. It's eleven at night now. There have been six or seven phone calls with the participants and I already know that getting them to deliver what I want is not going to be easy at all. Plus, there is so much that can go wrong! I must keep a detailed contingency plan ready.

I open a new word document on my laptop and name it 'Welfare Contingency Plan'.

Then I type 'Things that could go wrong' and make a list (with bullet points).

- Electricity cut
- Invertor / generator failure
- Microphone not working
- Microphone lost
- Collar microphone not working
- Collar microphone lost
- Background music CD stuck
- Filler Music (during the welcome and snacks) CD stuck
- CD Player not working

Okay.

This is pointless.

I should focus on the solutions instead.

I'm about to make a list of 'Solutions to things that could go wrong' when the fauji phone rings.

Who could be calling me this late?

Mrs Bhandari's voice is unsteady on the phone. 'Pia, there has been an incident,' she says, and suddenly I feel giddy.

It is six months back again, when she was over at my place, telling me there has been an accident.

At least this time she said 'incident'.

What does that mean?

Oh god, I might faint.

An hour later, I am sitting on my living room couch, surrounded by Naina, Mrs Singh and Mrs Sengupta. Mrs Bhandari must have sent them over after I threw the phone receiver and refused to answer my cell phone.

I hug my knees, thinking about what I've been told.

There has been an incident.

Arjun's cell phone is switched off.

There was an encounter in the outer districts of Sambha involving three terrorists and Arjun's patrol party. Somebody is badly hurt. The CO is busy making calls to several people, so are the other Unit officers, trying to get all the information possible. But no one is telling me anything.

Someone is hurt badly, Mrs Sengupta said when she came over.

God, please don't let it be Arjun.

Mrs Sengupta gets a call on her cell phone and she runs outside to talk. Great, I think, now they aren't even talking in front of me. Naina hands me a glass of water and I gulp it down. Mrs Sengupta returns.

'So,' she says to all of us, but mainly to me, I think. 'BSF got a tip-off about a group of anti-nation elements trying to sneak into a market to plant an IED device in a public vehicle.'

Mrs Singh gasps. Naina clutches my hand tightly. I think I might burst a vein.

IED device? Aren't those like, super-powerful and extremely dangerous?

My heart drops to my stomach.

I try Arjun's number once again. Switched off. I am about to press redial when Mrs Nair's number flashes on the screen.

'Hello?' I say into the phone. 'Do you know anything Mrs Nair? What's happening?' I cry.

'Relax Pia,' she says calmly. Why the fuck is she calm? 'Everything is great.'

Great?

Everything is great?

What is wrong with her?

'Our patrol party was informed about a planned attack and they immediately followed it up,' she is saying. Mrs Singh is pressing her ear to the phone and so is Naina so I put it on loud speaker mode. 'The terrorists, three of them, were surrounded by our team. Now this is where it got confusing for us. They were supposed to hold position and wait for reinforcements but something happened—maybe an escape attempt by the terrorists. It was late, so the marketplace was almost deserted and a few rounds were fired by both sides.'

I stop breathing.

Rounds were fired?

There was *firing* involved?

'One terrorist managed to escape. One is successfully caught and is in our custody. And one—' she says happily, '—we killed.'

Killed?

As in, dead? No more?

'The reinforcement party has reached the location now. One of our men—Ganga Singh—is shot and is currently unconscious. Another one has a bullet in his arm but is stable. Both are being transferred to the hospital as we speak.'

Shot?

Ganga bhaiya was shot?

I can practically hear my heart beating.

'And Captain Arjun has shot a terrorist,' Mrs Nair says.

Arjun has what?

'Captain Arjun successfully carried out a terrorist encounter, Pia. This is such a proud moment for the Unit, for you, for all of us!' she says.

Everyone around me hoots with joy. Naina hugs me happily and sings 'Congratulations, and celebrations' loudly. Mrs Sengupta claps with glee and Mrs Singh digs out a bowl of custard from my fridge and insists we eat some, to celebrate.

I feel exhausted.

Arjun is fine—I say out loud. He is okay.

I close my eyes. I'm too stunned to react just yet.

chapter twenty-seven

Part of the Plan

'And then—you won't believe it,' Mrs James pauses for effect and looks around at everyone's faces. Mrs Singh is leaning in, looking a bit off-balanced. Mrs Sengupta's hand, which is holding a glass of grape juice, has stopped midway to her mouth. I am clutching at my clutch (nude with silver crystals; very chic) so tightly that I think I might have chipped my nail paint (hot pink, what else?).

'She abused me,' Mrs James says at last. 'In Hindi.' She looks offended and excited at the same time.

'Hawwww,' says Mrs Singh.

'Really?' I ask in disbelief.

'What swear words did she use? Tell me!' demands Mrs Sengupta.

Mrs James whispers something in Mrs Sengupta's ears and she looks unimpressed.

'Nose Hair is a behenji, really,' she says.

'So do you hate Nose Hair now?' I ask Mrs James hopefully.

'Of course,' Mrs James says seriously. 'She's horrible. She just wanted to be queen bee, and I think I made it worse for you when I told her in the beginning that you were the go-to gal here. And then her influence on me was like a whirlpool. I wanted out, but I kept getting sucked in.' She stares into space. I can't help smiling.

We are standing in the brightly-lit garden of the Brigade Officers' Mess, listening to old English music, talking animatedly about a million things, dressed in our best sarees and I am extra-radiant tonight because:

a.) I'm wearing my brand new Manish Malhotra-inspired saree—subtle golden chiffon with delicate crystal work all over, and
b.) The party is being thrown by the Brigade commander in Arjun's honour.

Yes.

I feel like I'm floating on air.

Just a few days ago I was trembling with fear and praying for Arjun's safety. I've lived with terrorism—the bomb blasts in Delhi, the terror attacks in Mumbai. But it had never been so personal; it had never been my reality.

Obviously, I know all the dangers and risks that an Army officer might face, and I thought I was mentally prepared for it. But how can you ever be prepared for fear?

Hell, I don't even understand terrorism. I mean, how do you get used to the fact that at any time, any place, some fanatic can just decide to kill people? I guess the only way to keep our sanity in such times is to not let fear overcome us.

That's easier said than done, obviously. It took me the entire night and almost half a day to be able to speak in complete sentences after the encounter, even after Arjun arrived home—exhausted but euphoric—later that night.

Things have only gotten better since then. In fact, these have been the best days of my life, no doubt about that. It is like I am a sudden celebrity.

Can you believe it?

Ever since the terrorist-killing-and-capture operation, Arjun has become a hero in the entire station. I've attended congratulatory calls from—oh, pretty much everyone, including Manpreet, Mrs Chandok and even the deputy GOC's wife. All the ladies have been congratulating me as if I'm responsible for Arjun's accomplishment.

When Mrs Nair congratulated me for the fifth time, I told her that I had done nothing and that it's entirely to Arjun's credit. But she shook her head and said that Army wives are the backbone of the Army and its soldiers. She said that it's not just the brave husbands, but also their spouses who each day live the unwritten codes; the wives are equally heroic and deserve all the credit possible.

'Never say you did nothing. You are his strength,' Mrs Nair said.

What is that sound I hear? Oh, that's me—patting myself on the back. I am Arjun's strength.

My brave husband has killed (killed; this one still needs some time to sink in) a dangerous terrorist in an unforeseen encounter and in some bizarre way, I am the valiant one, receiving all the accolades. Not that I'm complaining.

In fact, I'm hoping all this lasts for a while. I could use the positive energy and the rave reviews of my amazing Army-wife qualities to even out the bad times from not-that-very-long-ago.

Things that have changed dramatically:

- No more a transfer-worthy liability, Arjun is now the celebrated hero of the Unit, the distinguished celebrity of the Brigade.

- The CO threw a big party at his residence to honour Arjun and his feat the very next weekend of the operation and said: 'Arjun is my bachha! I remember when I was a major and he had just joined the Unit—I was certain of his exemplary ability right then. Today he has proved me right and how! Arjun is our shining star!'

- We have completed one year of marriage!

- No more a cruel frenemy that's a sidekick to a spiteful bitch, Mrs James is now back to being friends with me and the others. She apologized to me several times and let's just say that I'm pleased with being the 'right one' all along.

- Nose Hair is still the same, but at least she is alone for now. No sidekick. Plus, she has managed to rub Mrs Sengupta the wrong way—she apparently talked about Mrs Sengupta's alleged affair to Mrs James, who has obviously spilled the beans—and God alone can help Nose Hair now. She has not been attending any of Arjun's celebration parties, claiming bad health. As if.

Anyway.

Like a Bollywood movie, this is the super happy ending that gives the viewers a misty far-away look in their eyes. Naina not being here is the only negative in my happiness. But I have a feeling we'll never lose touch; after all she's my AW-BFF!

I'm giggling over something that Mrs Sengupta has just said, when Arjun walks over.

'Tomorrow night dinner at the GOC's residence,' he whispers in my ear as soon as he gets close.

'Oh . . .' I look up at him. I take a step in front and my heels dig into the wet garden soil. I become a bit unsteady and bump against him. He steadies me with a firm hand at my back.

'The CO and Ma'am. You and me,' he whispers again. I look into his eyes. No smug smile, no trace of conceit. In fact, he looks so cool and unruffled that you'd think he shoots down terrorists on a one-per-day basis.

Feeling fresh tingles of joy and pride, I smile at him. He smiles back. Then my eyes travel down to his collar where I bumped into him a few seconds ago. There's a bright pink lipstick mark, looking like it was carefully planted there instead of by accident.

For a split second I consider telling him about it, but then better sense prevails and I decide against it. What's the use anyway? It's not like he can run home and change right now.

So I just say, 'Okay, dinner date tomorrow at GOC's house', wink at him and turn back to the ladies.

'What were the love birds talking about?' Mrs Singh teases. Mrs Bhandari and Mrs Nair have also joined the group by now.

'Nothing . . .' I say with a smile. Why the hell am I blushing? 'There's another dinner tomorrow.'

'Oh, it will last for a while Pia,' Mrs Bhandari says happily. 'Every senior officer in the station wants to congratulate Captain Arjun and his wife.'

'Speaking of honours—' Mrs James says, coming up to us after visiting the Ladies' Room, '—I just passed the commander and our CO at the bar.' She points towards the bar area. 'And I heard something. Something *huge*!' She looks at everyone and stops at me. Huge? What huge thing could the commander and CO be talking about to get Mrs James so excited? All the ladies are now gazing at her, naked curiosity obvious on their faces.

'Out with it!' Mrs Singh says.

'I heard that Captain Arjun's name can be recommended for a medal, along with Ganga Singh,' Mrs James says in a low, dramatic tone and I exhale sharply.

'Medal?' I say in a shaky voice.

'On Republic Day!' Mrs Singh says excitedly.

'Awesome!' Mrs Sengupta whispers in awe.

'It's only fitting,' Mrs Bhandari says, nodding cheerily.

'What an immense honour for the Unit!' Mrs Nair says, looking elated.

The group immediately launches into a discussion about what the chances are of Arjun getting selected for a medal, what a big deal it is for the Unit, etcetera, etcetera.

And me?

I'm thinking I'll have to buy a new saree for the ceremony.

Something that's elegant and subtle, but not drab.

How cool is this! Arjun will get a medal! And Ganga bhaiya too!

And—oh my god—it will be in Delhi, right?

Maybe I can take a few friends with me to the Republic Day parade. Being the wife of a brave medal-recipient I should be allowed to get a few people in, right?

And I'll get to meet all the big politicians! Not that I want to, but what's the harm? I'll be there anyway.

'Pia?' someone is saying.

'Pia!' Mrs James is nudging me slightly.

I smile at her vaguely, still lost in my train of thoughts.

I really hope that the guest for this year's Republic Day celebration is that handsome French president.

And what about the TV cameras? When Arjun marches up to receive the medal, they might zoom in on me, right? I can wave at the camera then.

No. How stupid will that look!

I will sit tight and smile serenely at the camera then, giving my best strength-behind-the-husband Army wife smile.

I look around and catch Arjun's eye from across the garden. He flashes a dazzling smile at me and my heart does a little flip. I smile back, feeling my cheeks get a little warm. He raises his glass to me and winks. Both of us take a sip from our glasses and . . . yuck.

My orange juice is bitter! I stick my tongue out and look down at it. It's not orange and it's not mine. I think I might have picked up Mrs Sengupta's glass by mistake. And the horrible taste is almost choking me.

I look back at Arjun whose eyes are flashing with amusement, and I feel an unwilling grin spread across my face. I shrug and calmly place the glass on a tiny table in the most dignified Army wife-like manner possible.

'Juice, Memsaab?' comes a voice from behind me, instantly reminding me of my first day in the Army Cantt, when being called Memsaab seemed like the most unusual thing to happen to plain old civilian me. And look where I am today, having been through so much more than I could have ever imagined at that moment, almost a year ago. Now being addressed as Memsaab feels like the most normal thing in the world.

I smile at the realization, nod at the waiter, and pick up a glass of juice.

There's never a dull moment in Army, I realize. And it suits me just fine. With the glass in my hand, I join the animated group of my fellow Army wives.

Yes. I'm an Army wife, and it feels just right.

Acknowledgements

This story is a work of fiction. Seriously, I completely made it up. But it wouldn't have been possible without inspiration and encouragement from a lot of people. Here's the short version of that list.

A huge thanks to my parents for passing down the undying love for books.

Thank you, Arti Jain, who loved the plot when it was just an idea for a blog post and said, 'Write a book, silly.' A million thanks to Deepthi Talwar—the coolest editor ever.

I can't thank my husband enough, who is the reason I was able to finish writing this story. He was also my first and only beta reader. He only reads books on military history, so it's a big deal.

And the biggest thank-you goes to the all the amazing army wives I know. Each and every one of you has inspired me to tell this story. I am proud to be a tiny part of this grand world of Indian Army wives, and all of you are my strength. You girls are true rocks stars, and I salute you.

This book is dedicated to the Indian armed forces, and the resilient army wives, also known as the 'silent ranks', who hold the fort when the soldier is away at duty.

Jai Hind.